W0266763

FAQs – Häufige Fragen zur Abiturprüfung

Wie ist die Prüfung aufgebaut und wie viel Zeit habe ich?

Die schriftliche Abiturprüfung besteht aus den Teilen **Hörverstehen**, **Sprachmittlung** und **Textaufgabe**. Als erstes findet der *listening comprehension test* statt, im Anschluss daran erhalten Sie die Sprachmittlungsaufgabe. Beim dritten und letzten Prüfungsteil, der Textaufgabe, können Sie zwischen zwei Vorschlägen auswählen.

Prüfungsteil	Zeit
Hörverstehen	30 Minuten
Sprachmittlung	60 Minuten
Textaufgabe (2 Vorschläge zur Auswahl)	225 Minuten (einschließlich Auswahlzeit)

Welche Hilfsmittel darf ich verwenden?

In allen Prüfungsteilen stehen Ihnen sowohl ein **einsprachiges** als auch ein **zweisprachiges Wörterbuch** zur Verfügung. Anstelle der gedruckten Wörterbücher kann auch ein elektronisches Wörterbuch verwendet werden, sofern es bereits in der Qualifikationsphase eingeführt wurde und für jeden Prüfling ein Exemplar bereitsteht.

Welche Textsorten und Aufgabentypen können vorkommen?

Genaue Informationen zu den Textsorten und Aufgabenformaten, die Sie in den einzelnen Prüfungsteilen erwarten können, erhalten Sie im Kapitel „**Hinweise, Tipps und Übungsaufgaben zu den Prüfungsteilen**“. Dort finden Sie auch Schritt-für-Schritt-Anleitungen zum richtigen Vorgehen in der Prüfung sowie Übungsaufgaben, mit denen Sie die „Theorie“ gleich praktisch anwenden können.

Gibt es inhaltliche/thematische Schwerpunkte?

Die Abiturvorbereitung im Englischunterricht stützt sich auf das **Kerncurriculum**, das wesentliche Unterrichtsinhalte und -methoden festlegt. Folgende Themenfelder werden danach in der Oberstufe behandelt und sind Grundlage für das Abitur:

- *Beliefs, values and norms in society – tradition and change:*
  Britishness; the American experience; Postcolonial/Neo-colonial experiences; migration effects on the world of work
- *Individual and society:*
  identity; ethnic, cultural and linguistic diversity; gender and sexual diversity
- *Globalisation:*
  effects on the world of work; impact on personal lives; global responsibility concerning e. g. politics, the environment, economy; English as a global language
- *Science and technology:*
  chances and risks; visions of the future; the media, e. g. the influence of the media on public opinion and personal life; the digital revolution
- *Shakespeare: the world that made him; modern adaptations*

Ergänzend veröffentlicht das Kultusministerium eine Liste mit **verbindlichen Materialien**, die im Unterricht behandelt werden müssen. Diese sind speziell für den Prüfungsteil „Textaufgabe" relevant: Zwar entstammt der Prüfungstext im Abitur nicht einer der Pflichtlektüren – es kann aber sein, dass von Ihnen verlangt wird, den Prüfungstext in Bezug zu den verbindlichen Materialien zu setzen. Für das Abitur 2024 wurden folgende Texte und Filme als verbindliche Materialien festgelegt:

Verbindliche Materialien	verbindliche Unterrichtsaspekte
Roman: Ian McEwan, *Atonement* (2001)	Britishness; innocence and guilt; perception(s) of reality
Kurzprosa (allgemeinbildende Schulen): Nafissa Thompson-Spires: "Heads of the Colored People: Four Fancy Sketches, Two Chalk Outlines, and No Apology" (2018); Camille Acker: "Mambo Sauce" (2018)	ethnic identity; discrimination
Film (zusätzlich nur für berufliche Gymnasien): John Lee Hancock (Regie), *The Founder* (2016)	American Dream; ethics in the world of business
Film: Joel Edgerton (Regie), *Boy Erased* (2018)	coming of age; sexual diversity; tolerance and discrimination
Kurzdrama (nur für allgemeinbildende Schulen): Jasmine Lee-Jones, *seven methods of killing kylie jenner* (2019)	ethnic identity; the influence of social media on personal life and public opinion
Drama: Auszüge aus William Shakespeare, *Hamlet* (ca.. 1600)	fate vs. free will; the role(s) of women; questions of morality

Wie werden die einzelnen Prüfungsteile bewertet?

Sie bekommen für jeden der drei Prüfungsteile eine Note. Aus diesen drei Teilnoten wird am Ende durch prozentuale Gewichtung Ihre Gesamtnote für die schriftliche Prüfung ermittelt (siehe Tabelle unten).
Die Bewertung des **Hörverstehens** erfolgt über sog. Bewertungseinheiten (BE). In den Prüfungsteilen **Sprachmittlung** und **Textaufgabe** werden Sprache und Inhalt zunächst getrennt voneinander bewertet.

Folgende Kriterien sind für die Bewertung der **sprachlichen Leistung** relevant:
- kommunikative Textgestaltung:
  Textaufbau, Textsortenspezifik, Situationsangemessenheit und Adressatenbezug
- Ausdrucksvermögen/Verwendung sprachlicher Mittel:
  eigenständige Bearbeitung, angemessener und reichhaltiger Wortschatz, Verwendung idiomatischer Konstruktionen, abwechslungsreicher und angemessen komplexer Satzbau, korrekte Zitiertechnik
- Sprachrichtigkeit:
  korrekte Rechtschreibung/Grammatik/Satzbau/Wortschatz; Verständlichkeit

Bei der Bewertung der **inhaltlichen Leistung** werden folgende Kriterien angelegt:
- Aufgabenerfüllung:
  Umsetzung der Aufgabenstellung, Textsortenspezifik, Situations-/Adressatenbezug
- Erläutern kulturspezifischer Aspekte (bei der Sprachmittlung)
- Text- und Problemverständnis:
  Durchdringung der Textvorlage, Problemverständnis/ggf. Einordnen in größere Zusammenhänge
- Darstellung und Gliederung:
  Umsetzung des Operators; selbstständige und differenzierte Entfaltung des Themas; Verständlichkeit, Klarheit und Schlüssigkeit der Darstellung

Prüfungsteil	Ermittlung der Teilnote	Anteil der Teilnote an Gesamtnote
Hörverstehen	Bewertung über Bewertungseinheiten (BEs): Pro richtige Antwort 1 BE; für eine ausreichende Leistung (5 Notenpunkte) ist das Erreichen von 45 % der BE notwendig	20 %
Sprachmittlung	60 % auf Sprache, 40 % auf Inhalt	25 %
Textaufgabe	60 % auf Sprache (wird ganzheitlich für alle Teilaufgaben ermittelt) 40 % auf Inhalt (wird zunächst einzeln für jede Teilaufgabe ermittelt und danach entsprechend der prozentualen Vorgabe in der Prüfung gewichtet)	55 %

Zur Veranschaulichung hier ein **Beispiel, wie Ihre Note errechnet wird:**
Nehmen wir einmal an, Sie haben bei der Textaufgabe für Ihre Arbeit im Bereich „Sprache" 11 Punkte bekommen. Im Bereich „Inhalt" ergibt sich für Sie bei drei Aufgaben und prozentualer Gewichtung ein Mittelwert von 9,3 Punkten. Für das Endergebnis multiplizieren Sie Ihre sprachliche Note mit 0,6 und die inhaltliche Note mit 0,4 und addieren dann beide Ergebnisse. Es ergibt sich 10,32 – dieser Prüfungsteil wird also mit „noch gut (10 Punkte)" bewertet.
Nehmen wir zudem an, Sie haben im Hörverstehen eine Teilnote von 9 Punkten erzielt und in der Sprachmittlung eine Teilnote von 8 Punkten. Multiplizieren Sie nun die 10 Punkte aus der Textaufgabe mit 0,55, die 9 Punkte aus dem Hörverstehen mit 0,2 und die 8 Punkte aus der Sprachmittlung mit 0,25 und addieren Sie anschließend die drei Werte. Es ergibt sich ein Wert von 9,3. Ihre Gesamtnote für die schriftliche Prüfung ist also „befriedigend (9 Punkte)".

Wie bereite ich mich am besten auf die Prüfung vor?

Inhaltliche Vorbereitung

Sie werden in der Abiturprüfung Texte und Aufgaben vorgelegt bekommen, die für Sie neu sind, die Sie also noch nicht zuvor im Unterricht behandelt haben. Für Ihre Vorbereitung bedeutet das Folgendes:

- Arbeiten Sie vor allem an Ihrer **Methodik**. Trainieren Sie also, wie man an die verschiedenen Aufgabenstellungen herangeht – das ist insbesondere für die Sprachmittlung und Textaufgabe von entscheidender Bedeutung. Die nachfolgenden Kapitel enthalten detaillierte Informationen, was Sie in den einzelnen Prüfungsteilen beachten müssen und wie Sie in der Prüfungssituation am besten vorgehen. Diese Abschnitte sollten Sie unbedingt genau durchlesen. Mit den Übungsaufgaben haben Sie anschließend die Möglichkeit, Ihr methodisches Wissen in der Praxis zu testen.
- Für die Textaufgabe ist zudem wichtig, dass Sie mit den **Pflichtlektüren bzw. -filmen** vertraut sind. Neben der Vorbereitung im Unterricht hilft Ihnen hier das „**AbiturSkript Englisch Niedersachsen 2024**" (Bestell-Nr. 3546S4). Sie finden darin knapp zusammengefasst alles Wichtige zu Handlung, Figuren und relevanten Themen sowie nützliche Schaubilder, mit denen Sie sich das Gelernte besser einprägen können.

Sprachliche Vorbereitung

Mindestens ebenso wichtig wie die inhaltliche Vorbereitung ist die sprachliche Vorbereitung auf die Prüfung. Im *listening comprehension test* müssen Sie mit dem normalen Sprechtempo von *native speakers* zurechtkommen. In den Prüfungsteilen Sprachmittlung und Textaufgabe fließt Ihre sprachliche Leistung mit 60% in die Teilnote ein und wird damit sogar stärker gewichtet als Ihre inhaltliche Leistung. Eine flüssige Ausdrucksweise, ein vielseitiger Wortschatz sowie grammatikalische und orthografische Richtigkeit sind hier von besonderer Bedeutung. Länger- und mittelfristig können Sie u. a. folgende Strategien zur Vorbereitung anwenden:

2024

Abitur

Original-Prüfungsaufgaben
mit Lösungen

Niedersachsen

Englisch eA

STARK

18. neu bearbeitete und ergänzte Auflage
www.stark-verlag.de

Inhaltsverzeichnis

Textaufgabe

Original-Prüfungsaufgaben

Abiturprüfung 2018

Abiturprüfung 2019 (Auszug)

Abiturprüfung 2021

Abiturprüfung 2022

Sobald die Original-Prüfungsaufgaben 2023 freigegeben sind, können sie als PDF auf der Plattform MyStark heruntergeladen werden (Zugangscode vgl. Umschlaginnenseite).

MP3-Dateien

Sprecher*innen (MP3-Dateien)

Eva Adelseck, Daniel Beaver, Clare Gnasmüller, Daniel Holzberg, Rees Jeannotte, Jennifer Mikulla, Veronica Stivala

FAQs: Redaktion

Hinweise, Tipps und Übungsaufgaben zu den Prüfungsbereichen:

Hörverstehen: Redaktion (Aufbau des Prüfungsteils, Vorgehen)
Dorothée Just (Set 1, Task 1; Set 2, Task 3)
Paul Jenkinson (Set 1, Tasks 2/3; Set 2, Tasks 1/2)

Sprachmittlung: Redaktion (Aufbau des Prüfungsteils, Vorgehen; Übungsaufgabe 2)
Mareike Hasselmann (Übungsaufgabe 1)

Textaufgabe: Redaktion (Aufbau des Prüfungsteils, Vorgehen; Übungsaufgabe 3)
Rainer Jacob (Übersicht Stilmittel, hilfreiche Wendungen zu Cartoons/Statistiken)
Karin Feldner (Übungsaufgabe 1)
Birgit Holtwick (Übungsaufgaben 2 und 4)

Lösungen zu den Original-Prüfungsaufgaben

Abitur 2018: Redaktion (Hörverstehen)
Robert Klimmt (Sprachmittlung)
Christian Fischer (Textaufgaben)

Abitur 2019: Redaktion (Hörverstehen)
Johannes Schmidt-Wellenburg/Gertrude Weber (Sprachmittlung)

Abitur 2021: Redaktion (Hörverstehen)
Rainer Jacob (Sprachmittlung)
Christian Fischer (Textaufgaben)

Abitur 2022: Dorothée Just (Hörverstehen)
Robert Klimmt (Sprachmittlung)
Christian Fischer (Textaufgaben)

Vorwort

Liebe Schülerinnen, liebe Schüler,

dieses Buch (und seine digitalen Zusätze, siehe Folgeseiten) soll Sie auf dem Weg zu einer erfolgreichen Abiturprüfung im Fach Englisch begleiten. Es ist folgendermaßen aufgebaut:

- Die **FAQs** enthalten alles Wichtige rund um die Abiturprüfung in aller Kürze. Hier können Sie sich einen ersten Überblick verschaffen, was Sie in der Prüfung erwartet.
- Im zweiten Teil des Buches finden Sie **Hinweise**, **Tipps** und **Übungsaufgaben zu den Prüfungsbereichen Hörverstehen**, **Sprachmittlung** und **Textaufgabe**. Zu Beginn jedes Kapitels erfahren Sie, welche **Aufgabenformate** auf Sie zukommen können und wie Sie in der Prüfung am besten **vorgehen**. Außerdem finden Sie hier nützliche **Übersichten** zu Operatoren, Textsorten, hilfreichen Wendungen und vielem mehr. Nach dieser theoretischen Hinführung können Sie Ihre Kenntnisse in den **Übungsaufgaben** praktisch anwenden. Bei der jeweils ersten Übungsaufgabe bzw. dem ersten Übungsset werden Sie Schritt für Schritt angeleitet (bei der Textaufgabe in Form von Lernvideos). Die weiteren Übungsaufgaben enthalten keine solche zusätzliche Hilfestellung. Wenn Sie möchten, können Sie sich auch ein vollständiges Abiturprüfungsset (bestehend aus je einer Übungsaufgabe Hörverstehen, Sprachmittlung und Textaufgabe) zusammenstellen und damit den „Ernstfall" simulieren.
- Am Ende des Buches finden Sie **Original-Prüfungsaufgaben** der letzten Jahre, die Ihnen einen Eindruck vermitteln, wie die zentral gestellte Abiturprüfung aussieht. Beachten Sie, dass sich einzelne Aufgabenstellungen im Bereich „Textaufgabe" auf die damals gültigen Pflichtlektüren beziehen. Die Aufgaben eignen sich dennoch weiterhin gut zum Üben.
- Zu allen Übungsaufgaben und Original-Prüfungen gibt es ausführliche **Lösungsvorschläge**. In den Tippkästen finden Sie nützliche Hinweise zum Bearbeiten der Aufgaben bzw. wesentliche Aspekte, die in Ihrer Lösung enthalten sein sollten. Hier können Sie also bei Bedarf nachschlagen, wenn Sie Hilfestellung benötigen. Anschließend können Sie Ihre Lösung mit unserer (Beispiel-)Lösung vergleichen.

Wir wünschen Ihnen schon jetzt viel Erfolg in der Prüfung!

Hinweise zu den digitalen Zusätzen

Auf alle digitalen Zusätze können Sie online über die Plattform **MyStark** zugreifen. Ihren persönlichen Zugangscode finden Sie auf der Umschlaginnenseite (vorne im Buch).

PDF der Original-Prüfungsaufgaben 2023

Um Ihnen die Prüfung 2023 schnellstmöglich zur Verfügung stellen zu können, bringen wir sie in digitaler Form heraus. Sobald die Original-Prüfungsaufgaben 2023 freigegeben sind, können Sie sie als PDF auf der Plattform MyStark herunterladen.

MP3-Dateien

Über die Plattform **MyStark** können Sie außerdem auf die Hörverstehenstexte der Übungsaufgaben und Original-Prüfungen zugreifen.

Lernvideos zur Textaufgabe

Textaufgaben sind Teil vieler Prüfungen und Klausuren – und machen oft einen Großteil der Prüfungsleistung aus. Mithilfe der **Lernvideos zum richtigen Umgang mit Textaufgaben** können Sie sich optimal auf die Anforderungen in diesem Bereich vorbereiten. Am Beispiel von zwei Texten mit je drei Aufgabenstellungen wird gezeigt, wie man an eine Textaufgabe herangeht und sie erfolgreich löst.

Die Lernvideos beinhalten:

- **Schritt-für-Schritt-Anleitungen** zum richtigen Vorgehen in der Prüfung
- einen **Sachtext** und **literarischen Text** als Grundlage
- nützliche Hinweise zu **häufigen Operatoren** und **Zieltextsorten**

Interaktives Training

Im **Online-Training „Basic Language Skills"** erhalten Sie Zugriff auf zahlreiche **interaktive Aufgaben** zu Grundlagen wie **Hörverstehen**, **Leseverstehen** und **Sprachverwendung im Kontext**. Dies sind ganz wichtige „Basics", die Sie für eine gute Sprachbeherrschung brauchen.

Das interaktive Training bietet Ihnen:

- „**Listening**" – authentische Audiodateien mit vielfältigen Aufgaben, die Ihr Hörverstehen testen
- „**Reading**" – abwechslungsreiche Lesetexte und dazugehörige Aufgaben
- „**English in Use**" mit gemischten Aufgaben rund um den Gebrauch der englischen Sprache
- Alle Aufgaben sind interaktiv, d. h., Sie können sie direkt am PC oder Tablet bearbeiten und erhalten sofort eine Rückmeldung zu Ihren Antworten.

Web-App „MindCards"

Mit der Web-App „**MindCards**" können Sie am Smartphone Vokabeln lernen. Auf diesen interaktiven Karteikarten finden Sie hilfreiche Wendungen, die Sie beim Schreiben von Texten oder im mündlichen Sprachgebrauch einsetzen können.
Scannen Sie einfach die QR-Codes oder verwenden Sie folgende Links, um zu den „MindCards" zu gelangen:
https://www.stark-verlag.de/mindcards/writing-2
https://www.stark-verlag.de/mindcards/speaking-2

Writing

Speaking

Video zur mündlichen Abiturprüfung

Teil Ihres Abiturs ist auch eine mündliche Prüfung (im fünften Prüfungsfach). Für viele Schülerinnen und Schüler sind solche Prüfungen mit Unsicherheit und Nervosität verbunden. Aber keine Panik, denn auch hier gibt Ihnen eine gute Vorbereitung die nötige Sicherheit. Über diesen QR-Code bzw. in der Plattform MyStark können Sie sich ein Video mit vielen praktischen Tipps zum mündlichen Abitur ansehen – egal, in welchem Fach Sie ins mündliche Abitur gehen.

FAQs – Häufige Fragen

- Schauen Sie englischsprachige Filme oder Serien, hören Sie englische Hörbücher oder Podcasts und lesen Sie Artikel oder Bücher auf Englisch.
- Speziell als Vorbereitung auf die Sprachmittlungsaufgabe sollten Sie außerdem üben, deutsche Zeitungsartikel für (imaginäre) englische Bekannte zusammenzufassen – das entspricht dem üblichen Szenario, das Ihnen auch in der Prüfung begegnet.
- Sehen Sie sich Ihre korrigierten Englisch-Klausuren an und notieren Sie, was Ihre häufigsten Fehler sind. Üben Sie diese Bereiche dann ganz gezielt. Zur Wiederholung von Grammatik und Wortschatz eignen sich beispielsweise die Abitur-Trainings-Bände „Englisch Grammatikübungen" (82452D) und „Englisch Themenwortschatz" (82451D).
- Auch mit dem interaktiven Training auf der Plattform MyStark können Sie sprachliche Grundlagen wie Hörverstehen, Wortschatz und Strukturen trainieren (Zugang vgl. Umschlaginnenseite, ganz vorne im Buch).

ÜBUNGSAUFGABEN

Hörverstehen

Aufbau des Prüfungsteils „Hörverstehen“

Der *listening comprehension test* im Abitur besteht meist aus **zwei bis vier einzelnen Hörtexten**, die jeweils **zweimal hintereinander abgespielt** werden. Häufig handelt es sich dabei um Radiobeiträge, Interviews, Nachrichtenmeldungen oder mehrere kurze Monologe. Die Themen der Texte können sehr vielfältig sein (von Politik über Kultur bis hin zu Umweltschutz) und müssen nicht in Bezug zu den Pflichtlektüren oder den Themen der anderen Prüfungsteile stehen. Die einzelnen Hörtexte sind in der Regel maximal fünf Minuten lang. Die gesamte Bearbeitungszeit beträgt **30 Minuten**. In diesem Prüfungsteil können **geschlossene** bzw. **halboffene Aufgabenformate** vorkommen, z. B. *multiple choice,* Zuordnung *(multiple matching)* und *table completion.* Dabei steht das reine Hörverstehen im Vordergrund. Deshalb werden Sie – wenn überhaupt – nur kurze Phrasen oder Sätze schreiben müssen. Sprachliche Fehler werden nur dann gewertet, wenn sie das Verständnis beeinträchtigen.

Aufgaben-format	Merkmale	Beispiel
multiple choice	• i.d.R. ist ein Satzanfang vorgegeben und Sie müssen aus mehreren möglichen Satzenden das richtige auswählen und abhaken • die Aufgaben können sich auf Detailinformationen oder den Text als Ganzes beziehen	*[…] tick (✓) the correct answer (a, b or c). There is only one correct answer.*
multiple matching	• Sie sollen mehreren kurzen Texten/Monologen von verschiedenen Sprechern die passende Überschrift oder Aussage zuordnen • häufig sind mehr Möglichkeiten vorgegeben als zugeordnet werden müssen	*[…] match the statements A to G with the speakers 1 to 6. There is one more statement than you need.*
table completion/ filling in information	• Sie müssen fehlende Informationen ergänzen (meist in einer Tabelle) • in der Regel sind keine vollständigen Sätze nötig • Sie können den Wortlaut des Texts übernehmen oder in eigenen Worten formulieren	*[…] fill in the missing information. You do not need to write complete sentences.*

Vorgehen in der Prüfung

Schritt 1 Vor dem ersten Hören: Aufgaben lesen

Meist haben Sie vor dem ersten Hören etwas Zeit, um sich mit den Aufgaben vertraut zu machen und sich auf das Thema des jeweiligen Texts einzustellen. Lesen Sie die Aufgabenstellung genau und unterstreichen Sie **Schlüsselbegriffe** oder Eigennamen mit Bleistift.

Schritt 2 Erstes Hören: möglichst viele Aufgaben lösen

Jetzt wird Ihnen der Text ein erstes Mal vorgespielt.

- Achten Sie beim Hören besonders auf die **Schlüsselbegriffe** aus der Aufgabe und damit verwandte Formulierungen (z. B. **Synonyme**, **Wörter derselben Wortfamilie** oder **aus demselben Wortfeld**). So erkennen Sie schnell die für die Lösung relevanten Stellen. Wird in der Aufgabenstellung beispielsweise das Wort „legislation" verwendet, ist im Hörtext möglicherweise von „laws" oder dem „legislative process" die Rede. Machen Sie bei *multiple choice*- und *matching*-Aufgaben aber nicht den Fehler, „automatisch" auf eine bestimmte Lösung zu schließen, nur weil ein bestimmter Begriff auch im Hörtext vorkommt. Manchmal enthalten die Aufgabenstellungen auch **Distraktoren**, also Antwortmöglichkeiten, die Sie auf eine falsche Fährte locken sollen. Beziehen Sie daher immer den **Kontext** mit ein, in dem ein Begriff im Hörtext genannt wird. Achten Sie außerdem auf die genaue **Formulierung in der Aufgabenstellung** (z. B. ob Verneinungen oder Relativierungen enthalten sind).
- Versuchen Sie während des ersten Hörens, sofort alle **Lösungen festzuhalten**, von deren Richtigkeit Sie überzeugt sind.
- Wenn Sie sich unsicher sind, dann halten Sie sich nicht lange mit einer Teilaufgabe auf. In der Regel sind die Aufgaben in der Reihenfolge angeordnet, in der auch die Lösungen im Text vorkommen. Sollten Sie sich also zu lange mit einer noch offenen Lücke beschäftigen, dann laufen Sie Gefahr, auch die nächste Lösung zu verpassen. **Markieren Sie** stattdessen **Aufgaben, bei denen Sie noch nicht ganz von Ihrer Antwort überzeugt sind**, mit Bleistift, damit Sie dort beim zweiten Durchgang ganz genau hinhören.
- Ist der erste Durchlauf beendet, gibt es eine kurze **Pause**, während der Sie Ihre Aufzeichnungen weiter **ergänzen** können.

Schritt 3 **Zweites Hören: Lösungen kontrollieren und vervollständigen**

Nun wird der Text ein zweites Mal vorgespielt.

- Sie haben jetzt die Gelegenheit, Ihre Lösungen aus dem ersten Durchgang noch einmal zu **kontrollieren**.
- Wenn Sie beim ersten Hören Informationen für eine Aufgabe verpasst haben, achten Sie jetzt besonders auf diese Stellen und **tragen Sie die Lösung(en) nach**.
- Auch nach dem zweiten Durchgang folgt meist eine kurze **Pause**. Nutzen Sie die Zeit, um Ihre **Lösungen** weiter zu **vervollständigen**. Sollten Sie die Antwort zu einer Aufgabe einmal gar nicht wissen, ist es besser, zu raten (etwa bei *multiple choice*- und *matching*-Aufgaben) als eine Aufgabe gar nicht zu bearbeiten. So besteht zumindest noch eine kleine Chance, einen Punkt zu bekommen.

Neben den Übungsaufgaben und Original-Prüfungen in diesem Buch können Sie Ihr Hörverstehen auch hervorragend mit den interaktiven Aufgaben im **Online-Training „Basic Language Skills"** trainieren. Das Training und alle Hördateien zu diesem Band stehen Ihnen auf der Plattform MyStark zur Verfügung (Zugangscode vgl. Umschlaginnenseite, ganz vorne im Buch).

Hörverstehen: Übungsset 1

Mit Schritt-für-Schritt-Anleitung

You will hear each recording twice. After each listening you will have time to complete your answers.

Task 1: Protecting the Climate

You will hear six people talking about climate change. Match each speaker (1 to 6) with one of the statements (A to G). There is one more statement than you need.

- **Before listening:** use the time before the recording starts to read through the statements below and underline the key words.
- **First listening:** if you are certain which statement goes with which speaker, write the letter in the table below. If you are not sure yet, write down the possible solution(s) in pencil first.
- **Second listening:** check your solutions and pay particular attention to those speakers where you haven't been sure yet which statement to choose. Don't just rely on the key words but also listen out for synonyms or paraphrases, and always take into consideration the context in which the terms are mentioned. In some cases, you can also find the correct solution by excluding statements that obviously don't fit a certain speaker *(Ausschlussverfahren).*

The speaker …

A believes that higher costs would make people change their habits concerning behaviour that is damaging to the environment.

B says politics will adopt measures to deal with the problem of climate change.

C is pointing the finger at individuals who refuse to bear responsibility for their actions.

D blames older generations and their blindness with regard to the future.

E wants politicians to take action but does not think the measures they take are sufficient.

F believes that everybody can do something to live a sustainable life.

G questions the impact an individual has and is against restricting people's freedom.

speaker	1	2	3	4	5	6
statement						

Task 2: Purple Door Coffee Shop: Changing lives one cup at a time

You will hear a recording about how a project is helping young homeless people in Denver. While listening, tick (✓) the correct answer (a, b or c). There is only one correct answer.

- **Before listening:** use the time before the recording starts to underline the key words and attune yourself to the topic.
- **First listening:** keep in mind that the tasks usually follow the order of the text. This helps you assess when the relevant passage might appear. If you miss an important passage or aren't sure which answer to choose, make a note next to the task with pencil.
- **Second listening:** check your answers and pay particular attention to the passages that you missed before.

1 The aim of the scheme is …

a ☐ to give homeless young people a job.
b ☐ to raise money to provide shelter for homeless young people.
c ☐ to give homeless young people a chance to change their lives.

2 The young people are found through …

a ☐ advertisements.
b ☐ suggestions by partner organisations.
c ☐ voluntary internships.

3 A big problem of young homeless people is that they …

a ☐ lack many basic life skills.
b ☐ often fight each other.
c ☐ do not eat healthily.

4 The coffee shop owners …

a ☐ provide an education for the young people.
b ☐ meet once a week to talk about their employees.
c ☐ help their employees to manage their lives.

5 What Kevin likes about working at the "Coffee Shop" is …

a ☐ gaining new ideas through the programme.
b ☐ the approach the owners adopt towards their employees.
c ☐ that employees can talk openly to the owners.

6 The owners feel that the best thing is seeing the people in the scheme …

a ☐ grow up.
b ☐ gain self-confidence.
c ☐ enjoy themselves.

Task 3: Teen Business Owner Creates Recipe for Success

You will hear a recording about a teenager who has started her own business. While listening, fill in the missing information. You need not write complete sentences. Unless otherwise specified, one aspect is enough. There is one example **(0)**.

- **Before listening:** begin by underlining key words and proper names in the task.
- **First listening:** the information that you need in order to fill the table will appear in the same order as in text. You only have to note down one aspect per line, except in tasks 3 to 5, where you are meant fill in two pieces of information. It is probably easiest to use the words from the text, but you may also use your own words.
- **Second listening:** check your answers and concentrate on passages you missed the first time round.

0	How Bree feels when baking:	innovative / creative / in another world
1	How her great-grandmother influenced Bree:	
2	What Bree's mother advised her daughter to do:	
3	What role Bree's mother has in the business today:	• •
4	What Leo Harrington thinks of Bree's work:	• •
5	What Bree has learnt through working in her bakery:	• •
6	What ingredient makes Bree's sweets special:	

Lösung

Transkript 1 Protecting the Climate

Speaker 1: For my generation – I'm 17 – climate change is a big issue. My friends and I have been to several demonstrations against man-made global warming. Politicians and lawmakers finally need a wake-up call to do more to protect the climate now. I mean, the older generations have lived at our expense! What about the future of the younger generations? We want to live on a planet that's still worth living in! I do hope we can make a difference and manage to change course.

Speaker 2: It worries me to see that the climate is changing at such a fast pace! In my opinion, individuals can do a great deal to contribute to protecting the climate and emitting less CO2, for example. I live in the city with my family – I'm a mother of two – so it's easy to do without a car – even with two little children. We use public transport, and when we go on holiday we take the train. You'd be surprised how far you can get by railway in Europe – and it can be much more comfortable than flying! We've also met a lot of lovely people on our train journeys – we're still in touch with some of them!

Speaker 3: I'm from the countryside and public transport there is dreadful. So I definitely need my car to get around. I don't know whether you can make a difference as an individual – it's the politicians who have to act. I asked the MP for my constituency to speak up for a regular bus connection to the nearest city, but nothing has been done. There's always a lack of funds. If the government increased its expenditure on rural infrastructure, the number of people who left their car in the garage would rise. That's for sure!

Speaker 4: In my opinion, both individuals and politicians need to act to slow or stop global warming. I only vote for parties that take global warming seriously and support legislation that gives incentives for environmentally friendly behaviour. And why isn't there a tax on jet fuel? If flying got more expensive, maybe fewer people would fly? I, for one, try to fly as little as possible – and what I also do is eat less meat. You know that the methane gas cattle emit contributes a great deal to global warming?

Speaker 5: I don't agree. What difference does it make if some people, say, avoid flying? Other people will take their places. And why should we cut back on our lifestyle? Don't I have the right to fly to Bali in winter when the weather is dreadful here? I can afford it and I just do it. Wouldn't it be unfair to less affluent people if the price of flying increased? They also have the right to fly to Majorca for their summer holidays, for example. And, by the way, if I feel like it, I also treat myself to a juicy steak. I can't make a difference anyway.

Speaker 6: I'm an MP from the south of England. I really understand that an increasing number of citizens are getting more and more impatient with politics as far as global warming is concerned. But I can assure people who are worried that the topic is high on my party's agenda. I know the legislative process can be lengthy and that compromises have to be made, but we're working hard on a ground-breaking legislative package. Both lawmakers and citizens should do their very best to tackle the pressing issue of global warming, however.

TIPP

These text passages will help you find the correct answer:

1 "I mean, the older generations have lived at our expense! What about the future of the younger generations?" (ll. 4/5)
In this case, the same keyword ("older generations") is used both in the task (statement D) and in the listening text.

2 "In my opinion, individuals can do a great deal to contribute to protecting the climate and emitting less CO_2, for example." (ll. 7–9)
Here, you might be tempted to choose statement C or G, as they both contain the keyword "individual(s)". However, neither of the two is correct. Statement C does not fit the text, because speaker 2 does not blame anyone. Statement G is wrong, because speaker 2 actually believes in the power of individuals to make a difference. Thus, statement F has to be correct: "Everybody" can be seen as a synonym of "individuals".

3 "it's the politicians who have to act. I asked the MP for my constituency [...], but nothing has been done. There's always a lack of funds." (ll. 17–19)
Speaker 3 mentions the terms "politicians", "MP" and "government", which indicates that either statement B or E could be correct. Now you have to take the context into consideration: Speaker 3 sounds disappointed with what politicians have done so far rather than optimistic about what they will do – thus, E is the right solution.

4 "And why isn't there a tax on jet fuel? If flying got more expensive, maybe fewer people would fly?" (ll. 25/26)
Here, statement A is correct. The phrase "more expensive" in the text corresponds to "higher costs"; "fewer people would fly" corresponds to "change their habit".

5 "What difference does it make if some people, say, avoid flying? Other people will take their places. And why should we cut back on our lifestyle?" (ll. 29–31)
The correct solution for speaker 5 has to be statement G. "[R]estricting people's freedom" corresponds to "cut back on our lifestyle" and the question "What difference does it make" corresponds to "questions the impact an individual has".

6 "But I can assure people who are worried that the topic is high on my party's agenda. [...] we're working hard on a ground-breaking legislative package." (ll. 38–41)
The word "party" indicates that the speaker is talking about "politics" and the expression "legislative package" corresponds to "measures" – thus, both B and E could be correct. Due to the speaker's positive view of politics (and because E has already been used for speaker 3), only statement B can be correct.

The speaker …

A believes that higher costs would make people change their habits concerning behaviour that is damaging to the environment.

B says politics will adopt measures to deal with the problem of climate change.

C is pointing the finger at individuals who refuse to bear responsibility for their actions.

D blames older generations and their blindness with regard to the future.

E wants politicians to take action but does not think the measures they take are sufficient.

F believes that everybody can do something to live a sustainable life.

G questions the impact an individual has and is against restricting people's freedom.

speaker	1	2	3	4	5	6
statement	D	F	E	A	G	B

Transkript 2 Purple Door Coffee Shop: Changing lives one cup at a time

Paula Vargas: Kevin Person had been homeless for a quarter of his life. Today, he works at this espresso bar and is transitioning into a home.

Kevin Person: The struggle to get a job even when you have a house nowadays, but when you don't have a house, trying to get a job is so much harder.

Paula Vargas: The mission of the Purple Door Coffee Shop goes beyond serving coffee. The owners want to turn lives around and for two years the non-profit has hired three to four young adults per year. They work with shelters like Urban Peak, where Kevin was staying, for recommendations on who to hire. Kim Easton, who runs Urban Peak, says the partnership is vital to this community.

Kim Easton: When someone has lived in chronic stress and trauma for as long as these young people have, everyday fighting for survival, they haven't had the opportunity nor the example of how to learn conflict management, how to manage money, how to cook a meal, how to pay their rent on time – nor do they understand even why that's important.

Paula Vargas: Purple Door co-founder, Madison Chandler, and her partner meet with each worker once a week. They discuss 52 topics ranging from mental health, finance, hygiene and customer service, and provide a life coaching tour; they will help their employees put their past behind them. But there are success stories.

Madison Chandler: Our very first guy that ever graduated from the programme; he's been working at an Auto Parts Warehouse since he left, which has been over a year now.

Paula Vargas: Kevin appreciates the chance to learn new skills. He says the programme is giving him things he never had.

Kevin Person: They seem to have the philosophy that they don't want to change us, they want to help us change ourselves and to have, like, a purpose and a goal that's, like, tangible.

Madison Chandler: The more rewarding things are watching somebody start to believe in themselves and to believe that they can achieve a life for themselves that they have dreamed of, or to believe that they are worth it.

Paula Vargas: As for Kevin, who turns 25 this month, living off the streets in a home and having a job will be the best gift he gives himself. For VOA news, Paula Vargas in Denver.

From: Paula Vargas, "Purple Door Coffee Shop: Changing Lives One Cup at a Time".
In: Voice of America News, *29 May 2015.*

TIPP

These text passages will help you find the correct answer:

1 "The mission of the Purple Door Coffee Shop goes beyond serving coffee. The owners want to turn lives around" (ll. 5/6)

2 "They work with shelters like Urban Peak, where Kevin was staying, for recommendations on who to hire." (ll. 7/8)

3 "they haven't had the opportunity nor the example of how to learn conflict management, how to manage money, how to cook a meal, how to pay their rent on time – nor do they understand even why that's important." (ll. 11–14)

4 "Purple Door co-founder, Madison Chandler, and her partner meet with each worker once a week. They discuss 52 topics ranging from mental health, finance, hygiene and customer service, and provide a life coaching tour; they will help their employees put their past behind them." (ll. 15–18)

5 "They seem to have the philosophy that they don't want to change us, they want to help us change ourselves and to have, like, a purpose and a goal that's, like, tangible." (ll. 24–26)

6 "The more rewarding things are watching somebody start to believe in themselves and to believe that they can achieve a life for themselves that they have dreamed of, or to believe that they are worth it." (ll. 27–29)

1 The aim of the scheme is …

c ☑ to give homeless young people a chance to change their lives.

2 The young people are found through …

b ☑ suggestions by partner organisations.

3 A big problem of young homeless people is that they …

a ☑ lack many basic life skills.

4 The coffee shop owners …

c ☑ help their employees to manage their lives.

5 What Kevin likes about working at the "Coffee Shop" is …

b ☑ the approach the owners adopt towards their employees.

6 The owners feel that the best thing is seeing the people in the scheme …

b ☑ gain self-confidence.

Transkript 3 Teen Business Owner Creates Recipe for Success

Faith Lapidus: For Bree Britt nothing is more enjoyable, soothing and fulfilling than working in the kitchen.

Bree Britt: I can be in the worst of moods and … once I get started baking it's just … something turns on where I'm just … in my whole … another world.

Faith Lapidus: Here she says she can be innovative and creative.

Bree Britt: I'd like to compare myself to an artist, sort of a painter for his canvas which … I'm the baker so, of course my cupcakes and cookies, and all my sweet desserts are my canvas. I think I'm going to do something with, maybe, a banana.

Faith Lapidus: Bree started cooking with her great-grandmother when she was five years old.

Lillie Walter (great-grandmother): Well, I've always tried to help them learn to cook.

Faith Lapidus: Bree perfected her great-grandmother's recipes and came up with her own. When she was 12, she told her mother she wanted to open a bakery.

Bree Britt: She told me to really think about, you know, the sacrifices and the things that I'll have to go through. You know … I wasn't going to be just a normal teenager … or a normal kid anymore. So, she told me to really think about it.

Charmaine Britt (Bree's mother): I thought it was going to be fly-by-night. Something that she just would get tired of eventually and once she saw how much work it would be. So my deal was we'll start online – the only way we can start making money is we'll do it online.

Faith Lapidus: It made enough money that Charmaine Britt became her daughter's business partner. They rented a shop and opened Bree's Sweet Treats. Charmaine runs the store during the day until Bree gets out of school.

Leo Harrington (customer): I guess it's going to be key lime today.

Faith Lapidus: Leo Harrington, a neighbouring barber shop owner, comes almost every day.

Leo Harrington: The flavour … she has all kind … a great assortment.

Faith Lapidus: He admires what Bree's accomplished.

Leo Harrington: I watch her diligence; school and then here – baking all evening, getting ready for the next day.

Faith Lapidus: It's challenging but Bree says studying and running a business taught her how to better manage her time.

Bree Britt: It has also taught me hard work and responsibility … and it has also taught me to be more aware of people and when they come into the store, more … friendlier, that I can say. It's … it's taught me a lot.

Faith Lapidus: Whether it's vanilla or chocolate, key lime or strawberry, there is a secret behind Bree's recipes.

Charmaine Britt: Her cupcakes are made … are flavoured with fresh fruits or more of the extracts, more so than of sugar.

Faith Lapidus: But sugar or not, Bree's treats are sweet enough to keep them coming back for more.

Customer: They're so pretty!

Faith Lapidus: For writer Faiza Elmasry, I'm Faith Lapidus, VOA news.

From: Faiza Elmasry, "Teen Business Owner Creates Recipe for Success."
In: Voice of America News, *17 April 2015.*

TIPP

These text passages will help you find the correct answer:

1 "I've always tried to help them learn to cook." (l. 11)

2 "She told me to really think about, you know, the sacrifices and the things that I'll have to go through. You know … I wasn't going to be just a normal teenager … or a normal kid anymore. So, she told me to really think about it." (ll. 14–16)

3 "It made enough money that Charmaine Britt became her daughter's business partner." (ll. 21/22); "Charmaine runs the store during the day until Bree gets out of school." (ll. 22/23)

4 "He admires what Bree's accomplished." (l. 28); "I watch her diligence; school and then here – baking all evening, getting ready for the next day." (ll. 29/30)

5 "Bree says studying and running a business taught her how to better manage her time." (ll. 31/32); "It has also taught me hard work and responsibility … and it has also taught me to be more aware of people and when they come into the store, more … friendlier, that I can say. It's … it's taught me a lot." (ll. 33–35)

6 "Her cupcakes are made … are flavoured with fresh fruits or more of the extracts, more so than of sugar." (ll. 38/39)

1 How her great-grandmother influenced Bree:	taught her to cook / taught Bree to bake / taught her great-granddaughter her recipes
2 What Bree's mother advised her daughter to do:	to think about the sacrifices / to really think about it
3 What role Bree's mother has in the business today:	• Bree's business partner • runs the store during the day
4 What Leo Harrington thinks of Bree's work:	• admires what she accomplished • admires her discipline / diligence
5 What Bree has learnt through working in her bakery:	• to better manage her time • hard work / (to take) responsibility / to be more aware of people / to be friendlier
6 What ingredient makes Bree's sweets special:	fresh fruits / flavoured with fresh fruits / the extract of fresh fruits

Hörverstehen: Übungsset 2
Niedersachsen Englisch

You will hear each recording twice. After each listening you will have time to complete your answers.

Task 1: Behavioural Economics

You will hear an interview with a young psychologist on how people tend to behave. While listening, fill in the missing information. You need not write complete sentences. Unless otherwise specified, one aspect is enough. There is one example (**0**).

0	What conflicts of interests are named at the beginning to attract the listener's attention:	• no activities to lose weight • postponing paying a parking fine
1	Why humans prefer short-term benefits to long-term ones:	• •
2	What areas of our life are influenced by short-term thinking:	• •
3	What is meant by "present buyer's preferences":	
4	What advantages older children have over younger ones according to the psychologist:	
5	What classical economics is about:	
6	What behavioural economics is about:	• •
7	What is meant by "time-inconsistent preferences":	

Task 2: Robotics

You will listen to two robotics experts talking about the potential for intelligent robots to transform society. While listening, tick (✓) the correct answer (a, b or c). There is only one correct answer.

1 The first expert, Alan Winfield, holds that …

- **a** ☐ autonomous robots will change the world of work.
- **b** ☐ intelligent robots are already doing a lot of important jobs.
- **c** ☐ the most important jobs are not yet done by intelligent robots.

2 The robot industry still struggles to …

- **a** ☐ provide better learning functions for toy robots.
- **b** ☐ create robots which are smart enough to make the right decisions.
- **c** ☐ invent more autonomous robots for the education sector.

3 The second expert, Adam Afriyie, believes that …

- **a** ☐ it is dangerous not to know what an intelligent robot is capable of.
- **b** ☐ the boundaries of what we allow intelligent robots to do need looking at.
- **c** ☐ intelligent robots will help old people a lot in the future.

4 In general, both experts warn that …

- **a** ☐ technological progress usually requires a long learning process.
- **b** ☐ robots might soon be able to outsmart their inventors.
- **c** ☐ researchers need to deal responsibly with technological possibilities.

Task 3: Renting a House or Apartment

You will hear four young people talking about renting a house or apartment. Match each speaker (1 to 4) with one of the statements (A to G). There are three more options than you need.

The speaker …

A was happy that they found a cheap, cosy apartment with a spacious garden and a big office.

B had a problem with the owner of the house and told him they were moving out.

C first thought they found their dream house, but now regrets the decision to move in.

D isn't renting yet and feels as if the situation will never improve.

E did something new by renting out a flat for holiday-makers.

F found a very caring landlord who put a lot of effort into making the apartment homelike before they moved in.

G moved back home in order to be able to afford the high costs of living.

speaker	1	2	3	4
statement				

Lösung

Transkript 1 Behavioural Economics

Chandy Nath: How many times have you not bothered to go to the gym even though you wanted to slim up in time for the summer holidays, or not paid a parking fine on time even though you knew that by putting it off you'd pay even more? The fact is that many of us are biased in favour of what we want in the short term rather than the long term. We're impatient. We want it now and we like quick wins; and this means that we don't always make decisions in our best interests.
My name's Chandy Nath from the Parliamentary Office of Science and Technology. In this podcast we'll be finding out how short-term thinking affects all aspects of modern life from our own health and well-being, right through to pensions and global warming. We'll be talking to economists, …

Daniel Read, Economist: People have what are called present buyer's preferences. They really focus on the pleasures and pains of the moment.

Chandy Nath: … neuroscientists, …

Trevor Robbins, Neuroscientist: The sub-cortical brain will grab the immediate opportunity without thinking …

Chandy Nath: … behavioural experts …

Theresa Marteau, Psychologist: Young children have much more difficulty deferring gratification than older children.

Chandy Nath: … about what makes us short-term thinkers. And whether there's anything we can do about it. We'll also be talking to Deputy Leader of the Liberal Democrats, Vince Cable MP, to find out why this subject interests policy makers.

Vince Cable: Economics is not a science and anybody who could bring new insights to bear would seem to me very much to the good.

Chandy Nath: To help me understand all this I'm going to talk to Laura Hayns, who's a PhD student in psychology at the University of Cambridge. Now Laura specialises in behavioural economics. Laura, do you want to start just by telling me what behavioural economics is?

Laura Hayns: Basically, behavioural economics integrates findings from psychology into classical economic theory.

Chandy Nath: How does it do that?

Laura Hayns: Well, classical economics is all about how ideal people in an ideal world make rational decisions. But there's a lot of evidence now that people are actually not always rational, and the ways in which we deviate from rationality are quite systematic. So, this is where behavioural economics comes in. How do real people in a real world make decisions and what are the biases that we have when processing information?

Chandy Nath: So, in practical terms, what does that mean? Can you give me an example?

Laura Hayns: Sure. So, for example, according to classical economists our preferences should be stable across time. So, say my long-term goal is to give up smoking. Classical economists would expect that my short-term goal would be not to smoke today. However, as any smoker knows, it's actually quite difficult to resist the temptation of a cigarette. And it turns out that contrary to classical economics, our preferences are what we call time-inconsistent, so they're not stable across time – they actually change. So, even though my New Year's resolution might be to give up smoking this year, chances are in the short term, so, even, disappointingly, on New Year's Day, I might actually prefer the immediate gratification of a cigarette. I think this pattern of decision-making comes into a lot of areas of our lives.

From: Chandy Nath/Laura Hayns, Parliamentary Recording Unit.
http://www.parliament.uk/audio/scienceinparliament/behaviouraleconomics/

TIPP

These text passages will help you find the correct answer:

1 "We're impatient. We want it now and we like quick wins" (l. 5)
2 "In this podcast we'll be finding out how short-term thinking affects all aspects of modern life from our own health and well-being, right through to pensions and global warming." (ll. 8–10)
3 "People have what are called present buyer's preferences. They really focus on the pleasures and pains of the moment." (ll. 11/12)
4 "Young children have much more difficulty deferring gratification than older children." (ll. 17/18)
5 "classical economics is all about how ideal people in an ideal world make rational decisions." (ll. 31/32)
6 "So, this is where behavioural economics comes in. How do real people in a real world make decisions and what are the biases that we have when processing information?" (ll. 34–36)
7 "And it turns out that contrary to classical economics, our preferences are what we call time-inconsistent, so they're not stable across time – they actually change." (ll. 43–45)

1 Why humans prefer short-term benefits to long-term ones:	• lack of patience • we like quick wins/want things now
2 What areas of our life are influenced by short-term thinking:	*Name two of the following:* • health/well-being • pensions • global warming
3 What is meant by "present buyer's preferences":	focus on pleasures/pains of the moment

4 What advantages older children have over younger ones according to the psychologist:	They are more patient./ They can defer gratifications.
5 What classical economics is about:	ideal people in an ideal world making rational decisions
6 What behavioural economics is about:	• real people in a real world making decisions • in how far people are prejudiced
7 What is meant by "time-inconsistent preferences":	preferences change over time

Transkript 2 Robotics

Alan Winfield: The new kind of robotics that really has not yet made a big impact in society but is on the verge, if you like … on the cusp of making a big impact is called intelligent robotics. So, intelligent robots unlike those old kind of robots that make cars. Intelligent robots are capable of deciding what to do next on their own. The word that we use is "autonomous". So, the … if you like, the autonomous robot industry is new. The best examples of autonomous robots are really, so far, are toys. So, for instance, you know the Sony Aibo, which was the pet robot dog – that was a very good example of an autonomous mobile robot. Of course, I've forgotten the biggest application of autonomous mobile robots, which is, of course, robot vacuum cleaners. Most of those robots that I've just described are not learning. The toy robots do have some learning functions. One of the reasons, of course, the toy robots can be more advanced is because the scope for things going wrong is smaller. In other words, the potential for it to do harm if it does the wrong thing is much smaller than if it's a robot that's driving your car, for instance. So, typically, we find that the more serious and safety-critical the application, then the less the intelligence or the learning. One of the big challenges that we face in the robotics research community is how to figure out how to make intelligence safe; and that's a problem that we haven't yet cracked. We're just beginning to solve that problem but my guess is it'll be another 10 or 20 years before we can really build intelligent robots that we can have good confidence … are both going to do the right thing and equally importantly, not do the wrong thing.

Chandy Nath: Alan Winfield pointed out that the autonomous robots we have today aren't really that bright. So, toy robot dogs, robot vacuum cleaners – but hopefully the technologies demonstrated at the reception which Lord Salisbury just referred to were at the forefront of current research. Now, we've heard how Lord Salisbury was particularly impressed by the robot arm; Adam Afriyie, was there anything at the reception that particularly caught your eye?

Adam Afriyie: What struck me most was actually – and what Alan raises there – which actually was the ethical debate around how far does one allow robots, these new technologies to make decisions? And one of the speakers pointed out that if, for example, you've got assistive living technologies and an iPad, for example, where an older person who needs some support – maybe they've got Alzheimer's … needs some reminders, needs some medical input – how far do we allow that to go before we say … actually people need human interaction. Now I'll pick one example which is actually that, in the computer industry, computer chips actually design the next generation of computer chips. And, in fact, most technologists will admit they actually don't know how these computer chips work anymore because the … other computers have designed them. So, we're already into this vein where actually we may require those laws of robotics that Asimov first came up with to be applied. […]

Chandy Nath, Parliamentary Recording Unit. http://www.parliament.uk/about/podcasts/scienceinparliament/robotics/

TIPP

The following clues will help you find the correct answer:

1 The first expert, Alan Winfield, talks about intelligent robots that are used today, such as toy robots and vacuum cleaners but also mentions that there is still a lot of research needed until more intelligent robots can be used (cf. ll. 1–10, 18–21).

2 Alan Winfield claims toy robots have "some learning functions" (l. 11) because they cannot do a lot of harm. Before autonomous robots can be used to drive cars, for example, their actions and reactions need to be a lot more reliable as far as safety is concerned (cf. ll. 12–21).

3 The second expert, Adam Afriyie, thinks that intelligent robots can already do more than the technicians that designed them can fully comprehend. But he does not see that as a threat in itself. He just points out that this is an issue that has to be taken into consideration (cf. ll. 34–39).

4 Both experts are convinced that scientists and researchers need to use what might already be possible from the technological point of view in a responsible way (cf. ll. 18–21, 28–30).

1 The first expert, Alan Winfield, holds that …

c ☑ the most important jobs are not yet done by intelligent robots.

2 The robot industry still struggles to …

b ☑ create robots which are smart enough to make the right decisions.

3 The second expert, Adam Afriyie, believes that …

b ☑ the boundaries of what we allow intelligent robots to do need looking at.

4 In general, both experts warn that …

c ☑ researchers need to deal responsibly with technological possibilities.

Transkript 3 Renting a House or Apartment

Speaker 1: We saw the ad in the summer, in about July, I think, but we weren't really serious about moving then so we didn't even go and see it. It wasn't until November when they re-advertised it that we got in touch with the agency and had a look. They'd put the price down since the summer too, I suppose because it had been empty so long, so that made it more affordable for us which helped us make up our minds. It was perfect – a bigger garden for the kids and enough space for an office. In winter it was lovely, very cosy, in fact, which is important to me as I really feel the cold, whereas my husband will open a window when it's minus temperatures outside! Anyway, in July when summer really started and we had that heatwave, we understood why no one had wanted to rent it over summer. It was boiling! All those lovely big windows that made the flat so light and open were like a greenhouse as soon as it got warmer. From about 8 in the morning until 7 in the evening, it was like living in a sauna! We couldn't stand being at home, and weekends were especially bad. No air conditioning, of course. If only we'd gone to see it when it was first advertised in July, we'd never have moved in!

Speaker 2: I always rent apartments when I go on holiday, rather than staying in hotels. Hotels are so impersonal, aren't they? This way you get to feel like you really live in the place you're visiting. It's the first time I've done it the other way round, though, and rented out my place … but it seemed like a good way of making some extra money. The website is really easy to use and they only charge five per cent commission, which is lower than a lot of the other holiday rental sites. It's all about the photos and the reviews. Get the photos right and the place can look really upmarket and spacious, but you don't want to make it look too much better than it really is or you end up with a bad review. It's better to undersell and overdeliver so guests are pleasantly surprised and leave an extra positive review. So far, I'm averaging three stars because of one bad review that brought my average down from four and a half stars, but hopefully I'll get it back up during the busy season.

Speaker 3: Buying a house seems so far out of my reach it's almost impossible, as it is for loads of people my age these days. My parents always told me renting was throwing money away, but it was different in their day. Then people could afford to buy a house on a normal salary, but nowadays house prices are so high and no bank will look at you unless you've got a huge deposit. The problem with my dream of buying is that it's never going to come true. Not unless my parents help me out, but I've got two sisters and we're all in the same position. At least they've both got good jobs. Not good enough to buy a house, but at least they can afford to rent places of their own in nice areas. I just don't earn enough to rent around here. Even if I get promoted to manager, it'll be tough to find somewhere unless I share, and call me fussy, but there aren't that many people I want to share a bathroom and kitchen with. Some days I think I'll be stuck living with my parents forever – even renting is like a dream to me.

Speaker 4: At first our landlord was really helpful, couldn't do enough for us. You hear stories of nightmare landlords and we felt like we were really lucky, or so we thought anyway. He redecorated the whole place, from top to bottom, and let us keep all the bills in his name so we didn't have the bother of contacting all the companies ourselves. He even offered to come round and do the gardening as he knew we both worked long hours and might not have time. That's where the problems started now I look back. Then he'd pop round 'just to check everything's OK for you' once a month, then twice a month. Soon he was coming every week with some excuse or other. In the beginning we'd invite him in for tea, but it was only encouraging him, so when we realised, we'd try to have the conversation on the doorstep instead. It got so bad we pretended to be on our way out if we saw him coming up the path. We'd grab our coats and walk round the block until he'd gone. I don't know if he was just lonely or just didn't trust us not to ruin his precious house. In the end we gave our notice and found somewhere else. It's a shame because we really loved that house, but at least it's more peaceful in the new place.

Adapted from: British Council, https://learnenglish.britishcouncil.org/skills/listening/advanced-c1/renting-a-house

TIPP

These text passages will help you find the correct answer:

1 "It was perfect" (l. 6), "If only we'd gone to see it when it was first advertised in July, <u>we'd never have moved in</u>!" (ll. 14/15)
The speaker first mentions her positive impression of the flat (e. g. "bigger garden", "enough space", "cosy"), which could hint at statement A, but later she clearly points out that they "couldn't stand being at home".

2 "It's the first time I've done it the other way round, though, and <u>rented out my place</u> …" (ll. 18/19) Here, the mentioning of "renting out" is the key to the correct solution.

3 "Some days I think I'll be stuck living with my parents forever – <u>even renting is like a dream to me</u>." (ll. 39/40)
The speaker still seems to live with her parents ("stuck living with my parents") and does not mention moving back in with them (as in statement G). Moreover, she is not talking about the high costs of living in general (as mentioned in statement G), but about high rents and the impossibility of buying a house.

4 "In the end <u>we gave our notice</u> and found somewhere else." (l. 54) Although the speaker talks about a caring landlord, which could point towards sentence F, he later talks about "problems" and that "it got so bad".

speaker	1	2	3	4
statement	C	E	D	B

Sprachmittlung

Aufbau des Prüfungsteils „Sprachmittlung“

In der Abiturprüfung werden Ihnen **ein oder mehrere Ausgangstexte auf Deutsch** vorgelegt. Ihre Aufgabe besteht darin, den Inhalt des Texts bzw. der Texte **auf Englisch zusammenzufassen**. Eine Sprachmittlung ist also keine wörtliche Übersetzung – vielmehr sollen Sie die Kernaussagen eines Texts **sinngemäß** in die andere Sprache übertragen. In der Regel ist die Aufgabenstellung in einen **Kontext** eingebettet, d. h., es ist genau vorgegeben, für wen, zu welchem Anlass und in welchem Textformat Sie den deutschen Text zusammenfassen sollen. Wichtig beim Verfassen einer Sprachmittlung ist also nicht nur, dass Sie alle inhaltlich relevanten Aspekte in die Fremdsprache übertragen, sondern dass Ihre Lösung genau an die Situation und den Adressatenkreis angepasst ist.
Für die Bearbeitung der Sprachmittlungsaufgabe haben Sie **60 Minuten** Zeit.

Vorgehen in der Prüfung

Lesen Sie sich zunächst die Aufgabenstellung und den Ausgangstext (bzw. die Ausgangstexte) einmal ganz durch, um sich einen **groben Überblick** über den Inhalt zu verschaffen. Gehen Sie dann folgendermaßen vor:

Schritt 1 Aufgabenstellung genau lesen

Analysieren Sie die Aufgabenstellung in Hinblick auf die folgenden Aspekte:

- In welcher Form sollen Sie den Text wiedergeben (**Textsorte**)? Damit sind in der Regel bereits bestimmte formale Vorgaben verbunden. Bei einer E-Mail müssen Sie beispielsweise eine passende Anrede- und Schlussformel verwenden, ein Artikel weist immer eine Überschrift auf usw.
- Für wen sollen Sie den Text zusammenfassen (**Zielgruppe/Adressat*in**)? Das hat u. a. Auswirkungen auf den Sprachstil, den Sie verwenden.

- In der Regel enthält die Aufgabenstellung einen sogenannten **Operator**. Dabei handelt es sich um ein Aufforderungsverb, an das bestimmte formale Vorgaben geknüpft sind. Bei den Operatoren „sum up" oder „outline" etwa sollen Sie knapp und präzise die Kernaussagen bzw. wesentlichen Aspekte wiedergeben. Manchmal sind auch mehrere Operatoren miteinander kombiniert – dann müssen Sie die Vorgaben jedes einzelnen Operators berücksichtigen.

Operator	Dos and Don'ts	Beispiel
write [+ text type]	textsortenspezifische Vorgaben beachten (siehe Tabelle auf der folgenden Seite)	*[…] Using the information from the text,* ***write an article*** *for the English project website in which you present the drawbacks of digital language assistants such as Alexa. (ÜA 2)*
sum up / summarise / outline / present	• die wichtigsten Aspekte knapp und präzise zusammenfassen • ggf. kulturspezifische Aspekte erklären	*[…] Using the information from the text, write an article for the English project website in which you* ***present*** *the drawbacks of digital language assistants such as Alexa. (ÜA 2)*
explain	• Zusammenhänge darlegen • ggf. kulturbezogene Unterschiede miteinbeziehen	*[…] write an e-mail to your friend in which you* ***explain*** *why campervan holidays have become increasingly popular.*

- Manchmal müssen Sie nicht den Text als Ganzes zusammenfassen, sondern sollen sich nur auf bestimmte Teilaspekte fokussieren (beispielsweise die Nachteile bestimmter Entwicklungen). Achten Sie also genau auf den **inhaltlichen Fokus** der Aufgabenstellung.

Schritt 2 Schlüsselstellen markieren und Notizen machen

Lesen Sie sich nun den Ausgangstext noch einmal aufmerksam durch und markieren Sie sich die für die Aufgabenstellung relevanten Textstellen. Machen Sie sich neben den Stellen Notizen (idealerweise bereits auf Englisch).

Schritt 3 Notizen strukturieren

Gehen Sie Ihre Notizen noch einmal durch und bringen Sie sie in eine logische Reihenfolge – beispielsweise, indem Sie sie nummerieren. Fertigen Sie anschließend aus Ihren Notizen und den Überlegungen zur geforderten Textsorte eine Grobgliederung an.

Schritt 4 Lösung ausformulieren

Formulieren Sie Ihre Lösung anhand der Grobgliederung aus. Ihr Text sollte dabei deutlich kürzer sein als der Ausgangstext. Führen Sie sich noch einmal vor Augen, welche Zieltextsorte gefordert ist und welche formalen und sprachlichen Aspekte es dabei zu beachten gilt. Eine Übersicht über die Merkmale der häufigsten Zieltextsorten finden Sie in der folgenden Tabelle.
Denken Sie außerdem daran, ggf. **kulturspezifische Ausdrücke und Phänomene**, die einer englischsprachigen Person vielleicht nicht geläufig sind, zu **erklären**. Das können Begriffe aus der deutschen Medienlandschaft sein (z. B. „… *Tatort*, a very popular TV crime series“), technische Termini (z. B. „… cars have to pass the *TÜV* – an inspection to ensure that they meet the safety requirements“) usw. Auch dieser Aspekt – also Ihre Fähigkeit, zwischen Kulturen zu vermitteln und verbale Brücken zu bauen – fließt in die Bewertung der Sprachmittlung mit ein.

Textsorte	Aufbau	Sprachstil
Artikel	• Überschrift • Einleitung mit Hinführung zum Thema • klar gegliederter Hauptteil (z. B. Vor- und Nachteile, Chancen und Risiken)	• neutrales Register • bei jugendlicher Zielgruppe nicht zu förmlich
E-Mail	• passende Anrede • Einleitung mit Bezugnahme zum Kontext • klar gegliederter Hauptteil • evtl. abschließender Satz mit Bezugnahme zum Kontext • Schlussformel und Name	• formelle E-Mails: sachlich-nüchtern; meist Verwendung von Langformen • persönliche E-Mails: umgangssprachlich; Verwendung von Kurzformen
Blogeintrag	• Überschrift (+ ggf. mehrere Zwischenüberschriften) • Anrede der Leserschaft mit Bezugnahme zum Kontext/Anlass des Schreibens • klar gegliederter Hauptteil • kurze Abrundung (z. B. mit Aufforderung zum Kommentieren o. Ä.)	• oft eher umgangssprachlich; bei Blogs von Organisationen o. Ä. etwas sachlicher • häufig Verwendung der 1. Person Singular („I“) • meist direkte Anrede der Leserschaft („you“)

Auf der folgenden Seite finden Sie eine Liste mit hilfreichen Wendungen für die Sprachmittlungsaufgabe. Weitere Formulierungshilfen enthalten übrigens die digitalen „**MindCards**“.

Wenn Sie mit dem Formulieren Ihrer Lösung fertig sind, lesen Sie sich Ihren Text noch einmal in Ruhe durch und verbessern Sie Rechtschreib- und Grammatikfehler.

Hilfreiche Wendungen – Strukturieren eines Artikels / Blogeintrags etc.

Aspekte aufzählen	*First of all, ... / To begin with, ...* *Firstly, ... Secondly, ... Thirdly, ...* *In addition, ... / Moreover, ... / Furthermore, ...* *Finally, ... / Lastly, ... / To conclude, ...*
Gründe angeben	*As ... / Since ...* *... because ...* *Due to ...*
Folgen aufzeigen	*Thus, ... / Therefore, ...* *As a result, ... / As a consequence, ...*
zusammenfassen	*To conclude, ... / To sum up, ... / All in all, ...*

Hilfreiche Wendungen – E-Mails

formelle E-Mail	Anrede und Schluss, wenn man die Ansprechperson nicht kennt: *Dear Sir or Madam,* *[...]* *Yours faithfully,* *[first and last name]* Anrede und Schluss, wenn man die Ansprechperson kennt: *Dear Mr Smith, / Dear Mrs Smith, / Dear Ms Smith,* *[...]* *Yours sincerely,* *[first and last name]*
persönliche E-Mail	Anrede und Schluss: *Dear Sam, / Hi Sam, / Hello Sam,* *[...]* *Yours, / Take care, / All the best, / Hugs,* *[first name]*

Hilfreiche Wendungen – Blogeintrag

die Leserschaft einbeziehen	*Did you know ...? / Have you ever ...? / Would you ...?*
um Kommentare bitten	*Tell us about your experiences in the comment section.* *Please leave a comment below and let me know what you think.* *I'd love to hear what you think about this topic. Please leave a comment below.*

Sprachmittlung: Übungsaufgabe 1

Mit Schritt-für-Schritt-Anleitung

Aufgabenstellung

Your English friend Jake is planning to spend a year abroad in Recife, a town in the northeast of Brasil. He has heard that flying kites is a very popular pastime in Brasil, and is looking forward to trying it out himself. You have read the following two articles about this sport. You think it is interesting, but are also a bit worried about your friend.

Write an e-mail to your friend, outlining the main features of kite flying as well as its positive and problematic aspects.

Text 1 **Kampf der Drachenläufer**

In Brasilien beginnt die Hochsaison für ein seltsames Hobby

Sommerferien in Brasilien. Hochsaison der Drachenläufer, der kleinen und der großen. Die einen stehen auf einer freien Wiese, andere lassen ihre Drachen hoch oben über den Dächern der Favelas steigen. Wo man hinsieht, flattern bunte Papierdrachen am Himmel. Meiner ist aus verblasstem, rotem Seidenpapier mit einem lilafarbenen Totenkopf drauf. Er hängt im Schrank, und ich traue mich nicht, ihn endlich mal steigen zu lassen, weil ich mir sicher bin, nach ein paar Minuten wäre er weg.

Auf Anfänger wie mich nehmen die Profis an den Drachen nämlich keine Rücksicht. Sie kappen alles, was an einer Schnur durch die Luft weht [...].

Noch ein Grund, warum ich meinen Drachen erst gar nicht startklar machen muss: Das Drachen-Steigen-Lassen ist in Brasilien in fester Männerhand. Frauen und Mädchen sieht man selten inmitten der begeisterten Drachenläufer. Das Ziel ist einfach, jedenfalls beim Wettstreit mit den Drachen: Je mehr Exemplare eines anderen Teams gekappt und eingesammelt werden können, desto besser. Dafür werden die Drachenschnüre sogar ordentlich frisiert. Sie werden durch eine klebrige Masse gezogen, das so genannte Cerol. Es ist eine Mischung aus Leim, Zahnpasta und vielen fein gemahlenen Glassplittern. Danach schneidet so eine Drachenschnur wie ein Messer. Nicht selten liest man in brasilianischen Zeitungen von Unfällen mit den fast kaum zu erkennenden Schnüren, die über hunderte Meter auch Straßen kreuzen. Motorräder haben in Brasilien extra eine Art Antenne am Lenker, die die Drachenschnüre durchtrennen, bevor sie den Motorradfahrer verletzen.

Doch nicht immer dienen die Papierflieger nur dem Vergnügen. Eben weil sie so ein gewohntes und unauffälliges Bild am brasilianischen Himmel sind, haben die Drogengangs früh begonnen, sie für ihre Zwecke zu nutzen. Die Drachen werden teilweise als Kommunikationssystem genutzt, mit dem sich Drogenhändler untereinander verständigen. Drachen kündigen die Ankunft einer neuen Ladung Kokain an, warnen vor der Polizei oder melden Fremde in der Favela. Wer die Zeichen der Papierdrachen zu deuten weiß, ist schneller und sicherer informiert als mit jedem Funkspruch.

Dass das Drachenstiegen vor allem bei den unteren Einkommensklassen so populär ist, hat seinen Grund: Neben dem hohen Spaß- und Wettkampffaktor ist das Hobby mit den Papierdrachen sehr kostengünstig. Für zwei Euro bekommt man die komplette Ausrüstung mit Schnur und Drachen. Hunderttausende gehen pro Saison über die Ladentheken der kleinen Geschäfte. [...]

Der starke Küstenwind in Rio de Janeiro und die schnellen Manöver mit den Drachen verlangen jedem Mitspieler vollen Einsatz ab, und das heißt, fest zupacken, auch wenn die Schnur voller Glassplitter ist. Gelingt es, einen gegnerischen Drachen zu kappen, muss auch noch einer aus dem Team hinterherhetzen und ihn einsammeln. Wenn es dabei über Gräben, Mauern und Flüsse geht – Pech gehabt, da muss ein echter Drachenläufer durch. [...]

Quelle: Solveig Flörke, „Kampf der Drachenläufer", in: DIE WELT, *Springer A. Berlin. http://www.welt.de/print/die_welt/sport/article123940300/Kampf-der-Drachenlaeufer.html*

Text 2 Drachen für alle

Für den normalen Touristen gibt es in Brasilien viel zu sehen. Diejenigen von ihnen, die mehr über die brasilianische Kultur herausfinden wollen und sich nicht mit den ausgetretenen Pfaden zufriedengeben, können besonders viel entdecken. Dies gilt im speziellen für den Bereich der Jugendkulturen. Eine sehr beliebte Freizeitbeschäftigung für Kinder und Jugendliche ist Drachen steigen lassen. Gerade bei gutem Wetter kann man sehr viele Drachen, auf Portugiesisch Papagaios oder Pipas, über brasilianischen Vorstädten fliegen sehen. [...]

Überall auf der Welt lassen Kinder Drachen steigen, aber in Brasilien machen dies besonders viele. Weiterhin die Frage nach dem wieso? Es ist sicherlich ein billiges Vergnügen und kann somit von vielen Kindern ausgeübt werden. Es mag auch des Menschen Streben nach dem Unmöglichen, einem vogelgleichen Fliegen ausdrücken. Für manchen kann es die Verbindung der Erde oder des selbst zu etwas im Himmel oder dahinter darstellen. All dies oder nichts davon mag es sein, aber es gibt weitere Erklärungsversuche. Wenn brasilianische Großstädte aus der Fernsicht von Google Earth betrachtet werden, ist unschwer zu erkennen, dass sie sehr zugebaut sind, viel mehr als vergleichbare westliche Großstädte. Beispielsweise hat Sao Paulo weniger als ein Prozent Grüngebiete. Da bleibt für Kinder nicht viel zu entdecken. Der einzige Freiraum, der noch bleibt, ist der Raum über ihren Köpfen. Diesen erobern sie sich mit ihren Pipas. [...]

Quelle: Peter Michalski. Artikel: „Claiming the Sky", in: Graffiti Magazine, *S. 4–8, https://issuu.com/graffiti-magazine/docs/graffiti-magazine6*

1 Analyse the task. What do the text form, addressee, command term ("operator"), and focus mean in terms of the structure or language of your mediation? Write your notes in the grid below.

Write an <u>e-mail</u> to your <u>friend</u>, <u>outlining</u> the <u>main features of this pastime</u>, its <u>positive</u> and <u>problematic aspects</u>.

text form: e-mail	**target group/ addressee: friend**	**"operator": outline**	**focus: main features, positive and negative aspects**
⇩	⇩	⇩	⇩

2 Read the texts again carefully, highlight relevant passages and take notes. You may want to use different colours or symbols such as "~" for general information on flying kites, "+" for positive aspects and "–" for problematic aspects.

3 Use your notes from tasks 1 and 2 and sort them to get a rough structure for your e-mail.

4 Use your rough structure and write your e-mail in complete sentences.

Lösungsvorschlag

1 **TIPP**

If you are having difficulties, read the information in the introductory chapter again ("Vorgehen in der Prüfung").

text form: e-mail	**target group/ addressee: friend**	**"operator": outline**	**focus: main features, positive and negative aspects**
⇩	⇩	⇩	⇩
proper address and salutation; reference to year abroad, worries	friendly, informal tone	short/concise, no unnecessary details, no quotations	main body could be divided into three parts

2+3 **TIPP**

The example answer also contains line references, so that you can compare them with the passages you highlighted in task 2.

Hi Jake,	address
Happy to hear about year abroad/interest in flying kites; bit worried	introduction
~ kites called "pipas" or "pagagaios" (T 2, l. 6)	main features of flying kites
~ mainly done by men/boys (T 1, ll. 10/11)	
+ cheap (T 1, ll. 29–31; T 2, ll. 9/10)	positive aspects
+ not much space left in cities → claim sky (T 2, ll. 14–19)	
+ feeling like flying (T 2, ll. 10–13)	
– very competitive: aim to cut strings/collect trophies (T 1, ll. 7/8, ll. 11–14)	problematic aspects
– strings prepared with glass, very sharp, invisible → often accidents (T 1, ll. 14–20)	
– used as a means of communication by drug dealers (T 1, ll. 22–27)	
Sure about it? Please take care!	conclusion
Hugs,	salutation
Kristin	name

4 **TIPP**

Your rough structure is meant to guide you through the process of writing. You may want to re-read some passages in the texts if you are not sure how to express a certain aspect.
Remember that you are writing to a friend. Your language should thus be rather informal and you can also use short forms. Don't forget that you are meant to express worries about your friend's decision to try out kite flying. In the end, go through your e-mail again, check it for spelling or grammar mistakes and correct them.

Hi Jake, **address**

It was very exciting to hear about your plans for your year abroad in Recife. Your enthusiasm about becoming a "pipa guy" was contagious and so I informed myself about this interesting hobby. What I read left me a bit worried, so I'd like to give you some information I've found in two German newspaper articles. **introduction:** reference to year abroad, interest in kite flying, worries

In summer, the Brazilian sky is full of kites, also called pipas or papagaios. Mainly men or boys, particularly the youngsters from poor areas, are into pipas. **main part:** main features

It's a cheap hobby so everyone can afford it. Furthermore, there's not much natural space left to explore for poor kids in Brazilian cities and that's why they claim the sky. You might even feel like a part of the elements, or flying yourself, when using the kite. positive aspects

Still, for some people, it's the competitive factor they like best: This means cutting the strings of as many other kites as possible and collecting the trophies. And this is where my concerns come in. The competitors take flying kites too seriously: they are ruthless and strengthen their strings by gluing bits of broken glass to them so that they're razor-sharp! I think it's awful that non-participants are exposed to the nearly invisible strings, which frequently cause accidents in the streets. Besides, I really dislike the thought that drug dealers also use kites as a quick and efficient means of communication. problematic aspects

Are you sure this is the right hobby for you? I wish you'd think it over again – at least take care, please. **conclusion:** worries

Hugs, **salutation**

Kristin **name**

Sprachmittlung: Übungsaufgabe 2

Niedersachsen Englisch

Aufgabenstellung

You are taking part in an international youth project on "The Impact of Digitisation and AI".
Using the information from the text, write an article for the English project website in which you present the drawbacks of digital language assistants such as Alexa.

Text

Experten warnen vor Sprachassistenten: Diese Risiken birgt Alexa für Kinder

Minderjährige geben Alexa, Siri und ähnlichen Sprachassistenten zu viel von sich preis, zeigt ein Gutachten. Auch Datenschützer äußern Kritik.

Ein Junge, sechs Jahre alt, wünscht sich ein Kinderlied, ruft „play Digger, Digger" ins Mikrofon. Und was tut Amazons Sprachassistentin „Alexa"? Sie schlägt ihm verschiedene Porno-Titel vor. Diese Geschichte ist nicht die einzige Panne vergangener Jahre, die Eltern schockiert. Zu sehen auf Youtube. Jetzt warnt sogar der Wissenschaftliche Dienst des Bundestags.

In einem Gutachten wird bemängelt, dass Kinder und Jugendliche persönliche Informationen von sich preisgeben oder eben Inhalte abrufen können, die sie nicht hören sollten. Außerdem stelle sich die Frage, was eigentlich mit Besuchern sei, die nicht wüssten, dass die Software gerade ihre Sätze aufzeichnet. Amazon dürfte der Pflicht zur Informationsvermittlung bei der Datenerhebung von Nutzern zwar ausreichend nachkommen, heißt es – „offen bleibt jedoch, wie unbeteiligte Dritte und Minderjährige von der Datensammlung ausgeschlossen werden können".

Mit Blick auf die USA sei außerdem unklar, „zu welchen weiteren Zwecken Amazon seine Daten zukünftig nutzen könnte". Dass sich Kriminelle Zugriff zu den Daten in der Cloud verschaffen könnten, sei ebenfalls nicht auszuschließen.

Eine Reihe von Kritikpunkten. Das Bundesinnenministerium fühlt sich in der Sache aber nicht zuständig. Ein Sprecher erklärte auf Anfrage der Deutschen Presse-Agentur: „Die Nutzung der Sprachassistenten betrifft Datenverarbeitungen durch nichtöffentliche Stellen." Für diese lasse die Datenschutz-Grundverordnung der EU den nationalen Gesetzgebern so gut wie keinen Regelungsspielraum.

„Wir müssen darauf dringen, dass die Einwilligungserklärung für den Nutzer auf die Gefahren und Möglichkeiten hinweist, die mit der Übertragung und Nutzung der Daten sowie der Daten von Dritten, die sich zufällig im Raum befinden, hinweist", meint hingegen der fraktionslose Bundestagsabgeordnete Uwe Kamann. Dies müsse detailliert erfolgen, „und nicht indem man nur einmal ein Häkchen für alles setzt".

Kamann war es, der die Frage aufgeworfen hatte, ob es zulässig ist, dass Amazon die Spracheingaben der „Alexa"-Nutzer auswertet. [...]

Der Hamburgische Datenschutzbeauftragte Johannes Caspar ist ebenfalls empört. Er teile die Befürchtungen des Wissenschaftlichen Dienstes des Bundestags. Probleme würden sich „aus der hohen Zahl von Fehlaktivierungen bei automatischen Sprachassistenten" ergeben.

Diese führten dazu, dass Gespräche immer wieder übertragen werden, weil das System das Aktivierungswort fälschlicherweise verstehe. „Von diesen Datenerhebungen sind ausnahmslos alle Personen im Haushalt betroffen, ohne dass die relevanten rechtlichen Vorgaben vorliegen dürften", sagte Caspar zu Tagesspiegel Background Digitalisierung & KI.

Insbesondere dürften „Kinder kaum einwilligungsfähig sein". Ein weiteres Problem ist aus seiner Sicht „die fehlende Zugriffskontrolle durch eine personalisierte Steuerung, mit der eine Nutzung des Sprachsystems durch dritte unbefugte Personen verhindert werden könnte".

Amazon bietet den Nutzern zwar neuerdings mit dem Befehl „Alexa, lerne meine Stimme" die Möglichkeit, ein persönliches Stimmprofil einzurichten. Diese werden nach Angaben eines Amazon-Sprechers aber nur genutzt, „um das individuelle Nutzererlebnis zu verbessern". Auf den Befehl „Computer, spiele Musik!" hin würden für verschiedene Profile unterschiedliche Titel abgespielt. Das Gerät für Kinder zu sperren, erlaubt die neue Stimmerkennung nicht. [...]

Der Sprachassistent wird nicht zum ersten Mal als Übel für Kinder angesehen. Im vergangenen Jahr veröffentlichte die britische Childwise Agency eine Untersuchung mit dem Ergebnis: Da Alexa Anweisungen ohne Wörter wie „bitte" oder „danke" ausführt, fürchten Experten, dass Kinder zu unhöflichen Wesen heranwachsen, die bloß noch befehlen.

Alexa, lies mir eine Gute-Nacht-Geschichte vor! Alexa, ich will ...! Im April 2018 brachte Amazon tatsächlich eine Version für Kinder auf den Markt. Diese formuliert ihre Antworten kindgerechter, sagt der Hersteller. Außerdem bekamen Kinder ein Lob, wenn sie bitten und sich bedanken.

Ein anderes Alexa-Problem untersucht nun die Otto-von-Guericke-Universität Magdeburg. Nicht einmal jede vierte KI-Fachkraft sei eine Frau. Daraus ergebe sich die Frage, ob sich dies auch in Denkmustern bei der Künstlichen Intelligenz widerspiegele. Die Unesco hatte bemängelt, dass Siri und Alexa Gender-Stereotype reproduzieren.

Demnach seien sie unterwürfig, gehorsam und stets freundlich. Vor dem Hintergrund, dass Kinder mit der Technologie aufwüchsen und Sprache ein Geschlechtsmarker sei, bestehe die Gefahr, dass bestimmte Vorstellungen von Frauen transportiert würden – als dienende Maschinen.

Quelle: Sonja Álvarez, Marie Rövekamp: „Experten warnen vor Sprachassistenten – Diese Risiken birgt Alexa für Kinder", Tagesspiegel *vom 09. 07. 2019, https://www.tagesspiegel.de/wirtschaft/experten-warnen-vor-sprachassistenten-diese-risiken-birgt-alexa-fuer-kinder/24573516.html*

Lösungsvorschlag

TIPP

To solve the task, you should start by analysing the assignment in order to find out which formal requirements your solution must fulfil and which aspects you have to focus on:

- text form: article → interesting heading, several well-structured paragraphs
- target group: participants of an international youth project
  → style: should show expertise, but not be overtly formal
- "operator": "present" → give a concise account of the main aspects
- focus: disadvantages and problems mentioned in connection with Alexa, Siri and other digital language assistants

The following aspects could come up in your solution:

- two main points of criticism: data protection issues and dangers Alexa and other similar devices might pose to children
- child protection and educational issues:
  - children could be presented with inappropriate content (cf. ll. 1–3, 7/8)
  - children's data are saved and used without them giving their consent (cf. ll. 6/7, 11/12, 37, 45/46)
  - children learn that commands yield the desired results → their language becomes impolite (cf. ll. 49–51)
  - children learn gender stereotypes because language assistants have female names and reproduce an image of women as obedient servants (cf. ll. 59–64)
- data protection issues in general:
  - indiscriminate recording of everyone (with or without explicit permission), especially because activation of technologies is prone to errors (cf. ll. 8–12, 32–35)
  - insecurity as to what happens with the recorded data (cf. ll. 13–15)
  - lack of legal data protection framework in Germany for private commercial providers (cf. ll. 16–20)

Is Alexa a danger for children as well as for data security?	**heading**
In many German households, digital language assistants like Siri or Alexa have become a part of everyday life. While they might make some tasks easier, some experts also regard them with growing suspicion.	**introduction**
One of the most pressing issues is data protection. A voice assistant records thousands of pieces of information and so far there are no clear-cut rules as to what happens with these. Criminals potentially accessing the data are only the tip of the iceberg. With a private company involved in the data collection, many of Alexa's potentially unauthorised uses are not even considered in European data protection laws.	**data protection issues:** no legal framework, potentially criminal uses of data
Voice assistants do not limit their data collection to those who have explicitly given their permission. Instead, as soon as the assistant is activated – a process that despite experiments with voice recognition is still prone to errors –, everyone in the vicinity is recorded indiscriminately.	lack of consent of those being recorded
This is especially relevant in connection with child protection laws. Children cannot be considered to have given their permission to be recorded. Additionally, Alexa might inadvertently provide them with content that is inappropriate for their age.	**child protection and educational issues:** no consent, inappropriate content
There are further concerns when it comes to Alexa's educational side effects: Alexa does what you want her to do without being asked politely. This might lead to children becoming used to a commanding and impolite language.	communicating by giving commands
Secondly, Alexa, Siri and co. could reproduce harmful gender stereotypes: with their female names and their obedient behaviour, they could convey an image of women as docile servants.	gender stereotypes
Thus, for all her alleged progressiveness and user-friendliness, Alexa might also be a danger lurking in your living room.	**conclusion**

Textaufgabe

Aufbau des Prüfungsteils „Textaufgabe“

In der Abiturprüfung werden Ihnen **zwei Textaufgaben zur Auswahl** gestellt. Als Prüfungstexte kommen sowohl **Sach- als auch literarische Texte** infrage (Umfang: maximal 1 000 Wörter), die theoretisch durch weitere Materialien (etwa einen Cartoon oder eine Statistik) ergänzt werden können. Die Texte werden Ihnen in der Prüfung erstmals vorgelegt, d. h., sie entstammen nicht den Unterrichtslektüren. Eventuell wird aber in einer der Teilaufgaben verlangt, einen Bezug zwischen dem Prüfungstext und den **Pflichtlektüren bzw. -filmen** herzustellen. Mit dem „**AbiturSkript Englisch Niedersachsen 2024**“ (Bestell-Nr. 3546S4) können Sie sich darauf optimal vorbereiten. Es enthält knapp zusammengefasst alle wichtigen Informationen zu den verpflichtenden Materialien.
Für die Bearbeitung der Textaufgabe stehen Ihnen (einschließlich Auswahlzeit) **225 Minuten** zur Verfügung. Lesen Sie sich beide Textaufgaben durch und wählen Sie am besten denjenigen Vorschlag, zu dem Ihnen spontan mehr einfällt und dem Sie sich auch sprachlich am besten gewachsen fühlen. Achten Sie darauf, sich die Bearbeitungszeit sinnvoll einzuteilen. Planen Sie etwa die letzten 45 Minuten für das Korrekturlesen ein. Verteilen Sie die restliche Arbeitszeit sinnvoll auf die Einzelaufgaben (einen Anhaltspunkt dafür gibt Ihnen die prozentuale Gewichtung der jeweiligen Teilaufgabe).

Die **Aufgabenstellung** besteht in der Regel aus drei Teilen, die dem folgenden Schema entsprechen:

- Teilaufgabe 1: Textverständnis
- Teilaufgabe 2: Textanalyse/Vergleich o. Ä.
- Teilaufgabe 3: Transfer (hier können Sie zwischen Aufgabe 3.1 und 3.2 wählen)

Auf den folgenden Seiten finden Sie nützliche Hinweise zur Vorgehensweise bei jeder der drei Teilaufgaben – mit „Dos and Don'ts“, Formulierungshilfen und vielem mehr. Zusätzlich stehen Ihnen auf der **Plattform MyStark** sechs **Lernvideos** zur Verfügung, in denen das Vorgehen am konkreten Beispiel eines Sach- und eines literarischen Texts gezeigt wird (Zugangscode vgl. vorne im Buch).

Vorgehen bei Teilaufgabe 1

Mit der ersten Teilaufgabe soll überprüft werden, ob Sie den Text wirklich verstanden haben. Häufig wird daher von Ihnen verlangt, dass Sie den Text (oder bestimmte Aspekte daraus) **in eigenen Worten zusammenfassen**. Am besten gehen Sie dabei nach dem Schema vor, das Sie bereits aus dem Kapitel zur Sprachmittlung kennen:

Schritt 1 Aufgabenstellung genau lesen

Lesen Sie zunächst die Aufgabenstellung aufmerksam durch:

- Wichtig ist zum einen der **Operator** (also das verwendete Aufforderungsverb), da damit bestimmte formale Vorgaben verbunden sind, die Sie befolgen müssen. In der folgenden Tabelle sind die häufigsten Operatoren für die Textverständnisaufgabe zusammengefasst.

Operator	Dos and Don'ts	Beispiel(e)
sum up/ summarise/ outline/ state	• die wichtigsten Aspekte knapp und in eigenen Worten zusammenfassen • keine Zitate oder Zeilenangaben • keine persönliche Wertung	• *Summarise the text.* • *Outline the author's view on social media. (Video-Set 1)*
describe	bestimmte Aspekte detailliert wiedergeben	*Describe what happens at the party.*

- Als Zweites sollten Sie auf den **inhaltlichen Fokus** der Aufgabenstellung achten, also ob Sie den Text als Ganzes zusammenfassen müssen oder sich nur auf bestimmte Teilaspekte konzentrieren sollen (etwa „the author's view on social media").

Schritt 2 Schlüsselstellen markieren und Notizen machen

Gehen Sie den Text noch einmal durch, unterstreichen Sie die für die Aufgabenstellung relevanten Passagen und machen Sie sich dazu Notizen. Wenn Sie eine Zusammenfassung des ganzen Texts schreiben sollen, unterteilen Sie den Text in Sinnabschnitte und versuchen Sie, den Inhalt jedes Abschnitts in wenigen Worten zusammenzufassen.

Schritt 3 Notizen strukturieren

Sehen Sie sich nun Ihre Notizen (und ggf. die markierten Textstellen) noch einmal an und überlegen Sie, in welcher Reihenfolge Sie die Aspekte in Ihrem Text anführen möchten. Oft können Sie sich in Ihrer Lösung an der **Textchronologie** orientieren. Manchmal macht es aber auch Sinn, bestimmte **Aspekte zu bündeln** oder sie in der Lösung umzustellen. Dann können Sie die Aspekte z. B. entsprechend nummerieren und haben so bereits eine Art Grobgliederung für das anschließende Ausformulieren der Lösung.

Schritt 4 Lösung ausformulieren

Verwenden Sie Ihre strukturierten Notizen und Unterstreichungen im Text als Grundlage und formulieren Sie daraus Ihre Lösung in ganzen Sätzen.

- Beginnen Sie Ihren Text am besten mit einem sogenannten **Basissatz**. Darin nennen Sie den Autor bzw. die Autorin, den Titel des Texts, das Erscheinungsdatum (und ggf. den Erscheinungsort) sowie das zentrale Thema.
- Achten Sie in Ihrem Hauptteil darauf, Ihre Notizen sinnvoll miteinander zu verknüpfen, etwa durch **Konjunktionen**.

Hilfreiche Wendungen

Basissatz formulieren	*In his/her article "…", published in … on …, the author deals with/focuses on/describes/criticises/… .* *The extract from the novel/short story "…", written by … and published in …, deals with/is about …*
die Sicht des Autors/der Autorin wiedergeben	*According to the author, …* *The author emphasises/points out/…*
Aspekte aufzählen	*First of all, … / To begin with, …* *Firstly, … Secondly, … Thirdly, …* *In addition, … / Moreover, … / Furthermore, …* *Finally, … / Lastly, … / To conclude, …*
Gründe angeben	*As … / Since …* *… because …* *Due to …*
Folgen aufzeigen	*Thus, … / Therefore, …* *As a result, … / As a consequence, …*
Gegensätze herstellen	*However, … / Yet …* *While …* *…, whereas …* *Although …* *On the one hand … On the other hand …*

Weitere hilfreiche Wendungen finden Sie in den digitalen „**MindCards**“.

Vorgehen bei Teilaufgabe 2

Im zweiten Teil der Textaufgabe müssen Sie sich detaillierter mit dem Text auseinandersetzen. In der Regel wird hier eine **Analyse** verlangt (Operatoren „analyse“ oder „examine“): Sie sollen dabei nicht nur wiedergeben, **was** im Text gesagt wird, sondern auch **wie** und **warum**, also welche Funktion oder Wirkung bestimmte Textelemente haben. Weitere mögliche Aufgabenstellungen in diesem Teil der Prüfung sind **Vergleiche** oder **Gegenüberstellungen**.

Gehen Sie auch bei der zweiten Aufgabe nach dem gewohnten Schema vor:

Schritt 1 Aufgabenstellung genau lesen

- Auch hier gibt Ihnen der **Operator** wieder Aufschluss, was Sie genau tun müssen. Besonders wichtig bei allen unten genannten Operatoren ist, dass Sie Ihre Untersuchungsergebnisse durch **Textbelege** untermauern.

Operator	Dos and Don’ts	Beispiel
analyse / examine	bestimmte Textmerkmale oder Aspekte detailliert untersuchen	*Analyse the means the author uses to convey his attitude and the effect they have on the reader. (Video-Set 1)*
compare	Unterschiede und Gemeinsamkeiten aufzeigen	*Compare the protagonist’s situation with the situation of LGBTQ+ youths depicted in materials studied in class.*
contrast	Unterschiede zwischen zwei oder mehr Dingen herausarbeiten	*Contrast the authors’ views on innocence and guilt.*
explain	Zusammenhänge verdeutlichen / Ursachen und Wirkungen aufzeigen	*Explain the protagonist’s inner conflict.*
illustrate	etwas anhand von Beispielen erklären	*Illustrate how the author criticises the lack of ethical standards in business.*

- Achten Sie außerdem auf den **inhaltlichen Fokus** der Aufgabenstellung, d. h., ob bestimmte Aspekte genannt werden, auf die Sie in Ihrer Lösung zwingend eingehen müssen (z. B. „the **means** the author uses […] and their **effect on the reader**“).

Schritt 2 Schlüsselstellen markieren und Notizen machen

Gehen Sie den Text noch einmal systematisch in Hinblick auf die in der Aufgabenstellung genannten Aspekte durch.

- Angenommen die Aufgabenstellung lautet folgendermaßen (vgl. Video-Set 1, Teilaufgabe 2):

  Analyse the means the author uses to convey his attitude on social media and the effect they have on the reader.

  Überlegen Sie sich als Erstes, welche Haltung der Autor gegenüber sozialen Medien zum Ausdruck bringt (das „**was**" des Texts). Machen Sie sich dann neben dem Text Notizen, welche sprachlichen Mittel diesem Zweck dienen, und wie genau sie das tun. Sie können auch auf einem separaten Blatt eine **Stoffsammlung** anlegen – z. B. eine Tabelle mit den Spalten „attitude", „means (+ Zeilenverweise)" und „effect". Zu „means" zählen beispielsweise Aufbau des Texts, Wortwahl oder rhetorische Mittel. Eine Übersicht über häufig verwendete rhetorische Mittel finden Sie auf der übernächsten Seite.
- Wenn Sie einen **Vergleich** anstellen sollen (Operator „compare"), suchen Sie nach Gemeinsamkeiten und Unterschieden und kennzeichnen Sie diese z. B. durch entsprechende Symbole (z. B. = und ≠) oder legen Sie sich ebenfalls eine Tabelle an. Bei einer **Gegenüberstellung** (Operator „contrast") reicht es, wenn Sie sich auf die Unterschiede konzentrieren.

Schritt 3 Notizen strukturieren

Gehen Sie Ihre Notizen noch einmal durch und überlegen Sie sich davon ausgehend, wie Sie Ihre Lösung aufbauen könnten:

- Bei einer Analyseaufgabe haben Sie meist mehrere Möglichkeiten. Manchmal bietet es sich an, der **Textchronologie** zu folgen. Im erwähnten Beispiel könnten Sie z. B. auch sprachliche Mittel aus verschiedenen Textpassagen **bündeln**, die eine ähnliche Wirkung auf die Lesenden haben.
- Bei einem Vergleich können Sie Ihre Lösung oft in **zwei große Blöcke** unterteilen und zunächst alle Gemeinsamkeiten beschreiben, dann alle Unterschiede. Oder Sie gehen anhand einzelner **Vergleichspunkte** vor und arbeiten jeweils heraus, ob sich hier eine Ähnlichkeit oder ein Unterschied feststellen lässt.

Schritt 4 Lösung ausformulieren

Wenn Sie Ihre Notizen strukturiert und sich einen groben Aufbau überlegt haben, können Sie an das Ausformulieren Ihrer Lösung gehen. Untergliedern Sie Ihren Text in **Einleitung**, **Hauptteil** und **Schluss**.

- In der **Einleitung** nehmen Sie kurz auf die Aufgabenstellung Bezug. Im bereits genannten Beispiel sollten Sie also erwähnen, welche Haltung der Autor gegenüber sozialen Medien einnimmt („was?") und dann zu Ihrer Analyse der sprachlichen Mittel („wie?") und deren Wirkung („wozu?") überleiten:

  In his article, the author Matt Haig assumes a rather negative attitude on social media. He employs different means to warn the reader of its dangers and make them adopt his critical stance.

- Im **Hauptteil** führen Sie der Reihe nach Ihre **Untersuchungsergebnisse** aus. Orientieren Sie sich dabei an Ihren strukturierten Notizen. Nennen Sie zu Beginn jedes neuen Absatzes zunächst eine Ihrer **Thesen** und untermauern Sie diese anschließend mit einem **Beispiel** bzw. **Textbeleg**. Als Textbelege eignen sich wörtliche Zitate oder Zeilenverweise.

Firstly, Haig uses rhetorical devices such as metaphors.	These
He compares social media to the fast food and tobacco industries (cf. ll. 46/47) and claims that its effects can be as harmful as "secondhand smoke or a bad diet" (l. 50).	Beleg(e)
Since most readers would agree that smoking and eating junk food can be dangerous, they are likely to agree with his argument.	Schlussfolgerung (hier: *effect*)

- Im **Schlussteil** runden Sie Ihre Lösung ab, indem Sie noch einmal kurz auf die Aufgabenstellung eingehen.

  In sum, through his clever use of rhetorical devices […], Haig manages to convince the reader of his argument and make them reflect critically on their own stance on social media.

Hier noch einmal zusammengefasst einige Tipps zum richtigen Zitieren:

Textbeleg	Dos and Don'ts	Beispiel
direktes Zitat	• in Anführungszeichen, mit Zeilenangabe dahinter in Klammern • wenn in den Satz eingebunden: auf grammatikalische Richtigkeit achten • Änderungen oder Auslassungen durch eckige Klammern kenntlich machen	*The author stresses that "[i]t's high time we realised the consequences of our […] behaviour" (ll. 8/9).*
indirektes Zitat	• Inhalt der Textstelle in eigenen Worten paraphrasieren • Zeilenangabe in Klammern mit „cf." (steht für „confer" = vergleiche)	*The author urges us to be aware of the effects of our way of living (cf. ll. 8/9).*

Die folgende Tabelle bietet Ihnen einen Überblick über häufig verwendete Stilmittel. Achten Sie bei einer Analyse darauf, die Stilmittel nicht einfach nur zu benennen, sondern ihre Funktion und Wirkung im jeweiligen Kontext zu erläutern.

Stilmittel	Definition	Beispiel
alliteration	Mehrere Wörter beginnen mit dem gleichen Laut.	*[…] face the fire at freedom's front.* (Ronald Reagan)
antithesis	Gegenüberstellung gegensätzlicher Begriffe und Gedanken	*To err is human, to forgive divine.* (Alexander Pope)
ellipsis	Auslassung eines Wortes oder Satzteils	*Mastercard accepted.*
euphemism	Beschönigung; Unangenehmes mit angenehmen Worten sagen	*early retirement = unemployment*
hyperbole, exaggeration	Übertreibung	*He nearly died laughing.*
irony	Man sagt das Gegenteil von dem, was man meint.	*You broke that window really well!*
metaphor	Wort in übertragener Bedeutung; Bild, Vergleich (ohne „as" oder „like")	*All the world's a stage.* (Shakespeare, *As You Like It*)
parallelism	gleichartiger Satzbau	*What a day may bring, a day may take away.*
paradox	scheinbar falsche Aussage	*Fair is foul and foul is fair.* (Shakespeare, *Macbeth*)
personification	Vermenschlichung, Verkörperung (in Gestalt einer Person)	*The day has eyes, the night has ears.*
pun	Der witzige Effekt beruht auf der Doppeldeutigkeit des gebrauchten Wortes.	*We shot two bucks, but that was all the money we had.* (*buck* = 1. Bock; 2. Dollar)
repetition	mehrmaliges Aufführen desselben Wortes /Ausdrucks zur Verstärkung einer Aussage	*Tomorrow and tomorrow and tomorrow.* (Shakespeare, *Macbeth*)
rhetorical question	Scheinfrage, auf die keine Antwort erwartet wird	*How is it that a country that prides itself on its economic success could have so many very poor people?*
simile (comparison)	Form des Bildes; direkter Vergleich (mit Vergleichswort)	*My love is like a red,red rose.* (Robert Burns)

Die folgenden Formulierungen können Sie für „klassische Aufgabenstellungen“ wie Analysen und Vergleiche einsetzen:

Hilfreiche Wendungen – Textanalyse und Vergleich	
Stilmittel benennen	*The author uses/employs …* *The author refers to … /provides examples of …* *This is shown by…/is further exemplified by…/becomes apparent in … / becomes obvious in …/manifests itself …/is hinted at …*
Funktion/Wirkung auf die Leserschaft beschreiben	*This serves to illustrate/emphasise/add credibility to the argument/ convince the reader/evoke the readers' sympathies …* *The author wants to make the reader aware that …* *The reader is made to feel …* *The author appeals to the reader to …* *The text is like a wake-up call …* *By directly addressing the reader, …*
Vergleiche anstellen	*Compared to/with … / In comparison to/with …* *Similarly, …* *By contrast, …* *In contrast to … / Unlike …*
Beispiele anführen	*For example, …* *…, for example. / …, for instance.* *…, such as … / …, e. g. …*

Theoretisch ist es auch möglich, dass Ihnen in der Prüfung neben einem Text zusätzliches Material vorgelegt wird – etwa in Form eines Cartoons oder einer Statistik. Das kann in Teilaufgabe 2 der Fall sein, aber auch in anderen Teilaufgaben. Bei der Auswertung helfen Ihnen die folgenden Ausdrücke und Wendungen:

Hilfreiche Wendungen – Cartoon	
das Dargestellte beschreiben	*The cartoon shows … / In the cartoon, you can see …* *In the background … / In the foreground … / In the centre of the cartoon …* *On the left … / In the top right-hand corner you can see … / The left half shows …* *The cartoon has a/no caption …* *The caption reads …*
die Botschaft interpretieren	*The cartoonist/artist illustrates …/wants to express the fact that …* *The cartoonist/artist makes clear/criticises/emphasises …* *The cartoon is a reference to …/refers/alludes to …/is a criticism of …* *The message of the cartoon is … / The cartoon might suggest that …* *To get across this message, the cartoonist …*

Hilfreiche Wendungen – Statistik

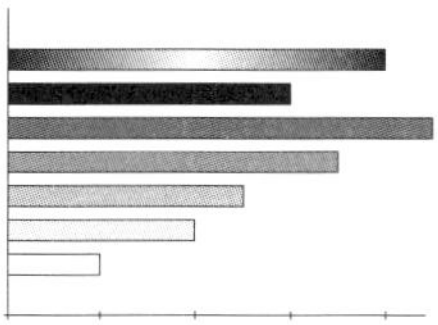

bar chart/graph (Balken-, Säulendiagramm)

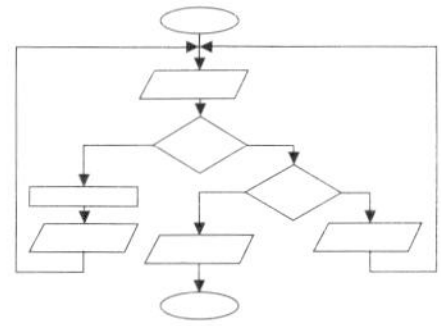

flow chart (Flussdiagramm)

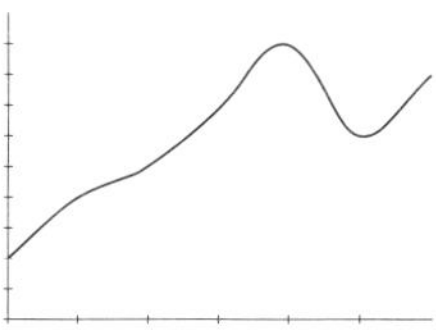

line graph (Kurvendiagramm)

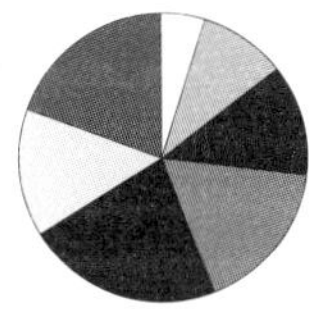

pie chart (Kreisdiagramm, Kuchendiagramm)

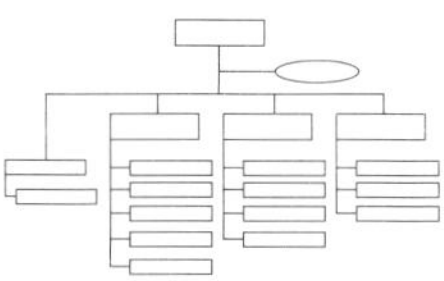

organisation(al) chart (Organigramm)

Thema / Modulreihe	12.1 The Challenge of Individualism	12.3 Tradition and Change
GK verb.	Presentations	Presentations
GK verb.	I USA	Work and Industrialization
GK verb.	II Science and Technology	United Kingdom
GK fakultativ	III Them and Us	Extreme Situations

table (Tabelle)

Statistiken allgemein beschreiben	*The pie chart shows/compares …* *As you can see from the line graph …* *The bar graph demonstrates …* *This table gives information about …* *Its most significant feature is …* *The figures in the table show that …* *The figures prove that … / This implies that …* *The statistics suggest that …* *The diagram makes it clear that …* *There is evidence that …*
eine Zunahme beschreiben	*to rise/go up/increase by … to …* *to rise/go up/increase from … to …* *an increase/a rise of …*
eine Abnahme beschreiben	*to drop/go down/decrease/fall by … to …* *to drop/go down/decrease/fall from … to …* *a drop/decrease/fall of …* *a drop/decrease/fall in …*

Weitere hilfreiche Wendungen finden Sie in den digitalen „**MindCards**".

Vorgehen bei Teilaufgabe 3

Die dritte Teilaufgabe im Abitur schließt zwar an das Thema des Prüfungstexts an, geht aber meist über die reine Textarbeit hinaus. Sie müssen hier also einen **Transfer** leisten und können zwischen zwei Aufgabenstellungen (3.1 und 3.2) wählen. Meist müssen Sie eine **Stellungnahme** oder **Erörterung** zu (Teil-)Aspekten des Prüfungstexts schreiben oder aber eine **kreativere Aufgabenstellung** bearbeiten. Es kann auch von Ihnen verlangt werden, einen **Bezug zu einer Pflichtlektüre** bzw. zu „materials studied in class" herzustellen. Gehen Sie wie folgt vor:

Schritt 1 Aufgabenstellung genau lesen

Mindestens eine der beiden Aufgabenstellungen in Teil 3 wird in einen **Kontext** eingebettet sein – ähnlich wie Sie das auch von der Sprachmittlungsaufgabe kennen. Es wird Ihnen also eine bestimmte Situation vorgegeben, die Sie zwingend in Ihrer Lösung berücksichtigen müssen. Dabei sollten Sie auf folgende Aspekte achten:

- Welche **Textsorte** ist vorgegeben?
- Wer ist (ggf.) die **Zielgruppe** bzw. **der Adressat/die Adressatin** des Texts?
- Auf welche **inhaltlichen Aspekte** sollen Sie eingehen?
- Welcher **Operator** wird verwendet? Häufig werden auch mehrere Operatoren miteinander kombiniert – in diesen Fällen müssen Sie die Vorgaben jedes einzelnen Operators berücksichtigen.

Operator	Dos and Don'ts	Beispiel
write [+ text type]	textsortenspezifische Vorgaben beachten	*As a contribution to its monthly topic "Science Meets Literature," your online book club has asked its members to contribute a blog entry, commenting on the following statement by software programmer Justin Rosenberg: "[…]". **Write the blog entry** […]. (2022-10)*
discuss / assess / evaluate	hier müssen zwingend Pro- <u>und</u> Kontraargumente angeführt werden, die zu einer begründeten Schlussfolgerung führen	*You have to hand in an article about the struggles of integration, **discussing** the statement "It is not easy to be stranded between two worlds, the sad truth is that we can never be completely comfortable in either world" by the novelist Sharon Kay Penman. (2022-7)*
comment (on)	die eigene Meinung begründet darlegen (Argumentation kann „einseitig" sein oder Pro- und Kontraargumente umfassen)	*[…] Write a letter to the editor in which you **comment on** the author's claim that "multiculturalism has failed" (l. 8).*
justify	eine nachvollziehbare Begründung für eine Entscheidung geben	*Imagine you are the protagonist. Write an e-mail to your friend **justifying** your decision to decline her offer.*

Schritt 2 Notizen machen / Stoffsammlung anlegen

Aus der Analyse der Textsorte, Operatoren etc. in Schritt 1 ergibt sich bereits ein Grundgerüst, wie Sie Ihre Lösung aufbauen müssen. Um nun Aspekte bzw. Argumente für den Hauptteil Ihrer Lösung zu sammeln, sollten Sie eine **Stoffsammlung** anlegen: Sie können dazu beispielsweise eine **Mindmap** erstellen, in der Sie Ihre Ideen sammeln, eine **Tabelle** mit Pro- und Kontraargumenten anlegen usw.

Schritt 3 Notizen strukturieren

Gehen Sie Ihre Stoffsammlung noch einmal durch, bündeln Sie ggf. ähnliche Aspekte und überlegen Sie, in welcher Reihenfolge Sie die einzelnen Punkte anführen möchten. Wenn Sie in einer **Stellungnahme** Pro- und Kontraargumente anführen müssen (z. B. Operatoren „discuss“ oder „assess“), haben Sie zwei Möglichkeiten: Sie können Pro und Kontra entweder in **zwei separaten Blöcken** abhandeln oder jeweils **einzelne Argumente einander gegenüberstellen**. Auch wenn Sie linear argumentieren dürfen (z. B. „comment on“) kann es sich anbieten, auf mögliche Gegenargumente einzugehen und diese zu entkräften.

Schritt 4 Lösung ausformulieren

Formulieren Sie jetzt Ihren Text aus:

- Rufen Sie sich noch einmal ins Gedächtnis, welche formalen und stilistischen Vorgaben Sie in Hinblick auf die vorgegebenen **Textsorten** und ggf. **Zielgruppen** beachten müssen.
- Vergessen Sie bei einer **Stellungnahme** nicht, Ihre Argumente durch Beispiele zu untermauern. Die einzelnen Absätze Ihres Hauptteils sollten also nach dem Muster „**These – Beleg / Beispiel**“ aufgebaut sein.

  One of the biggest dangers of social media is cyberbullying. These
  According to recent studies, about half of all teenagers and adolescents have already been threatened or insulted online on platforms such as Instagram or Facebook. This can have serious consequences on their mental or physical health, performance in school, etc. Beleg / Beispiel

- Achten Sie bei **kreativen Aufgabenstellungen** (z. B. „write an interiour monologue“) besonders darauf, aus welcher **Perspektive** Sie schreiben sollen bzw. an welche **Informationen aus dem Ausgangstext** Sie anknüpfen können.

Textsorte	Aufbau	Sprachstil
Artikel / Essay	• Überschrift • Einleitung mit Hinführung zum Thema • klar gegliederter Hauptteil	• neutrales Register • bei jugendlicher Zielgruppe nicht zu förmlich
E-Mail	• passende Anrede • Einleitung mit Bezugnahme zum Kontext • klar gegliederter Hauptteil • evtl. abschließender Satz mit Bezugnahme zum Kontext • Schlussformel und Name	• formelle E-Mail: sachlich-nüchtern; Verwendung von Langformen • persönliche E-Mail: informell / umgangssprachlich; Verwendung von Kurzformen
Leserbrief	• Anrede • Nennung des Artikels, auf den man sich bezieht • klar gegliederter Hauptteil • Name und Wohnort	• meist eher förmlich
Rede	• Begrüßung des Publikums • strukturierter Hauptteil • Verabschiedung / Dank	• direkte Anreden • Verwendung rhetorischer Mittel • Stil je nach Thema und Zielgruppe emphatisch / locker / aufrüttelnd / …
innerer Monolog	• assoziativer Aufbau (Gedankenstrom) • Bezugnahme auf Themen oder Ereignisse, die im Ausgangstext oder der Aufgabenstellung genannt wurden	• 1. Person Singular (Ich-Perspektive) • mündlicher Stil • Sprache muss zur Figur passen
Fortsetzung / Ende einer Geschichte	Wiederaufgreifen von Handlungssträngen und Figurendarstellung des Ausgangstexts	• Erzählperspektive / Sprachstil wie im Ausgangstext
Dialog zwischen zwei Figuren	Wiederaufgreifen von Handlungssträngen und Figurendarstellung des Ausgangstexts	• jeweils Name der Figur, gefolgt von direkter Rede • mündlicher Stil • Sprache muss zu den Figuren passen

Hilfreiche Wendungen – Leserbrief	
Anrede	*Sir/Madam, / Dear Sir or Madam, / Dear Editor,*
Bezug nehmen	*I am writing in reference to the article …* *In the article …, the author wrote about …*
Meinung ausdrücken	*I would like to congratulate you on the article …* *I (wholeheartedly) agree with the author that …* *However, the author fails to mention that …* *What the author does not take into account is …*

Hilfreiche Wendungen – Rede	
Publikum begrüßen	*Ladies and gentlemen,* *Good evening, / Good afternoon,* *It's an honour and privilege to speak to you today….* *I am proud to stand here in front of you today …*
sich bedanken	*Thank you for your attention.*

Weitere nützliche Formulierungen für verschiedene Zieltextsorten finden Sie im Kapitel zur Sprachmittlung sowie in den digitalen „**MindCards**".

Textaufgabe: Lernvideos

Mit Schritt-für-Schritt-Anleitung

Auf **MyStark** (www.stark-verlag.de/mystark) stehen Ihnen sechs **Lernvideos** zur Verfügung, in denen die Vorgehensweise bei der Textaufgabe an konkreten Beispielen gezeigt wird. Die Texte und Aufgabenstellungen finden Sie ebenfalls auf MyStark. Am besten lesen Sie sich die Texte zunächst einmal genau durch und überlegen sich bei jeder Teilaufgabe, wie Sie sie lösen würden. Erst danach sollten Sie sich das zugehörige Video ansehen.

Video-Set 1: Sachtext

Text: "I used to think social media was a force for good. Now the evidence says I was wrong" by Matt Haig

Aufgabenstellung

1 **Outline** the author's view on social media. *(Video 1)*

2 **Analyse** the means he uses to convey his attitude and the effect they have on the reader. *(Video 2)*

3 **Write** a **letter to the editor/blog entry/speech** expressing your own opinion on the chances and dangers of social media. *(Video 3)*

Video-Set 2: literarischer Text

Text: *The Hate U Give* by Angie Thomas (extract from the novel)

Aufgabenstellung

1 **Describe** the night of the shooting as it is presented in the interview and as Starr remembers it. *(Video 1)*

2 **Characterise** the police officer as he is presented in this abstract. Take into account the narrative perspective. *(Video 2)*

3 "'His life always matters more!' […] 'That's the problem!'"
Discuss the statement referring to the general situation of African Americans in the US. *(Video 3)*

Textaufgabe: Übungsaufgabe 1

Niedersachsen Englisch

Aufgabenstellung

1 Outline the development of segregation since the 1960s.

2 Analyse the author's attitude towards the segregation that influences her private life and how it is conveyed.

3 Imagine you read the article below on *The Guardian*'s website.
Write an entry for the comment section in which you express your own thoughts as to the current state of segregation in the US and to Allen's opinion about it.

Text Our 21st-Century Segregation: We're Still Divided by Race

Even now, there are two Americas: one for brown people, one for whites. The difference is that we choose it today.

Many Americans don't want to admit it, but I'll say it: segregation is still around. Sometimes by design. And sometimes by choice.

Let me be clear, this isn't the segregation of my parent's era. It's not a legally mandated and enforced system backed by public figures like former Alabama George Wallace, who famously said, "Segregation today. Segregation tomorrow. Segregation forever," to resounding applause, in 1963. The "whites only" signs have ceased to <u>lurk</u> over water fountains, bathrooms, and restaurant counters.

Yet, 21st-century segregation exists overtly in our school systems, communities, and prisons. It also <u>permeates</u> our society in ways we don't even realize.

We need to continue the conversation about the shocking segregation in our schools and neighborhoods. According to a study last year, 43 % of Latinos and 38 % of blacks go to schools where less than 10 % of their peers are white. But beyond that, we often fail to talk about how segregation impacts us personally. How it <u>permeates</u> not only many of our public and private institutions, but American culture at large. We less easily talk about cultural or social segregation, an area that we have control over, via the restaurants we patronize, the bars we drink at and the places where we worship.

It's time for us to face the reality that for many Americans, even if we live and work around "diversity", our best friends and spiritual leaders, the people we invite into our lives and homes, often look like we do, reinforcing a de facto segregation. This social and cultural segregation isn't restricted to "uneducated" people living in the country. It is equally prominent in environments where smart, educated people are supposed to "know better". People who have studied race, spent months abroad in India or Africa, tasted the best fufu and mofongo, read Ralph Ellison, James Baldwin and Pablo

Neruda, and who may even have black "friends" or lovers, still too often manage to have a community that doesn't reflect diversity in their broader city or nation.

[…]

My knee-jerk reaction is to blame racism and discrimination. To complain about all the times that I've felt odd being the only brown face in the crowd. To get mad about how all the television shows that have casts that look like my family are segregated to the so-called "cable ghettos". To get angry at all the bouncers who say they have a racial quota in hotspots. And to wonder why all the books I like are sitting in a "separate" section … until of course, I realize, I'm guilty of many of the same offenses: I segregate, too.

I think about all the nights I plan out that were based on the racial and ethnic make-up of the crowd I am going out with. If I am hanging with black friends, I likely go to an all-black establishment, where I know my friends will like the music, and the mating potential. If I am hanging out with an all-white crowd, I immediately cross all black locations off the list, not wanting anyone to feel uncomfortable. Instead, I relegate myself to being one of a few blacks in the crowd. If it's going to be a night with mixed company, the venue would be more likely to be up for grabs. But an all-black locale still would probably be out of the question.

This isn't secret intel: many blacks, whites, Latinos, and Asians seem to stick to these same guidelines, too, particularly in New York City, America's supposed great melting pot. There are still two Americas: one for brown people and one for whites, and both are heavily segregated.

If our social worlds were more integrated, perhaps we would see it trickle down to the way we govern and the way we dispense justice. Having some sort of connection, a shared experience is the only way I believe that we can get politicians, police officers, and everyday citizens […] to truly understand race.

It may seem silly to connect major state and federal policies to something as simple as a night on the town, but our experiences are shaped not just by legalese and policy, but also by understanding and interacting with each other. Segregation in the 21st century is not just about being legally and physically separated, but about a cultural separation that still feels like it divides more than it binds.

From: Reniqua Allen, "Our 21st-century segregation: we're still divided by race",
on: theguardian.com, *3 April 2013.*
http://www.theguardian.com/commentisfree/2013/apr/03/21st-century-segregation-divided-race

Annotations

6 to lurk: to wait quietly or secretly for sth to happen or sb to appear, usually with bad intentions
9, 13 to permeate: to be present everywhere
27 knee-jerk reaction: way of automatically responding to sth
42 intel: short for intelligence, "insider" information acquired by well-informed sources
47 to dispense justice: to decide whether or not sb is guilty of a criminal act and how this person should be punished
51 legalese: all the special words and expressions that belong to the terminology of judges and lawyers

Lösungsvorschlag

1 **TIPP**

In this task, you are supposed to outline a development, which means that you should summarise it concisely. It might be helpful to structure your text by contrasting the state-enforced segregation of the 1960s with the "voluntary" cultural and individual segregation that the author claims exists today.

- segregation in the 1960s:
  - prescribed by law
  - Black and White people separated spatially
- segregation today:
  - overt segregation in institutions
  - self-imposed segregation in personal lives
    → more implicit, often not admitted
  - tendency to surround oneself with people from same ethnicity
    → impact on social and cultural life
  - could be overcome through more interaction with people from other backgrounds

introduction: source and topic

The article "Our 21st-Century Segregation: We're Still Divided by Race" by Reniqua Allen was published on the website of *The Guardian* in April 2013 and is about segregation in the US. According to the author, segregation still exists in the 21st century but it is a culturally motivated separation that people choose freely.

main part: segregation in the 1960s

Up until the 1960s, segregation was prescribed by law: Black and White Americans were not allowed to eat at the same places or use the same toilets, for example.

segregation today

While it is no longer state-enforced, the author claims that segregation is still found in public institutions, such as schools or prisons. Even more importantly, however, it exists in people's private lives, impacting society and culture. The reason for this is that people tend to surround themselves with members of their own ethnicity and go to places where they are among "their own". As this new segregation comes from the inside rather than the outside, people are likely to deny it because by admitting to its existence, they would have to admit that they contribute to the phenomenon as well.

On the other hand, the author claims that it could be overcome through individual effort, by means of common experiences and more social interaction with people from other racial backgrounds.

2 **TIPP**

This analysis task is twofold: You should both present Reniqua Allen's attitude towards segregation and explain how she conveys it. It is probably a good idea to structure your answer with regard to content (her general assessment of segregation, her initial angry reaction, her blaming of herself) and substantiate each point with evidence from the text.

- personal attachment to the subject:
  - use of first-person pronoun; reflection on her position as a Black person (cf. e. g. ll. 38/39)
  - repetition of "permeate" (ll. 9, 13) to show the all-pervasiveness of the topic
- wish to raise awareness and call for change
  - address to readers to take action (cf. ll. 10, 17)
  - reference to a study about school segregation (cf. ll. 11/12) → further increases credibility
  - dismantling of politically correct behaviour as a mere pretence: interest in other cultures (cf. ll. 17–25), foreign foods (cf. l. 23) and literature about race/ethnicity (cf. ll. 23/24), but segregation in private life
- anger about modern segregation, but also self-criticism
  - examples of her own experiences with segregation (cf. ll. 27–32)
  - repetition/enumeration of verbs (ll. 27–31) → underlines frustration
  - use of verb "to segregate" in active rather than passive voice (l. 33) → stresses individual responsibility
  - examples of how she segregates, too (ll. 34–41)
- conclusion: call for more interaction (cf. ll. 46–54)

introduction

The author's attitude towards the modern kind of segregation is conveyed in different ways.

main part: personal attachment

First of all, Allen writes in the first-person singular, which emphasises how deeply she is affected by the subject of racial segregation. Being Black herself (cf. e. g. ll. 38/39), her private life is as much influenced by segregation as the society she lives in; that this influence is extensive is hinted at by the repeated use of "permeate" (ll. 9, 13). Like everybody else, she claims not to have been particularly aware of the presence of segregation in everyday life (cf. l. 9), which makes it very difficult to fight against. The result is a society that lacks the diversity it officially ensures.

wish to raise the readers' awareness

Now that the author has realised that there are "two Americas" (l. 44) existing next to each other without overlapping very often, she wants to make society aware of the lie many Americans are living: her article is like a wake-up call to make her fellow citizens see what they refuse to acknowledge (cf. l. 1). She urgently wants to force them to take action now. Thus, she writes that "[w]e need to continue the conversation about the shocking segregation in our schools"

(l. 10) and "[i]t's time for us to face [...] reality" (l. 17). To prove that this is not just her own possibly prejudiced perception of the world, she refers to a study conducted recently that revealed that schools are still heavily segregated (cf. ll. 11/12). Before talking about her own experiences, the author reveals the politically correct behaviour of the educated US middle class as a mere pretence: people talk about "diversity" (l. 18) and show interest in other cultures without really mixing with them in their private lives (cf. ll. 17–25). She enumerates foreign-sounding foods (cf. l. 23) and intellectually demanding authors who deal with the subjects of race and ethnicity (cf. ll. 23/24). Through her description of how "smart, educated people [who] are supposed to 'know better'" (ll. 21/22) include these in their lives, while still staying in their own small, segregated world, she further exemplifies this pretence.

anger about modern segregation

The author does not exclude herself from sharing the responsibility for segregation, although her metaphorical "knee-jerk reaction" (l. 27) – in other words her first impulse – would be to feel victimised. Her fury at the injustice and the fact that people do not seem to have learned from history is still perceptible when she lists her personal experiences (cf. ll. 27–32). That anger is especially emphasised by her use of language: she starts her sentences with the infinitives "[t]o complain about", "[t]o get mad about", "[t]o get angry at", "[a]nd to wonder why" (ll. 27–31) to let off steam about the everyday segregation she is confronted with.

self-criticism

However, she counters that enumeration of verbs which express her anger and frustration by blaming herself, using the half-sentence, "until of course, I realize, I'm guilty of many of the same offenses" (l. 32) and the simple, but impressive statement, "I segregate, too" (l. 33). While the verb "to segregate" is normally not used in the active voice, this personalisation of its use underlines her main point: She herself and most Americans are responsible on a very individual level; they get angry but stay passive and fail to change anything. In the subsequent lines (ll. 34–41), she provides examples of her own "offenses" of segregation. Obviously, she leads a very active social life with friends of different races and carefully selects locations according to the ethnic background of the people she meets. The reasons she gives for her choices are that she does not want non-Black people to feel uncomfortable in an all-Black crowd and that she is rather willing to be the outsider instead (cf. ll. 37–41).

conclusion: call for more interaction

Especially in the light of her own experiences, her final conclusion becomes understandable: change must come from the individual level and "trickle down" (l. 46) to state institutions. In other words, Reniqua Allen believes that political and legal guidelines are only theory as long as they are not based on real-life, multiracially shared experience. By including examples from her own life and her own mistakes, Reniqua Allen makes her article an appeal to herself and others to be that driving force for change.

3 **TIPP**

In this task, you are free to express your own ideas as to the subject of ongoing racial segregation. However, you should pay attention to the characteristics of a comment entry, which you are supposed to write. Therefore, you should clearly refer to Reniqua Allen's point of view by agreeing with her, by opposing some of her arguments and by making further suggestions etc.
Possible arguments:
- agreeing with Allen on the progress achieved through the Civil Rights Movement, but also on the de facto ongoing segregation and inequality
- approving of her point that segregation is mainly happening in people's minds
- however, to change that, politics and especially the media have the responsibility to present positive role models
- subconscious prejudices have to be broken down
- tightrope act between affirmative action and discrimination

First of all, thank you very much, Ms Allen, for your enlightening article. I would say that I wholeheartedly agree on most points. As you correctly point out, segregation should be a thing of the past by now. The Civil Rights Movement has achieved so much and legally there is no reason why people of different skin color should still lead "separate, but equal" lives. Discrimination has been outlawed, we even elected an African American as President of our country and yet it would be too simplistic to interpret all these positive developments as ending inequality.

points of agreement: progress through Civil Rights Movement

Statistics speak a different language and it simply cannot be denied that there still is blatant inequality between Black and White when it comes to wealth, education, housing, the criminal justice system etc. And if no discriminatory laws can be blamed for these conditions, as was the case in the 1960s, what or who is to blame?

inequality still persists

Once more, I wholeheartedly agree with you that it is not enough to point an accusing finger at others, while in our own minds we all continue to categorise people according to their skin color, their religion, their sexual orientation or what have you. So, we have to break down those boundaries in our minds in order to effect the real change in our society that is overdue.

necessity to overcome barriers in the mind

As to how to break down these boundaries, I slightly disagree with your opinion, however. You wrote that people interacting with people from other ethnic backgrounds in a natural and "color-blind" way would influence larger political decisions. In an ideal world I would agree, but in an ideal world, people would not even have to write articles like yours to bring the ongoing prejudices to the world's attention. The differences between various social and ethnic groups would not even be noticed and people would not categorise establishments as either "Black" or "White".

points of disagreement: idea of colourblindness too idealistic

Unfortunately, however, we do not live in an ideal world. That is why I think politics and especially the media have a duty to act as positive role models for the society at large. In my opinion, it will not work the other way round. Of course, I admit that strategies like affirmative action, racial quotas or politically correct discourse are often tightrope acts because they might lead to an even more strained atmosphere between different social or ethnic groups. Yet, I think they are necessary in order to overcome our subconscious fears of what is unknown and foreign.

politics and media must be agents of change

All in all, I believe that only by giving people time, by facilitating multiracial encounters and especially by constantly showing them as something positive can the segregation in our minds be overcome. Through your article, you have made the first important step in the right direction by addressing the problem and facing reality instead of pretending that an ideal world with no differences has already arrived.

conclusion

Textaufgabe: Übungsaufgabe 2

Niedersachsen Englisch

Aufgabenstellung

1 State why the author claims that Shakespeare does not belong in the classroom.

2 Analyse the way the author uses argumentative techniques and language to persuade the readers of his view.

3 You have been invited to take part in an international workshop on Shakespeare's plays. Your task is to write an essay evaluating Powell's view that "most of the kids have no concept of the vitality of [Shakespeare's] youth" (ll. 8/9). Refer to materials studied in class, such as the play *Hamlet*.

Text **Kill Bill: Why We Must Take Shakespeare out of the Classroom**

Shakespeare wrote to put money in his pocket, food on the table and fire in the bellies of his audiences, not strike modern teenagers with fear. Most of Shakespeare's audiences were illiterate. His words were chosen to be spoken or heard, not to be read and deadened behind a desk – they wither when performance is removed.

Our schools are full of Shakespeare, but often in completely the wrong places. Old uncle Bill has become the relative that we invite to family gatherings out of habit, not because we actually want to. He sits there in the corner sharing his stories with anyone who'll listen; the adults lend a patient ear out of a sense of duty and most of the kids have no concept of the vitality of his youth.

Even before, and most definitely since, the recent <u>plummet</u> in drama's status as a specialist subject in schools, many young people's first experience of Shakespeare is in an English classroom taught by enthusiastic purveyors of imagination, but primarily non-theatre practitioners. It's an English teacher's remit to analyse language, but pick apart every word of Shakespeare and you've dissected the butterfly – pretty in parts but a nonsensical whole and certainly unable to fly.

A well-meaning English teacher can take a student through the meaning of every word in a sentence and it soon becomes a drawn out and confusing process. Shakespeare's audience didn't know the meaning of every word uttered (uncle Bill was busily making new ones up) but the sounds and pictures they created kept viewers enthralled for hours.

English teachers agree that Shakespeare's language isn't intended to be desk-bound; it's crafted for stage. Simple. Well, not so simple these days. Recent governments have decreed that Shakespeare is so key to our national identity and intelligence that he should be studied by all the children in a specific year group. Great, you might say, but it's not.

Over the past few years I've welcomed fewer and fewer school groups to our theatre. The planning and paperwork involved is prohibitive. Consider as well the amount of staff needed to accompany such a group and the knock-on cost of cover needed back at school. Don't forget the travel time to get to a theatre for what is often a three hour show, plus travel time back. Trips can rarely happen in a school day because of other "core" subjects missed, and teachers can't be relied upon to give up their evenings to deliver what has become a luxury.

If a teacher does manage to get kids to a theatre for a rare visit, it's not always useful. Students who are inexperienced theatregoers think that a particular director's version is how Shakespeare intended his play to be done, when actually the personal interpretations can be brave, boring or bad enough to put a child off theatre for life. So, a teacher keeps the class in school and tries hard to explain the play.

Teachers are supposed to have all the answers, but dramatic literature is a playground of opinions: why does Juliet say this? Why would Macbeth do that? The real answer is that we don't know, but teachers are not encouraged to say just that: "I don't know." Their own suppositions are often reported back in essays as facts. Plays aren't meant to be taught like this. They are meant to be explored on their feet. Actors and audiences are supposed to argue over meaning, finding multiple ways of delivering word and deed.

Our <u>BTEC</u> acting course has just started work on *The Tempest*. These are engaged, talented young people from a range of secondary schools who auditioned to be on the course, but the majority expressed disdain, dislike and hatred for poor uncle Bill. They had all experienced him separately in schools, behind desks. Shakespeare had made them feel stupid rather than empowered.

Let's give English teachers a break, give drama teachers a boost and give young people an important sense of equality. You don't need an expensive education to understand the words, but you do need the luxury of time, space and specialism to put his words on their feet and try them out.

Powell, Mark: "Kill Bill: why we must take Shakespeare out of the classroom." In: The Guardian,
Copyright Guardian News & Media Ltd 2018

Annotations

10 plummet: Since 2012 various decisions in educational policy have severely decreased the status of drama as school subject.

45 BTEC (Business and Technology Education Council): it provides secondary school leaving qualifications and further education qualifications

Lösungsvorschlag

1 **TIPP**

Here you are meant to report the reasons the author gives for not dealing with Shakespeare in the usual school context.

- Shakespeare's plays are to be seen and heard but not to be read
- it has become more difficult to take school groups to the theatre for organisational reasons
- it is more of a duty than a real desire to study and teach Shakespeare
- decisions in educational policy have decreased the importance of drama as a school subject
- teachers analyse Shakespeare's words, which deprives the plays of their entertainment and may even lead to confusion
- teachers are believed to know how to interpret Shakespeare's plays but that is not true because there is no one truth about them, their meaning needs to be discussed
- dealing with Shakespeare in class makes students feel ignorant

In his article "Kill Bill: Why We Must Take Shakespeare out of the Classroom" published in *The Guardian*, Mark Powell argues that Shakespeare's plays should no longer be taught in school.

introduction: reference to source, topic

The most important reason he gives is that these plays are not to be read but to be seen and heard in a theatre. This, however, is becoming more and more difficult as the regulations for taking school groups to the theatre are getting stricter and stricter according to the author. Moreover, he complains that decisions in educational policy have decreased the importance of drama as a school subject in its own right.

main part: reasons

Furthermore, Powell holds the view that Shakespeare is taught more out of a sense of duty than a real desire to deal with the playwright. He adds that English teachers tend to analyse Shakespeare's words and thus deprive his plays of their entertainment. Actually he claims that this approach to Shakespeare makes it more difficult for students to understand the text and thus leads to even more confusion.

Finally, teachers are believed to know how to interpret Shakespeare's plays. As a result, the plays' meaning or, even better, meanings are not discussed but students just convey their teachers' understanding of the plays in their papers. Consequently, Powell's experience shows that students hate Shakespeare because he makes them feel ignorant.

So, Powell argues that plays should not be taught by English teachers but by drama teachers, who teach their students how to stage Shakespeare's plays.

2 **TIPP**

In this task you need to analyse how the author tries to persuade the readers of his view that Shakespeare should be removed from the classroom. You are meant to focus on argumentative techniques such as stating facts and displaying authoritative knowledge as well as on language, for example figurative speech, allegory, imperatives and contrasts. Make sure to not just describe what you find in the text but also to interpret how it affects the readers.

- argumentative techniques: Powell bases arguments on …
  - historical facts (cf. ll. 1–4) → stresses differences between Elizabethan age and the present
  - authoritative knowledge → refers to recent decisions in educational policy (cf. ll. 10/11, 22–25); explains why fewer and fewer classes go to the theatre (ll. 26–32)
  - personal experience (ll. 45–49) → students want to put Shakespeare on stage even though most of them learned to hate him at school

  Powell anticipates the readers' reaction and contradicts (cf. ll. 24/25) → refutes counterarguments
- Language (examples): Powell uses …
  - numerous contrasts to underline the difference between Shakespeare's plays as they were intended and received in the Elizabethan age and today (cf. e. g. ll. 1–4, 21/22)
  - figurative speech:
    - his plays "wither" (l. 4) like flowers without water if they are not performed → stresses importance of seeing the plays in a theatre
    - analysing Shakespeare is like "dissect[ing] the butterfly" (l. 14) → easier for the reader to imagine the detailed approach that is taken to deal with Shakespeare; also implies that the butterfly is dead; imagination can't fly
    - students have to explore Shakespeare "on their feet" (ll. 42, 53) → stresses importance of drama teachers
    - allegory (ll. 5–9) → the reader can easily imagine the situation described
  - imperatives/parallelism/enumeration in ll. 50–53 to underline the demand to have drama teachers teach Shakespeare and not English teachers
  - an enumeration of reasons why less and less school groups come to the theatre (cf. ll. 27–32) → it is virtually impossible to take students to the theatre
  - alliteration, enumeration (l. 36) → if one manages to take students to a play, it might even be a poor performance
  - enumeration ("disdain, dislike and hatred", l. 47) → studying Shakespeare in school makes students hate the bard
  - contrast ("stupid rather than empowered", l. 49) → Shakespeare makes them feel ignorant

The author stresses his view that Shakespeare should be removed from the classroom by employing different argumentative techniques which are supported by stylistic devices such as contrasts, figurative speech, allegory and imperatives.

introduction: thesis / reference to assignment

Throughout the whole text Powell emphasises that Shakespeare cannot be taught without acting his plays out, or at least seeing them in a theatre. To prove this assertion, he describes what Shakespeare intended to achieve with his plays when he wrote them 450 years ago, namely to "put [...] fire in the bellies of his audiences, not strike modern teenagers with fear" (ll. 1/2). The contrast underlines the counter-productive effect Shakespeare's plays have when taught inside today's classrooms. Further contrasts which stress that the plays belong on stage can be found for example in lines 3/4 and 21/22.

main part:

argumentative technique
→ reference to historical facts

language
→ contrasts

The author also claims that Shakespeare's plays are dead if their language is analysed and they are not put "on their feet" (l. 42). When he makes this point, he uses figurative speech. For instance, he employs the verb "wither" (l. 4) to describe what happens to the words "when performance is removed" (l. 4) and compares the analysis of the plays' language to "dissect[ing] the butterfly – pretty in parts but a nonsensical whole and certainly unable to fly" (ll. 14/15). The comparison to the butterfly allows the readers to vividly imagine the detailed approach that is taken when dealing with Shakespeare in the English classroom. Furthermore, most people probably would not want to dissect a butterfly as the beauty of the creature is slowly destroyed leaving but parts of a dead body. So it can be deduced that they would not want to analyse Shakespeare word by word either.

language
→ figurative speech

Powell uses different stylistic devices to stress the effect this approach has on the students. He employs an enumeration to show that students are left feeling "disdain, dislike and hatred" (l. 47) for the poet. Using a contrast he points out that dealing with Shakespeare's plays makes students "feel stupid rather than empowered" (l. 49). Thus, it seems entirely counterproductive to teach Shakespeare at school.

→ enumeration, contrast

Additionally, the author argues that Shakespeare is only dealt with out of tradition and not out of enthusiasm. To stress this argument Powell employs an allegory in which he calls Shakespeare "[o]ld uncle Bill" (ll. 5/6) and compares him to a relative who we invite "out of habit, not because we actually want to" (ll. 6/7). The reader can easily relate to this situation as it is a typical experience many families share.

→ allegory

Powell argues that the situation gets worse due to recent decisions in educational policy. Dealing with Shakespeare has become obligatory for students "in a specific year group" (l. 24). Powell assumes that many readers might agree with that decision and therefore he anticipates what readers might think and contradicts. "Great, you might say, but it's not" (ll. 24/25). Thus, he can refute possible counterarguments. The problem he perceives is that the status of drama as a subject in its own right has decreased. The word "plummet" (l. 10) emphasises the seriousness of the situation. To make things worse it also becomes harder and harder for teachers to take their students to a theatre because of the "planning and paperwork involved", which he calls "prohibitive" (l. 27). The adjective stresses the hopelessness of the situation. Furthermore, Powell lists numerous other reasons why less and less students come to the theatre (cf. ll. 26–32). On the rare occasion that a group attends a performance, they even risk seeing a poor one. Here Powell uses an enumeration and alliteration to make his point ("brave, boring or bad", l. 36). The readers readily believe the author as he has first-hand experience (cf. ll. 26–32) and therefore radiates authority. Increasing the importance of Shakespeare for the national curriculum while at the same time weakening drama as a subject in its own right, does not seem to make much sense.

argumentative technique

anticipates readers' reaction, refutes counterarguments

language
→ choice of words

lists reasons

→ enumeration, alliteration

argumentative technique
→ radiates authority

Finally, the author uses imperatives (cf. l. 50) and an enumeration (cf. l. 52) to summarise his demands in a nutshell. As he does so in the last paragraph of his comment, the readers can easily keep his demands in mind.

language
→ imperatives, enumeration

To sum it up, Powell uses the historical perspective, a humorous allegory and his personal experience to support his most important argument for taking Shakespeare out of the classroom: the fact that a play without performance is pointless.

conclusion

3 **TIPP**

Choose a suitable heading for your essay. You should start your evaluation by explaining the meaning of the given quotation. Afterwards you need to balance the pros and cons to finally form your own opinion.

- explanation: young people do not understand that Shakespeare's plays are still relevant
- pros:
  - their language is outdated
  - Shakespeare made up new words, which may be difficult to understand
  - characters and their values are old-fashioned (e. g. role of women)
- cons:
  - performing scenes themselves allows students to step into the shoes of the characters and better relate to their situation
  - discussing complex philosophical and moral questions can be very engaging for students
  - watching modern film or theatre adaptations (e. g. Michael Almereyda's film version of *Hamlet*, set in present-day New York City) invites students to draw parallels between Shakespeare's world and our own
- conclusion: young people do recognise the relevance of Shakespeare's plays if the works are dealt with in an interesting way

Shakespeare – Our Contemporary?

heading

In an article for *The Guardian*, the author Mark Powell claims that young people today fail to see that Shakespeare's plays are still relevant. According to him, they are bored by the plays because they do not grasp the energy and enthusiasm that is inherent in them. Whereas it is certainly true that it is difficult to fill young people with enthusiasm for Shakespeare, it is not impossible.

introduction: explanation of quote

The major reason why it is hard for young people to accept that Shakespeare's plays are still relevant is probably their language. These plays were written about 450 years ago in Elizabethan English and many of their words are outdated like "thee" and "thou". Also, Shakespeare made up many words, some of which have become part of everyday language but sometimes their meaning is difficult to grasp. Therefore, this language is hard to understand for British teenagers and all the more so for students who learn English as a second language. They need to decode the meaning of Shakespeare's words, which often means hard work, before they can grasp the ideas he wants to convey.

main part: pros outdated language

Some of his characters and their values also seem old-fashioned. In particular, the role of women has changed considerably. These days they usually are not dominated by their father or husband.

outdated role models

However, in my experience, a lot of students do recognise the relevance of Shakespeare's works if the plays are dealt with in an engaging way. Even a very long and complex play such as *Hamlet* can fascinate young people if the scenes are not just read in silence and "dissected" in class, but if the students are made to perform some of the scenes themselves, for example. This can make it easier to step into the shoes of the characters and relate to their experiences. The particular situation Hamlet is in – the question if and how to seek revenge for his father's murder – may be quite removed from the everyday realities of most teenagers. His self-doubt and the feeling of being overwhelmed by conflicting emotions and therefore finding himself unable to act, however, is something quite a few young people can relate to, at least to a certain extent. Moreover, young people's curiosity to deal even with complex philosophical and moral questions, such as whether "to be or not to be", should not be underestimated. Like Hamlet, they might have wondered what compromises they need to make to live a life worth living. They might have been in situations where they were worrying and thinking critically about something but did not really dare to act. If students are invited to bring their own perspectives and interpretations to the play, dealing with Shakespeare in the classroom becomes a very stimulating experience.

cons

activities that allow students to relate to Shakespeare's ideas → reference to *Hamlet*

Watching film or theatre adaptations can be another good means to give students an understanding of the modernity of Shakespeare's plays. Michael Almereyda's film version of *Hamlet* (starring Ethan Hawke), for example, is set in the present but still uses Shakespeare's words. The action takes place in New York City (rather than the Danish court) and Claudius does not inherit the crown, but a big company named Denmark Corporation. Comparing this version to the original play and discussing in how far this "translation" of the plot into contemporary times is convincing invites young people to look for parallels between Shakespeare's world and our own.

use of modern film versions (to show parallels to students' reality)

All in all, I believe that it is not generally true that young people have no concept of Shakespeare's vitality. A lot of students will readily accept the relevance of his plays if the works are dealt with in an interesting way – be it by performing scenes themselves, by discussing philosophical questions in class and relating them to their own experience, or by watching or comparing film adaptations.

conclusion

Textaufgabe: Übungsaufgabe 3
Niedersachsen Englisch

Aufgabenstellung

1 Outline problems the author sees with the way British children learn about Britain's colonial past at school.

2 Examine the means the author uses to convey her opinion that British colonial history should be part of the curriculum.

3 "Some regard teaching about colonialism as simply too political, as if the way we tell history now is somehow neutral." (ll. 53/54) Comment on that statement. In your answer refer to both this article and your coursework.

Text

Put Our Colonial History on the Curriculum – Then We'll Understand Who We Really Are

Britain's past weighs on our present: learning about it would mean a better debate about race and migration.

My mum came to the UK from India in 1973, after a chunk of time spent in Uganda, when she was only 13. Colonialism shaped her life, and that of my grandparents; growing up in Newcastle, it was the backdrop to mine too. I'd heard plenty about empire and anticolonial movements at home, but during 14 years in the UK's state education system I learned almost nothing about it. Now, over a decade later, little has changed: new research suggests that there still isn't much systematic teaching about empire.

The national curriculum says young people are supposed to learn about "how Britain has influenced, and been influenced by the wider world", but when it comes to a central part of this country's history, there can be near silence. It's contained in one-month of learning, or hived off from the "core curriculum" in the form of optional modules.

Why does this matter? A leaked draft of the independent review into the Windrush scandal earlier this year showed one reason. It recommended that all Home Office staff should "learn about the history of the UK and its relationship with the rest of the world, including Britain's colonial history".

If we were all taught about colonial history in school, we'd learn at a young age that many of the people who came here from colonies and former colonies did so as citizens, not as immigrants. We'd discuss how so-called immigration policies introduced from the 1960s onward were designed to make it more difficult for people of colour to come to this country, and we'd examine the forms of resistance that came with this.

In a manner similar to the implementation of the anti-Jewish Aliens Act of 1905, successive governments treated minorities as a threat to the UK. They enacted what the academic Gurminder Bhambra calls "policies of racialisation". "If we understood that," she told me, "we wouldn't just shift the boundary of citizen and migrant to include people from (former) colonies. To say that I'm not a migrant is not a lack of solidarity with those who are migrants ... If we were to accept that I am British, then that would mean that we would have to think differently about migration in the present."

History is not stuck in the past. What we remember, and how, helps us understand who we are. Learning about empire [...] would mean understanding that colonialists created race and the racial hierarchy to control and govern colonies around the world. Unpicking how and why race was constructed would make for a more sophisticated discussion about racism now and chip away at the idea that this was ever an exclusively "white" country.

It might also mean people on either side of the Brexit divide pausing before they demand "we" "take back control" or lament that the UK was a "tolerant" country before the EU referendum.

In a sanitised version of history that is spouted by politicians such as Boris Johnson, the UK grew rich not because of exploitation and resource extraction, [but] because of an innate ability to progress. This colonial thinking persists; the "backward" became the "underdeveloped", while the lives and knowledge of some are still considered more important than others.

Four billion people are not poor because of some unhappy accident or an inherent failing; legacies of colonialism, extractive capitalist economies and racialised hierarchies of power produce poverty. Against a history where supremacy often meant mastering the environment for profit – decimating indigenous communities in the process – it's not by chance that the climate crisis now impacts those least responsible for it.

As part of its race and faith strategy, the Labour party has committed to setting up an Emancipation Education Trust, which would ensure migration, colonialism and this country's multiracial past are taught in schools. So too would the legacy of slavery, including "how it interrupted a rich and powerful black history which is also British history".

Some regard teaching about colonialism as simply too political, as if the way we tell history now is somehow neutral. Relative quiet in our schools is paired with politicians glorifying empire as its realities are erased; nostalgia and amnesia sitting side by side. Britain's bloody colonial history is weighed up as both good and bad; the railways v the Bengal famine. One the UK can take credit for; the other is too far in the past to have much to do with "us". This country is the saviour, never really an oppressor.

[...] there is a chance to change this narrative. It's not about guilt or one-dimensional stereotypes: if histories of exclusion, colonialism and the fierce resistance to much of this were more widely known, it could mean a more nuanced, inclusive understanding of the present.

Maya Goodfellow: "Put Our Colonial History on the Curriculum – Then We'll Understand Who We Really Are", 05 December 2019, https://www.theguardian.com/commentisfree/2019/dec/05/britain-colonial-history-curriculum-racism-migration. Copyright Guardian News & Media Ltd 2022

Annotations

12/13 Windrush scandal: 2018 political scandal, in which former migrants were wrong-fully detained, denied their rights or even deported, even though many of them had arrived as British citizens or had become British citizens or long-term residents since their arrival

22 Aliens Act of 1905: parliamentary act to control immigration, specifically targeted against poor immigrants

38/39 Boris Johnson: British Conservative politician, Prime Minister (2019–2022)

57 Bengal famine: famine in the Bengal province of British India (now Bangladesh and eastern India) in 1943 that cost millions of lives

Lösungsvorschlag

1 **TIPP**

For this task, you should first describe the treatment of Britain's colonial past at school, as it is depicted in the article. Then mention problems the author sees as a result. Remember that for an assignment like "outline", you only have to mention the key points and do not need quotes from the text. Start your answer with a topical sentence in which you summarise the message of the article briefly and name its source, author, date of publication etc.

You could mention the following points:

- introduction
- treatment of Britain's colonial past at school:
  - Maya Goodfellow's own experiences: lack of formal teaching (cf. ll. 4/5)
  - situation today: still not much systematic teaching (cf. ll. 5/6), colonialism not part of the core curriculum (cf. ll. 8–11)
- problems resulting from the lack of formal teaching:
  - British multicultural identity often disregarded or misunderstood (cf. ll. 16–28)
  - incomplete knowledge about the origin of race ideologies (cf. ll. 29–34)
- conclusion: unbalanced glorification of Empire (cf. ll. 54–59, 61–63)

introduction

In her article, "Put Our Colonial History on the Curriculum – Then We'll Understand Who We Really Are", published in *The Guardian* in December 2019, Maya Goodfellow criticises the lack of education about colonialism in the British school system. She attributes a limited understanding of history to that lack.

main part: treatment of Britain's colonial past at school

Goodfellow herself has had little to no formal teaching on the subject of colonialism in her 14 years in the British school system. Apparently, very little has changed since the author's schooldays: British colonialism is hardly taught at all in schools. Goodfellow mentions that it is not part of the core curriculum. Instead, it is only treated very briefly or in optional modules, which the students can choose to attend or not.

problems resulting from the lack of formal teaching

The result of this is that despite its significance for British history, people often have only a fragmented view of Britain's colonial past and lack an overall understanding of the topic. Goodfellow deduces problems for the present from this omission of the past: she argues that if people knew more about the British Empire and its legacy, this could change their view on British multicultural society today. British identity might be better grasped and seen as something more inclusive, while race ideologies and discrimination could be challenged if people were well-informed about who is or was a British citizen and how and why race ideologies were formed.

conclusion As it is now, only carefully selected parts of the country's imperial history are commonly known, which leaves a lot of space for misguided interpretations. Consequently, Maya Goodfellow's thesis is that a more thorough historical knowledge would prevent the currently prevailing sentiments of the British as "bringers of civilisation" or of the country as only made up of White citizens.

2 TIPP

The author's own opinion is already given in the assignment: She thinks "that British colonial history should be part of the curriculum". Furthermore, you have described for task 1 why the British school system's ignorance of the country's imperial history could be seen as problematic. What is left to do now is a closer examination of how Maya Goodfellow expresses her ideas in a convincing manner. Typical means and strategies you could look out for include stylistic devices, sources the author quotes to give her text credibility or the way the readership is made to feel included.

The following aspects come up in the sample solution:

- introduction: summary of Maya Goodfellow's opinion
- strategies to create a feeling of inclusivity:
  - reference to the author's own background as a second-generation immigrant (cf. ll. 1–4)
  - use of the pronoun "we" (cf. heading, ll. 16–20)
  - British history / Britishness seen as inclusive (cf. ll. 27, 51 /52)
- quoting "authorities" to give her opinion credibility:
  - independent review (cf. ll. 12–15)
  - academic Gurminder Bhambra (cf. ll. 23–28)
  - Labour Party's Emancipation Education Trust (cf. ll. 48–52)
- use of metaphorical language:
  - "Britain's past weighs on our present" (introductory lines)
  - "History is not stuck in the past." (l. 29)
- current examples to stress relevance:
  - Brexit debate influenced by lack of knowledge about colonial history (cf. ll. 35–37)
  - climate crisis with connection to colonial history (cf. ll. 43–47)
- invalidating opposing views:
  - use of quotation marks to show opposing views as wrong (cf. ll. 36, 40/41)

  - opposing view as simplified in contrast to scientifically bolstered arguments: "Four billion people are not poor because of some unhappy accident [...]; legacies of colonialism, extractive capitalist economies and racialised hierarchies of power produce poverty." (ll. 43–45)
- criticism of glorification of Empire:
  - metaphor "nostalgia and amnesia sitting side by side" (cf. ll. 55/56)
  - personification: Britain as "the saviour" (l. 58)
- appeal to include colonialism in the curriculum: positive word "chance" (l. 60)

introduction

Maya Goodfellow's article is a strong appeal to include teaching about colonialism in the core curriculum of British schools. The author uses different strategies to convince the reader of the significance of such a step.

main part: strategies to create a feeling of inclusivity

Starting with the heading of her article, her use of the pronoun "we" (cf. also ll. 16–20, for instance) sends a strong message of inclusivity. Both she, who is a second-generation immigrant herself (cf. ll. 1–4), and the readers should be interested in defining British history in a new way. Apart from addressing the readers directly, this is also shown in the stress Goodfellow puts on the definition of Britishness. Academic Gurminder Bhambra emphasises that she is British (cf. l. 27) and Black history is also explicitly called "British history" by Labour's Emancipation Education Trust (ll. 51/52).

quoting "authorities"

Quoting the former two, an individual expert (cf. ll. 23–28) as well as a political committee (cf. ll. 48–52), Maya Goodfellow makes use of another strategy to give credibility and relevance to her opinion: she shows that experts agree with her that a more thorough teaching and understanding of the country's history would be beneficial. Another example of this strategy can be found in lines 12 to 15, when an official review is quoted as concluding that even a political scandal could have been prevented through more knowledgeable individuals.

metaphorical language

Goodfellow furthermore uses metaphorical language to illustrate her point. In the introductory lines, the past's "weight" on the present makes it clear that what happened cannot simply be forgotten, an argument which is taken up again in the sentence, "History is not stuck in the past" (l. 29).

current examples

The author further underlines the past's influence on the present when she mentions topics, such as Brexit (cf. ll. 35–37) or the climate crisis (cf. l. 47). These are currently of high relevance and were shaped in one form or the other by events during colonialism that were never genuinely addressed.

The Brexit example also illustrates another of Goodfellow's strategies, namely her way of treating opposing views. She does give them some room in her article, but by writing ideas like "we [have to] take back control" (l. 36) in quotation marks, she shows them as misguided. The same goes for people with persistently colonial attitudes, who call fellow human beings "backward" or "underdeveloped" (ll. 40/41). That their line of thought is wrong and overtly simplified becomes especially obvious when the understatement of "some unhappy accident" (l. 43) befalling those who are poor is contrasted with the more scientifically correct causes for their poverty, namely "legacies of colonialism, extractive capitalist economies and racialised hierarchies of power" (ll. 44/45).

invalidating opposing views

That ignorance of the true extent of colonialism can also be due to laziness and an unwillingness to leave one's comfort zone is further underlined by the metaphor of "nostalgia and amnesia sitting side by side" (ll. 55/56). It is so much easier and more comfortable to continue seeing Britain as "the saviour" (l. 58) than it is to confront history in its entirety.

criticism of glorification of Empire

However, the end of Goodfellow's article is a strong appeal to do the latter: By using the positive word "chance" (l. 60), the author makes it clear that not all is lost. There is a way to come to "a more nuanced, inclusive understanding of the present" (ll. 62/63) and this way is to be found in education. This is the perfect conclusion to her article, the main message of which is to put colonial history on the school curriculum.

appeal to include colonialism in the curriculum

3 **TIPP**

"Comment" means that it is sufficient to give arguments for your own opinion. You need not discuss all possible angles. So, in that case, it will probably prove the easiest to agree with Maya Goodfellow that the way history is taught now, incomplete and one-sided, is political too. However, it makes sense to start you're answer by explaining the given quote in your own words. Therefore, you might mention reasons why "teaching about colonialism [could be] too political".

The sample solution mentions the following points:

- introduction: explanation of quote in own words
- main part: agreement with Goodfellow's quote
  - argument 1: withholding information is political too
  - argument 2: exclusion of parts of the population when their history is not addressed
  - argument 3: critical discourse is always about seeing things from different perspectives

- conclusion: difficult subjects and mistakes are especially important as topics of history lessons because we should learn from them

Opponents of teaching British colonial history in a more profound way tend to bring forward the argument that this part of the country's past can never be treated in a neutral and objective way and thus should not be taught at all. Maya Goodfellow, however, counters that its omission from the curriculum is not neutral either. What she means by her criticism is that it is not only what you do, say, or teach that reveals your attitude, but also what you decide to keep quiet about.

introduction

I must say that I totally agree with Maya Goodfellow that not talking about colonialism at all will be almost exactly as bad as exploiting it for political propaganda. Of course, one way of spreading propaganda is to show past events in a particularly favourable or unfavourable light, whatever your political agenda demands. However, concealing parts of the truth or intentionally skimming over them can also lead to one-sided attitudes forming or becoming acceptable. That this has indeed happened in the UK can be seen from the fact that the Empire is too often glorified or only seen in a positive light because its unpleasant facts, such as the brutal oppression of and racist attitudes towards the colonised, are simply not widely known.

main part:
argument 1: withholding information is political too

Besides keeping the common public un- or misinformed, the silence over such a significant part of the UK's past also excludes large parts of the population by not acknowledging them, their history and often their suffering. The way history is told and the past is remembered always depends on the materials and perspectives which are dealt with in the classroom. Chinua Achebe, a Kenyan author and a prominent voice in postcolonial literature, once explained this phenomenon with the following example: "Until the lions have their own historians, the history of the hunt will always glorify the hunter." So, the colonised and their descendants will only get their say when their stories and voices are included in the official version of British history as well. If they are not, this will perpetuate their role as victims for whom others speak and who do not feel as true and equal members of their society.

argument 2: exclusion of parts of the population when their history is not addressed

Moreover, irrespective of the topic, students should always learn that a real discussion involves seeing different angles. Only this allows a more nuanced view of the world and fosters critical thinking as well as empathy. By acquiring these skills, students will be well prepared for current and future challenges they and society as a whole face. It is no use pretending that there is only one dimension or one accepted

argument 3: critical discourse always about seeing things from different perspectives view when this is simply not the whole truth. This will never solve any problems, but only generate division and hate.

In conclusion, especially for many White people (like myself), colonialism and its effects may be an inconvenient topic to talk about, since our ancestors often do not appear in a positive light in this context. That, however, makes it all the more crucial that this aspect of the past is taught and discussed in class. Mistakes are the worst when you are not prepared to learn from them. Then they can influence the future in a negative way. A well-informed mind, on the other hand, can be the first step towards a more open and inclusive society. **conclusion**

Textaufgabe: Übungsaufgabe 4

Niedersachsen Englisch

Aufgabenstellung

1 Outline what we learn about Amma's family background (see the excerpt from *Girl, Woman, Other* on the following pages).

2 Analyse how the changing self-image of women is presented in the excerpt. Focus on narrative perspective and use of language.

3 Choose one of the following tasks.

3.1 Assess the role family and social communities play in a person's development. Also refer to Amma's and Yazz's experiences in the novel.

3.2 You are doing an internship for an advocacy organisation whose aim is to inform the general public about the situation of LGBTIQ+ people world-wide. Write an article for the organisation's website commenting on the infographic below.

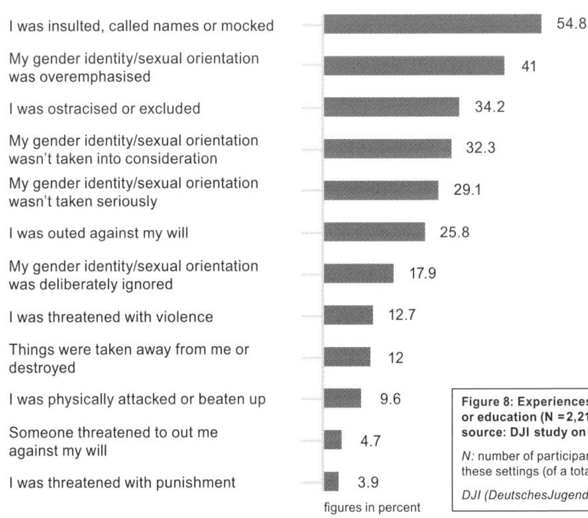

Figure 8: Experiences of discrimination in places of work or education (N =2,217) (multiple answers were possible); source: DJI study on coming out, 2015

N: number of participants who reported discrimination in these settings (of a total of 5,037 participants)

DJI (DeutschesJugend Institut): German Youth Institute

Source: Claudia Krell/Kerstin Oldemeier: Coming out – what next?! German Youth Institute, Munich 2015, https://www.researchgate.net/publication/324167887_Coming_out-what_next_A_DJI_research_project_into_the_lives_of_lesbian_gay_bisexual_and_trans_adolescents_and_young_adults_German_Youth_Institute, p. 20.
Translated by Fiona Potter and George Austin Cliff

Text Excerpt from Bernardine Evaristo, *Girl, Woman, Other*

These lines are taken from a chapter called "Amma".

they married and moved to Peckham

I was their last child and first girl, Amma explained, blowing smoke into the already thickening fug of the room

my three older brothers became lawyers and a doctor, their obedience to the expectations of our father meant I wasn't pressurized to follow suit

his only concern for me is marriage and children

he thinks my acting career is a hobby until I have both

Dad's a socialist who wants a revolution to improve the lot of all of mankind

literally

I tell Mum she married a patriarch

look at it this way, Amma, she says, your father was born male in Ghana in the 1920s whereas you were born female in London in the 1960s

and your point is?

you really can't expect him to 'get you', as you put it

I let her know she's an apologist for the patriarchy and complicit in a system that oppresses all women

she says human beings are complex

I tell her not to patronize me

Mum worked eight hours a day in paid employment, raised four children, maintained the home, made sure the patriarch's dinner was on the table every night and his shirts were ironed every morning

meanwhile, he was off saving the world

his one domestic duty was to bring home the meat for Sunday lunch from the butcher's – a suburban kind of hunter-gatherer thing

[…]

he doesn't know I'm a dyke, are you kidding? Mum told me not to tell him, it was hard enough telling her, she said she suspected when pencil skirts and curly perms were all the rage and I started wearing men's Levis

she's sure it's a phase, which I'll throw back at her when I'm forty

Dad has no time for 'the fairies' and laughs at all the homophobic jokes comedians make on telly every Saturday night when they're not insulting their mother-in-law or black people

[…]

The following lines are taken form a chapter called "Yazz", Yazz being Amma's daughter.

Yazz was allowed to wear exactly what she liked so long as she wasn't endangering herself or her health

she wanted her to be self-expressed before they tried to crush her child's free spirit through the oppressive regimentation of the education system

she has a photo of her daughter walking down the street wearing a plastic Roman army breastplate over an orange tutu, white fairy wings, a pair of yellow shorts over red and white stripy leggings, a different shoe on each foot (a sandal and a welly), lipstick smudged on her lips, cheeks and forehead (a phase), and her hair tied into an assortment of bunches with miniature dolls hanging off the ends

Amma ignored the pitying or judgemental looks from passers-by and small-minded mothers at the playground or nursery

Yazz was never told off for speaking her mind, although she was told off for swearing because she needed to develop her vocabulary

(Yazz, say you find Marissa unpleasant or unlikeable rather than describing her as a shit-faced smelly bottom)

and although she didn't always get what she wanted, if she argued her case strongly enough, she was in with a chance

Amma wanted her daughter to be free, feminist and powerful

later she took her on personal development courses for children to give her the confidence and articulacy to flourish in any setting

big mistake

Mum, Yazz said at fourteen when she was pitching to go to Reading Music Festival with her friends, it would be to the detriment of my juvenile development if you curtailed my activities at this critical stage in my journey towards becoming the independent-minded and fully self-expressed adult you expect me to be, I mean, do you really want me rebelling against your old-fashioned rules by running away from the safety of my home to live on the streets and having to resort to prostitution to survive and thereafter drug addiction, crime, anorexia and abusive relationships with exploitative bastards twice my age before my early demise in a crack house?

Amma fretted the whole weekend her little girl was away

adult men had been ogling her daughter since before puberty

there are a lot more paedophiles out there than people realize

a year later Yazz was calling her a feminazi when she was on her way out to a party and Amma dared suggest she lower her skirt and heels and raise the scoop neck of her top so that at least 30 % of her body mass was covered, as opposed to the 20 % currently given a decency rating

not to mention *The Boyfriend*, glimpsed when he dropped her off in his car

as soon as Yazz was in the door, Amma was waiting in the hallway to ask her the sort of harmless question any parent would ask

who is he and what does he do? hoping Yazz would say he was in the sixth form, a relatively harmless schoolboy then

Yazz replied with dead-pan insolence, Mum, he's a thirty-year-old psychopath who abducts vulnerable women and locks them in a cellar for weeks on end while he has his wicked way with them before chopping them into pieces and sticking them in the freezer for his winter stews

before waltzing upstairs to her room leaving a whiff of whacky-backy

nor is the child she raised to be a feminist calling herself one lately

feminism is so herd-like, Yazz told her, to be honest, even being a woman is passé these days, we had a non-binary activist at uni called Morgan Malenga who opened my eyes, I reckon we're all going to be non-binary in the future, neither male nor female, which are gendered performances anyway, which means your *women's* politics,

Mumsy, will become redundant, and by the way, I'm humanitarian, which is on a much higher plane than feminism

do you even know what that is?

Bernardine Evaristo, Girl, Woman, Other, *London: Penguin Books 2019, pp. 19–21, 37/38*

Annotations

1 Peckham: a district in southeast London
66 feminazi: (pej.) combination of the words "feminist" and "nazi"
79 whacky-backy: (sl.) cannabis

Lösungsvorschlag

1 **TIPP**

In this task you have to present briefly what you learn about Amma's family background, which implies both the family she was born into and her daughter, Yazz. It makes sense to structure your answer into paragraphs, focusing on her parents and siblings, herself and her daughter. Do not forget to write a short introduction, in which you mention the basic facts about the excerpt and reformulate the task.

The following points could come up in your answer:
- introduction: basic facts about the excerpt and reference to the task
- information on Amma's family members:
  - Amma's father:
    - at some point in his life living in Peckham, London (cf. l. 1)
    - socialist (cf. l. 8)
    - considered a patriarch (cf. ll. 10, 15, 20)
    - born in Ghana in the 1920s (cf. ll. 11/12)
    - homophobic, doesn't know about Amma's sexual orientation (cf. ll. 26, 30/31)
  - Amma's mother:
    - works full-time (cf. l. 19)
    - takes care of the family home and the children's education (cf. ll. 19–21)
    - does not take Amma's coming out as a lesbian seriously (cf. l. 29)
  - Amma's siblings:
    - three older brothers (cf. l. 4)
    - two lawyers, one doctor (cf. l. 4)
    - fulfilled their father's wish (cf. ll. 4/5)
  - Amma:
    - born in the 1960s (cf. l. 12)
    - acting career, not taken seriously by her father (cf. l. 7)
    - identifies as lesbian (cf. l. 26)
  - Amma's daughter, Yazz:
    - raised to be open-minded, independent, confident, feminist (cf. e.g. l. 51)
    - despite her free-spirited education, feels restricted by her mother (cf. e.g. l. 66)
    - calls herself humanitarian (cf. ll. 85/86)

In the extract of Bernardine Evaristo's novel *Girl, Woman, Other*, published in London in 2019, the reader meets the protagonist, Amma, and learns about her family background. This includes both the family Amma was born into and the one she later starts herself. **introduction**

Amma's father was born in Ghana in the 1920s. He moved to Great Britain and at some point during his married life to Peckham, London. He is a socialist but is also described as a patriarch and homophobe. Despite working full-time, Amma's mother also took care of the education of her now grown-up children and of their home. She never even complains about her husband not helping in the household duties. Amma has got three older brothers, who are lawyers and a doctor. According to Amma, this is what their father expected them to become. *Amma's parents and siblings*

Amma herself was born in the 1960s. She pursues an acting career, which is not taken seriously by her father. She self-identifies as lesbian, which her mother considers merely a phase and which her father is not meant to know. *Amma*

Amma has got a daughter of her own called Yazz, who she raises to be open-minded, independent, confident and a feminist. Despite being given lots of liberties, Yazz feels restricted by her mother's care and describes herself as humanitarian because she regards feminism as outdated. *Yazz*

2 **TIPP**

Here you are asked to analyse the image Amma's mother, Amma and her daughter Yazz have of themselves. The task already indicates that this image is not the same for all three of them, so you should point out the differences. In doing so, pay close attention to narrative perspective and language and the way they influence the presentation of the three women.

You can structure your solution in the following way:

- introduction
- narrative perspective:
  - excerpts from "Amma": mainly first-person narration (Amma) (exception: "Amma explained", l. 2)
  - excerpt from "Yazz": third-person narration (Amma's perspective as well):
    - "she wanted" (l. 36)
    - Amma's view on other mothers (cf. ll. 43/44)
    - "big mistake" (l. 54)
- Amma's mother:
  - traditional, working housewife and mother:
    - enumeration (cf. ll. 19–21) to stress her various chores
    - does not question her own role, understanding/supportive of her husband (cf. ll. 11/12, 14)

- traditional view of women:
  - says that she "suspected" that her daughter is lesbian because she does not follow the latest fashion trends (cf. ll. 27/28)
  - Amma's mother does not take her coming out seriously ("a phase", l. 29)
- words with a negative connotation to present Amma's critical view of her mother:
  - "apologist for the patriarchy" (l. 15)
  - "complicit in a system that oppresses all women" (ll. 15/16)
- Amma's criticism of her father, which is an indirect criticism of her mother as well:
  - "the patriarch" (l. 20) used in derogatory way
  - ironic/sarcastic metaphor: "a suburban kind of hunter-gatherer thing" (l. 24)
- Amma's hypocritical reproach:
  - Amma is not willing to even consider her mother's point of view (cf. short, aggressive question in l. 13)
  - she feels patronised when her mother tries to explain her view (cf. l. 18) although it is in fact rather Amma who patronises her mother (cf. ll. 15/16)

– Amma:
  - raises her own daughter completely differently from the way she was raised:
    - words with negative connotations when talking about other mothers (cf. l. 43) or "the system" (cf. "crush her child's free spirit", l. 36; "oppressive regimentation", l. 37)
    - comical detailed description of Yazz's attire (cf. ll. 38–42)
    - enumeration in l. 51 stresses her educational aims
  - Amma's education backfires:
    - comments on Yazz's education as a "big mistake" (l. 54)
    - Yazz seems verbally superior (cf. ll. 55–58)
  - Amma is not so very different to other mothers:
    - considers Yazz "her little girl" (l. 63)
    - worries a lot, especially when it comes to men ("paedophiles", l. 65; *"The Boyfriend"*, l. 70)

– Yazz:
  - looks down on her mother:
    - calls her "old-fashioned" (l. 59)
    - makes fun of her and provokes her with exaggerations (cf. ll. 60–62, 75–78)
    - calls her a "feminazi" (l. 66) because Amma thinks Yazz's clothes are too revealing (cf. ll. 66–69)

- considers herself progressive:
  - feminism is "herd-like" (l. 81)
  - looking at people as non-binary is the latest trend (cf. l. 83)
  - humanitarianism replaces feminism (patronising question in l. 87)
- conclusion: each generation judges the former one to be old-fashioned and thinks it knows better

introduction

In the excerpt three women from three consecutive generations are presented, Amma's mother, Amma and her daughter Yazz. Each of these three women has a self-image that differs completely from that of the other two, and the way the reader perceives these differences is influenced by the narrative perspective and language used.

narrative perspective: Amma's point of view

The excerpt is told from Amma's point of view. The parts taken from the chapter "Amma" are almost entirely told by Amma herself in the first person. In contrast, the part taken from the chapter "Yazz" is told by a third-person narrator. Still, even in that latter part, the reader sees the action through Amma's eyes because they learn what she wants (cf. l. 36) or what she thinks of others (cf. ll. 43/44) or her own educational decisions (cf. l. 54).

Amma's mother: working housewife and mother

Amma's mother is presented as a traditional working housewife and mother. To underline how many various chores she has, enumeration is used in lines 19 to 21: She has a full-time job and the education of her four children as well as the household are mostly her responsibility. Amma's mother does not question her role but is understanding and supportive of her husband. In lines 11, 12 and 14 she tries to explain the reasons for his attitude to her daughter.

traditional view of women

Her own view of women is very traditional too, not only when it comes to the gender roles she adheres to in her marriage, but also regarding the way a "typical" woman should look and be like: she "suspect[s]" (l. 27) her daughter to be a lesbian when she does not dress like most young women do (cf. ll. 27/28). Moreover, she does not take Amma's coming out seriously and calls it "a phase" (l. 29).

Amma criticises her parents

Accordingly, Amma's view of her mother is a rather negative one, which is underlined by the language Amma uses: She calls her mother "an apologist for the patriarchy" (l. 15) and "complicit in a system that oppresses all women" (ll. 15/16). The way Amma's father is depicted is further criticism on his wife who does not stand up to "the patriarch" (l. 20), as Amma derogatorily calls him. She also makes fun of her father's "domestic duty" (l. 23), which is metaphorically linked to prehistoric times as "a suburban hunter-gatherer thing" (l. 24).

When her mother tries to explain her and her husband's views, Amma feels patronised (cf. l. 18). Her reproach, however, is to be taken with a grain of salt because it has been rather Amma herself with all her highbrow words (cf. ll. 15/16) that patronised her mother. That she is not willing to even consider another view becomes apparent when she reacts to her mother's explanations only with the short, aggressive question, "and your point is?" (l. 13). As a result, the reader tends to sympathise with Amma's mother in that part of the excerpt.

Amma's hypocritical reproach

Amma herself seems to gradually realise the limitations of her progressiveness when she has a daughter of her own. She plans to raise her completely differently to what she experienced herself. A comical, very detailed description of what she allows Yazz to wear (cf. ll. 38–42) underlines her anti-authoritarian style. Her educational aims are enumerated and thus further stressed in line 51.

Amma:
very different style of education when it comes to her own daughter

When she talks about other mothers, she uses words with a negative connotation to express her own superiority to them. She considers them "judgemental" (l. 43) and "small-minded" (l. 43). In a similarly critical and condescending way she talks about the "system", which she accuses of "crush[ing] her child's free spirit" (l. 36) and of exercising an "oppressive regimentation" (l. 37).

words with negative connotations to describe other mothers or "the system"

However, at least parts of her education seem to have been a "big mistake" (l. 54), as the narrator herself comments. Yazz is verbally superior to her mother and uses Amma's own arguments and highbrow words against her (cf. ll. 55–58). Thus, Amma is made fun of and beaten at her own game.

education backfires

Also, she worries about her daughter a lot, which shows that she is not so different from other mothers in that respect. She panics, for example, about men, who are considered "paedophiles" (l. 65), and about *"The Boyfriend"* (l. 70). The capitals and italics indicate that Amma probably overestimates his importance. Despite all her efforts to promote Yazz's independence, Amma still sees her as "her little girl" (l. 63).

Amma not so very different to other mothers

Yazz, in return, considers her mother "old-fashioned" (l. 59). She looks down on her and calls her a "feminazi" (l. 66), because Amma thinks her daughter's clothes are too revealing (cf. ll. 66–69). According to Yazz, feminism is outdated and looking at people as non-binary is the latest trend (cf. l. 83). Humanitarianism has replaced feminism (cf. ll. 85/86), which is disqualified as being "herdlike" (l. 81). When Yazz feeds her mother's fears with highly exaggerated examples of what could happen to her (cf. ll. 60–62, 75–78)

Yazz looks down on her mother and considers herself progressive or patronisingly asks her whether she even knows what being humanitarian means (cf. l. 87), it is now Amma with whom the reader empathises.

To conclude, one can say that each woman in *Girl, Woman, Other* judges her predecessor to be old-fashioned and thinks she knows better. Through the generations, Amma's mother, Amma and Yazz have turned from traditional working housewife to independent, lesbian feminist and finally to outspoken non-binary humanitarian. As the reader follows this development through Amma's eyes and her often ironic words, they can see how easily each woman's perceived superiority can be challenged by even newer and more progressive ideas. **conclusion**

3.1 **TIPP**

In this evaluation task you need to assess in how far family and social communities influence a person's development. Apart from this rather general question you need to consider Amma's and Yazz's experiences. Make sure that in your solution you both refer to examples from the text and make some more general observations on the topic. When it comes to structuring your text, you can either use the examples from the excerpt as a starting point and develop some more general conclusions from these or start with the influence of family and social communities in general and use examples from the novel to bolster your view.

The sample solution uses the latter structure:

- introduction
- general role that family and social communities play in a person's development
  - family = primary source of socialisation
    - first place where a person learns about values, beliefs and norms
    - ideally providing emotional support and guidance, helping to develop a sense of self-worth and confidence
  - social communities shape the development further
    - sense of acceptance and belonging when adhering to a common set of rules and values
    - peers particularly important and influential at a certain stage in life
  - however, influence can also be negative: rejection and distance instead of acceptance and imitation
- Amma's experiences:
  - mother points out importance of social community (cf. ll. 11/12), daughter and father grew up completely differently, cannot understand each other
  - Amma attempts to distinguish herself from her parents
- Yazz's experiences:
  - also attempts to distinguish herself from her mother
  - influenced by university (= social community) (cf. ll. 81–86)

- her mother's education becomes apparent in the way Yazz expresses herself: Amma wants her to express herself well (cf. ll. 45/46, 52/53), Yazz is able to argue well (cf. ll. 55–62)
- conclusion: family and social communities are essential for a person's development, even if someone chooses to distance themselves from the influences around them

introduction

Families and social communities play a very important role in a person's development because they shape their identity. Amma and Yazz, two of the protagonists in the excerpt from *Girl, Woman, Other*, illustrate the different forms this influence can take very well.

family: values, beliefs, norms

One's family is the primary source of socialisation because it is the first place where a person learns about values, beliefs and norms. From very early on, children get to know both the values, beliefs and norms that a family adheres to and also those they dismiss. Ideally, families also provide emotional support and guidance and can thereby help a person to develop a sense of self-worth and confidence.

social communities: sense of acceptance and belonging

As children grow older, social communities shape their development further because they provide more social interactions and show which kind of behaviour is acceptable and which is not. When people adhere to a community's rules and norms, they may be rewarded with a sense of belonging. In this respect, peers are very influential, especially during puberty, when young people become more independent from their families and look for new social circles.

influence can also be negative

Thus, family and communities shape a person's identity and influence their attitudes, beliefs and behaviours. However, this does not mean that the influence of people's families or the other communities they find themselves in is always a positive one. Instead, from a certain age onwards, people can also individually decide to rebel against conformity and against values and beliefs they do not share.

Amma: protests against influence of social communities

This is also shown in *Girl, Woman, Other*: Amma's mother expresses the influence of social communities very clearly, when she tries to explain that Amma and her father cannot understand each other because the circumstances they grew up in are simply too different (cf. ll. 11/12). Amma protests against that view and does not seem to forgive her father for simply adhering to the traditions he grew up with. According to her, it is possible to shake off such limitations.

attempt to distinguish herself from her family

That is also what Amma herself does when it comes to her family ties: She clearly opposes her father's homophobic attitude. Fearing his reaction, she keeps her sexual orientation a secret from him (cf.

l. 26), but through her sarcastic descriptions of both her parents' lifestyles, she makes it obvious that she feels above their narrow-minded and old-fashioned views. Consequently, she turns into quite a different person from her mother precisely because she chooses to distinguish herself from the role model she offered. While Amma's mother was a traditional working housewife, Amma becomes an independent woman who seems to raise her daughter without a husband.

Yazz also tries to distinguish herself from her mother. It becomes apparent that it is mainly her social community, namely university, which has a big influence on her. There she gets in contact with the notion of humanitarianism, gender and considering people non-binary (cf. ll. 81–86).

Yazz: influenced by her social community

Yet, despite her alleged rejection of her mother's education, its influence also shows itself, for example in the way she expresses herself. Her mother put a lot of emphasis on language (cf. ll. 45/ 46) and even sent Yazz to "personal development courses for children" (l. 52) in order for her daughter to learn to be articulate. In discussions with her mum, Yazz proves that these courses were successful indeed (cf. ll. 55–62).

influenced by her education

All in all it can be said that family and social communities are essential for a person's development. They influence how people see themselves and define their values even if they choose to distance themselves from what they have grown up with.

conclusion

3.2 **TIPP**

In this task you need to write an article for the website of an LGBTIQ+ advocacy organisation. In this article you need to comment on the figures given. This means that you do not have to refer back to the narrative text you have analysed in the preceding tasks. Instead, study the given statistics closely and interpret their message. You will probably not mention all figures in detail, so ask yourself which ones are particularly striking and can best support the aim of your article. To answer the latter question, put yourself in the shoes of someone working for an LGBTIQ+ advocacy organisation and think about the aims you want to achieve with your article.

Possible aims of your article could be:

- to inform your readers about the situation LGBTIQ+ people face at school, at university or at work to create awareness of the problem
- to invite your readers to empathise with LGBTIQ+ people
- to demand change

When it comes to the formal elements necessary for the text form article, you need to come up with a headline and make sure that your language is rather formal. Use linguistic means to reach the aims of the article, e. g. evaluative adjectives or rhetorical devices. Your first paragraph should answer the wh-questions.

A possible structure for your answer could be:

- introduction: wh-questions
  - what: study by German Youth Institute among LGBTIQ+ people
  - when: 2015
  - who: 5,037 LGBTIQ+ people, of whom 2,217 reported being discriminated against in places of work or education
  - short summary of findings: the 2,217 respondents were affected by various forms of discrimination due to the widespread heteronormative assumptions about gender and sexual identity in society
- description of the main findings of the infographic:
  - overall message: many LGBTIQ+ people are discriminated against at places of education or at work, their gender identity / sexual orientation plays an enormous part in these places although it should not
  - particularly striking findings:
    - more than half of the 2,217 respondents were insulted, mocked or called names
    - often their gender identity/sexual orientation was either over-emphasised, ignored or not taken seriously
    - they experienced all kinds of threats or actual violence
- interpretation:
  - school, university, work are often no safe places for LGBTIQ+ people
  - it is made difficult for them to focus on their education or their work, which could have negative consequences for their career
  - LGBTIQ+ people's physical and psychological well-being is threatened
  - negative consequences for society at large
- demands:
  - everybody can help, either by facing people who threaten LGBTIQ+ people or by offering support (becoming allies)
  - diversity in educational institutions and workplaces needs to be encouraged
  - sexual and gender diversity needs to be addressed, e. g. in teaching materials, during awareness-raising projects
  - professionals need to be trained to be able to address the topic and to know how to react in various situations
- concluding appeal

Study shows sad truth — heading

In a study on coming out, which was conducted in 2015 in the name of the German Youth Institute, nearly half of all participants (2,217 out of the 5,037 overall) reported being discriminated against at school, university or work. It became apparent that they were affected by various forms of discrimination due to the widespread heteronormative assumptions about gender and sexual identity in society.

introduction: wh-questions

When we look at the findings and assume that not much has changed in recent years, it is hard to believe that someone's sexual orientation or gender identity can still play such an enormous role in places of education or work, where the focus should be a completely different one. More than half of the 2,217 respondents were insulted, called names or mocked. Often their gender identity or sexual orientation was either overemphasised (41 %), not taken seriously (29.1 %) or deliberately ignored (17.9 %). What is more, they experienced all kinds of threats or actual violence. Almost one person in ten was even physically attacked or beaten up.

description of the main findings of the infographic

This means that schools, universities and workplaces are often not safe for LGBTIQ+ people. While it does not become clear from the statistics whether the perpetrators of discrimination are peers or superiors, the impact of their behaviour can be dramatic in any case. In other words, it is very concerning that those who do not conform to heteronormative assumptions about sexual and gender identity have to worry about whether someone might beat them up or whether they will be discriminated against, and cannot therefore concentrate on their actual aims: studying or getting a job done. Sooner or later, this could have consequences on their career and/or their health. We know that bullying and discrimination have a negative impact on people's physical and psychological wellbeing. Health problems, sometimes even suicide, can be the results of such a mental burden.

interpretation of the findings

This is a situation we simply cannot tolerate because everybody has the right to be treated equally and to develop in a supportive and open environment, no matter their race, religion, ability status, gender or sexual identity. Discrimination is not only a problem that affects LGBTIQ+ people, but it goes right to the heart of our society.

relevance of the findings for society as a whole

But there is also good news: As we are all involved, we can all be part of the change as well. Everybody can help by standing up to people who bully LGBTIQ+ people or behave disrespectfully. Even if we might not always feel up to an open confrontation, we can at least offer support to those who are affected.

demands: on the individual

However, this is not enough. We need to stop discrimination before it happens. So, diversity in places of education and work needs to be encouraged. This means that non-heteronormative lifestyles must be both addressed and normalised, e. g. in teaching materials or through awareness-raising projects, but also by an open-minded employment practice. The more positive role models LGBTIQ+ people encounter, the safer and more welcome they will feel. In any case, professionals who work with young people need to be trained to be able to address the topic and to learn how to react when LGBTIQ+ teens want to talk about their sexual and gender identity or when they are challenged by others. on the system

The statistics show that it might still be an uphill struggle to reach the goal of non-discriminatory education. Yet, it is up to every single one of us to win this fight: Let's stand up to discrimination wherever and for whatever reason we witness it. For those who are suffering from discrimination at the moment, for those who might be affected by it at some point in the future and for a better society at large. **concluding appeal**

PRÜFUNGSAUFGABEN

HÖRVERSTEHEN

You will hear each recording twice. After each listening you will have time to complete your answers.

Task 1: Morning News (6 BE)

You will hear six pieces of news from the morning edition of a radio show. While listening, match the headlines **A** to **G** with the speakers **1** to **6**. There is one more headline than you need.

Headlines

A Well-known sight in need of repair
B Financial incentive for political participation
C Missing object brought back
D Angry creature defends living space
E Successful genius still a teenager
F Misfortune causes chaos
G Missing vehicle sighted repeatedly

Speaker	1	2	3	4	5	6
Headline						

Task 2: Cereal Killer Café

(6 BE)

Listen to a radio report by Leo Hornak about Whitechapel, London. While listening, tick (✓) the correct answer (a, b, c, or d). There is only one correct answer.

1 When Leo Hornak talks about "self-described anarchists", he is referring to people who

a ☐ see themselves as hipsters.
b ☐ meet in the Cereal Killer Café.
c ☐ took part in violent demonstrations.
d ☐ were born in the oldest part of London.

2 The Cereal Killer Café featured in the radio report

a ☐ is part of a global chain.
b ☐ will soon close due to high rents.
c ☐ attracts mostly people with money.
d ☐ serves reasonably priced breakfast.

3 "Class War" wants

a ☐ low-cost flats.
b ☐ social centres.
c ☐ fewer immigrants.
d ☐ more pubs and clubs.

4 Whitechapel, London

a ☐ used to be a safe neighbourhood.
b ☐ has always attracted mostly Bengalis.
c ☐ used to be the location for newcomers.
d ☐ was once home to workers from Southern Europe.

5 The demonstrators mentioned in the programme

a ☐ are relatively well off.
b ☐ throw paint at the police.
c ☐ are of South Asian origin.
d ☐ want the area to be redeveloped.

6 The main focus of this programme is on

a ☐ serious crime in London.
b ☐ urban change in London.
c ☐ racial tensions in London.
d ☐ violent demonstrations in London.

Task 3: Boredom

(13 BE)

Listen to an interview with psychologist Sandi Mann, who is speaking about her research on boredom. While listening, answer the questions. You do not need to write complete sentences.

1	Why might boredom be positive?	
2	What was the first thing people had to do in an experiment?	
3	What was special about this activity?	
4	What did people have to do in the second task?	
5	What was the result of this experiment?	
6	What happens when you daydream?	
7	When does boredom become a particularly unpleasant experience?	
8	What did a teacher do in meetings to overcome boredom?	
9	How does the psychologist explain behaviour like vandalizing?	
10	Which eating habits of bored people are mentioned? Name two.	a) b)
11	What is boredom often confused with?	
12	What does "positive boredom" imply?	

SPRACHMITTLUNG

Aufgabenstellung

You are a guest student at an American high school and your class is working on a project about popular fiction series. You have been asked to contribute an example from Germany.
Write an article for the project website using the information in both texts to describe the series and the reasons for its success.

Text 1 „Umsatzbringer ‚Die drei Fragezeichen': Da sieht Lady Gaga alt aus" (2013)

Seit Jahrzehnten lösen die kindlichen Krimihelden „Die drei Fragezeichen" einen Fall nach dem anderen – und es ist kein Ende in Sicht. […]

Die Superstars dieser Welt – sie alle kommen nicht gegen drei milchgesichtige Hobby-Ermittler an. Justus Jonas, Bob Andrews und Peter Shaw, besser bekannt als: „Die drei Fragezeichen". Sie stellen selbst Showbiz-Größen wie Lady Gaga in den Schatten.

Die Reihe aus Hörspielen und Büchern über die kindlichen Krimihelden bescherte dem Musiklabel Sony-Europa und dem Kosmos-Verlag seit ihrem Deutschland-Start 1968 einen Gesamtumsatz von fast einer halben Milliarde Euro, wie die *Wirtschaftswoche* am Samstag unter Berufung auf Branchenschätzungen berichtete. In Deutschland seien bislang mehr als 45 Millionen Tonträger und 16 Millionen Bücher der Reihe verkauft worden. […]

Die Geschichten funktionieren nach einem einfachen Grundprinzip: Verbrechensaufklärung mit einer Portion Grusel und einem hohen Wohlfühleffekt. *129 Wörter*

Quelle: mhe/afp, Der SPIEGEL Online *vom 30. 11. 2013, http://www.spiegel.de/kultur/literatur/die-drei-rekordumsatz-mit-den-kindlichen-krimihelden-a-936500.html.*

Text 2 „Kinderbuch als Bühnenshow: Die Live-Hörspiele der ‚Drei ???' befördern den Kult um sie. Ein Interview mit Jens Wawrczeck" (2015)

Drei Jugendliche, die in Kalifornien Kriminalfälle lösen: Justus Jonas, Peter Shaw und Bob Andrews sind Helden für jede Generation von Kindern in Deutschland seit 1968 – damals erschien der erste Band von „Die drei ???" in <u>deutscher Übersetzung</u>. Die Reihe wird wegen ihres Erfolgs hierzulande weitergeführt, obwohl sie in den USA 1994 eingestellt worden ist. Zur Popularität tragen die Hörspiel-Adaptionen der Krimis bei. Seit 2002 treten die Sprecher Oliver Rohrbeck (Justus), Jens Wawrczeck (Peter) und Andreas Fröhlich (Bob) zudem mit „Drei ???"-Bühnenshows auf. Dabei verwandeln sie jede noch so schnöde Halle in den fiktiven Sehnsuchtsort Rocky Beach.

Herr Wawrczeck, warum schreibt sich der Erfolg der „Drei ???“ derart fort?

Jens Wawrczeck: Wir werden vererbt. Menschen, die mit uns Kindheitserinnerungen verbinden, möchten uns in ihrem Leben behalten. Das klappt, wenn sie ihre Kinder „Die drei ???“ hören lassen. Auch wenn ich mir den Kultstatus nicht ganz erklären kann, fiel der Beginn in eine sonnenbeschienene Stunde des Hörspiels: Die Folgen spielten in Amerika. Das war damals ein weit entferntes Land, man konnte alles behaupten. Die Cover waren sehr einprägsam und stylish, nicht unbedingt wie bei Kinderhörspielen, daher konnten auch Erwachsene das kaufen, ohne rot zu werden. Inzwischen ist das ein Familien-Produkt, bei den Live-Auftritten versammeln sich die Generationen, jeder hat seine eigene Assoziation.

Die Geschichten bedienen Heldenfantasien von Heranwachsenden; zugleich kriegen Erwachsene erzählt, dass die Dinge in einer vermeintlich komplizierten Welt mit Tatendrang und Aufrichtigkeit ganz einfach zu regeln sind. Ist das der Trick?

Wir stehen in der Tradition erfolgreicher Kinderbücher, die den Erwachsenen zeigen: Ihr wisst nicht alles, ihr könnt nicht alles. Zudem sind Justus, Peter und Bob sozusagen Teile eines gesplitteten Menschen. Jeder steht für verschiedene Eigenschaften: Justus ist das Gehirn, Peter eher die Emotion, Bob erdet alles.

Haben sich die Hauptfiguren und ihre Geschichten über die Jahrzehnte verändert, vielleicht auch verändern müssen – um diejenigen zu bleiben, die sie sind?

Veränderungen sind nötig, um dem Zeitgeist gerecht zu werden – vor allem bei technischen Neuerungen. Aber alles, was diesen Kosmos zu sehr aus der Balance bringt – Freundinnen etwa – wird vom Publikum nicht akzeptiert und hat die Geschichten auch nicht befruchtet. […] Und je nostalgischer die Geschichten sind, desto besser funktionieren sie meines Erachtens. Auf keinen Fall wollen wir sprachlich hipp sein, wir verwenden keine extremen Schimpfwörter. Morde passieren eigentlich nie. Es ist dann vielleicht von Toten aus der Vergangenheit die Rede, aber es ist, glaube ich, noch nie richtig Blut geflossen.

Wie ticken Serienfiguren, damit sie für mindestens eine Generation das Potenzial zu Kindheitshelden haben?

Sie müssen authentisch sein. Meine Helden haben eine Haltung und enttäuschen mich darin nicht. Sie verkörpern ein Ideal, aber eines mit Schwächen. Glatte Helden sind uninteressant. Eine Identifikation muss schon möglich sein. Ein Held ist im Grunde jemand, der uns in einer idealen Form zeigt. Und „Die drei ???“ zeigen eine ideale Form der Freundschaft. *480 Wörter*

Quelle: Stefan Fischer, Jens Wawrczeck, Männerliebe, SZ.de *vom 23. 09. 2015, http://www.sueddeutsche.de/reise/synchronsprecher-maennerliebe-1.2657218.*

Anmerkung

14 amerikanischer Originaltitel: *The Three Investigators*

TEXTAUFGABE

Von den zwei Aufgaben ist eine auszuwählen und zu bearbeiten.

Aufgabe I: Aufgabenstellung

1 Sum up the reasons why writers turn to crime fiction according to Elizabeth George. (30 %)

2 Analyse the stylistic means the author uses and the effect they have on the reader. (30 %)

3 You are invited to take part in an international summer school project organized by the British Council, entitled "Why not crime? Opening up the curriculum in schools." Your task is to write an essay discussing whether crime fiction should be dealt with in school. Write this essay, referring to Elizabeth George's text and materials studied in class. (40 %)

Text I — Elizabeth George, "Introduction to *Crime from the Mind of a Woman*" (2002)

Whether the story is a murder mystery, a tale of suspense, a psychological study of the characters affected by a devastating event, the retelling of a famous criminal act, a courtroom drama, an exposé, a <u>police procedural</u>, or a truthful account of an actual offense, the question remains the same. Why crime? Whether the characters involved are FBI agents, policemen and women, forensic scientists, journalists, military personnel, the man or woman on the street, private detectives, or the little old lady who lives next door, the question remains the same. Why crime? [...] Why exists this fascination with crime and why, above all, exists this fascination with crime on the part of female writers?

I think there are several answers to these questions.

Crime writing is practically as old as writing itself and is consequently very much part of our literary tradition. The earliest crime stories come to us from the Bible: in a jealous rage, Cain kills Abel; in a jealous conspiracy, Joseph's brothers sell him into slavery in Egypt and fake his death for their devastated father [...].

Crime is mankind on the edge, <u>*in extremis*</u>, but more than that, crime is mankind stepping outside of the norm. For every Cain, there are a billion brothers who have co-existed throughout the centuries. [...] But this is what makes crime so interesting. It isn't what people normally do.

It would be nice to believe that cars slow down on the freeway when there is an accident because of the drivers' heightened sense of caution: everyone sees the flashing lights up ahead, the smoke, the flares, the ambulances, the fire trucks, and hits the brakes so as not to end up in the same condition as the unfortunates currently being extricated from mangled metal. But this is not generally why people slow down. They slow down to gawk, their curiosity piqued. Why? Because an accident on the freeway is an anomaly, and anomalies interest us. They always interest us: have done from the beginning of time and will do till the end of it. […]

For the writer who wishes to explore characters, there is nothing so catastrophically catalytic as the intrusion of a crime into an otherwise peaceful landscape. A crime places everyone into a crucible: […] the investigators, the perpetrator, and the victims. Within this crucible of life's most monstrous acts the mettle of the characters is tested. It is when characters confront the most serious challenges to their beliefs, their peace, their sanity, and their way of life that their pathology is triggered. And it is the pathology of the individual character clashing with the pathology of all the other characters that is the stuff of drama and catharsis. […]

What a crime does in a piece of literature is two-fold. First, it serves as a throughline for the story to follow: the crime must be investigated and solved within the twists and turns of the plot. But secondly and perhaps more importantly, the crime also acts as a skeleton for the body of the tale that the writer wishes to tell. On this skeleton, the writer can hang as much or as little as she likes. She can keep the skeleton down to the bones alone and tell a story that moves smoothly, concisely, and without deviation or decoration to its revelation and conclusion. Or she can hang upon the skeleton the muscles, tissues, veins, organs, and blood of such diverse elements of story-telling as theme, exploration of character, life and literary symbols, subplots, etc., as well as the specific crime-oriented story elements of clues, red herrings, suspense, and a list of time-honoured motifs peculiar to mysteries: the hermetically sealed death chamber (or locked room), the most obvious place, the trail of false clues left by the real killer, the fixed idea, and on and on. […]

Why, then, would a writer ever consider dabbling in anything else? There is no reason that I can see. For as long as a writer adheres to the notion that the only rule is there are no rules, the sky's the limit within this field. *679 words*

From: Elizabeth George. "Introduction." Crime from the Mind of a Woman: 26 Compelling Crime Stories from some of the 20th Century's Best Women Writers. *London: Hodder and Stoughton, 2002. 1–4.*

Annotations

3 police procedural: a subgenre of detective fiction
15 *in extremis:* to the highest degree
24 to gawk: to stare stupidly
28 catalytic: triggering a change
29 crucible: *here:* a situation in which people are tested
30 mettle of the character: a character's ability to cope with difficult situations
32 pathology: *G.: krankhaftes Verhalten*
34 catharsis: *(a literary term)* the creation of strong feelings as a way of providing relief
35 throughline: a connecting theme or plot in a movie, play, book, etc.
48 to dabble in sth: to do sth, but not very seriously

Aufgabe II: Aufgabenstellung

1 Summarize the text. (30 %)

2 Analyze how Mr. Yacobowski's behavior affects Pecola's self-esteem. (30 %)

3 Your school is taking part in a European project on "The Power of Imagery in Literature." You have decided to focus on the image of the "dandelion" used by Toni Morrison in *The Bluest Eye*. For the project's online journal you submit an article in which you assess whether the image of the dandelion is an appropriate literary symbol for Pecola as well as for other African-American characters in literature.
Write this article in which you refer to Toni Morrison's text and to materials studied in class. (40 %)

Text II Excerpt from Toni Morrison, *The Bluest Eye* (1970)

The protagonist of the following excerpt is Pecola, a young African-American girl living in the American Midwest in the late 1930s. The excerpt starts when Pecola is on her way to a small grocery store.

There is plenty of time to consider what to buy. Now, however, she moves down an avenue gently buffeted by the familiar and therefore loved images. The dandelions at the base of the telephone pole. Why, she wonders, do people call them weeds? She thought they were pretty. But grown-ups say, "Miss Dunion keeps her yard so nice. Not a dandelion anywhere." Hunky women in black babushkas go into the fields with baskets to pull them up. But they do not want the yellow heads – only the jagged leaves. They make dandelion soup. Dandelion wine. Nobody loves the head of a dandelion. Maybe because they are so many, strong […].

She climbs four wooden steps to the door of Yacobowski's Fresh Veg. Meat and Sundries Store. A bell tinkles as she opens it. Standing before the counter, she looks at the array of candies. All Mary Janes, she decides. Three for a penny. The resistant sweetness that breaks open at last to deliver peanut butter – the oil and salt which complement the sweet pull of caramel. A peal of anticipation unsettles her stomach.

She pulls off her shoe and takes out the three pennies. The gray head of Mr. Yacobowski looms up over the counter. He urges his eyes out of his thoughts to encounter her. Blue eyes. Blear-dropped. […] At some fixed point in time and space he senses that he need not waste the effort of a glance. He does not see her, because for him there is nothing to see. How can a fifty-two-year-old white immigrant storekeeper with the taste of potatoes and beer in his mouth, his mind honed on the doe-eyed Virgin Mary, his sensibilities blunted by a permanent awareness of loss, *see* a little black girl? Nothing in his life even suggested that the feat was possible, not to say desirable or necessary.

"Yeah?"

She looks up at him and sees the vacuum where curiosity ought to lodge. And something more. The total absence of human recognition – the glazed separateness. She does not know what keeps his glance suspended. Perhaps because he is grown, or a man, and she a little girl. But she has seen interest, disgust, even anger in grown male eyes. Yet this vacuum is not new to her. It has an edge; somewhere in the bottom lid is the distaste. She has seen it lurking in the eyes of all white people. So. The distaste must be for her, her blackness. All things in her are flux and anticipation. But her blackness is static and dread. And it is the blackness that accounts for, that creates, the vacuum edged with distaste in white eyes.

She points her finger at the Mary Janes – a little black shaft of finger, its tip pressed on the display window. The quietly inoffensive assertion of a black child's attempt to communicate with a white adult.

"Them." The word is more sigh than sense.

"What? These? These?" Phlegm and impatience mingle in his voice.

She shakes her head, her fingertip fixed on the spot which, in her view, at any rate, identifies the Mary Janes. […]

"Christ. Kantcha talk?"

His fingers brush the Mary Janes.

She nods.

"Well, why'nt you say so? One? How many?"

Pecola unfolds her fist, showing the three pennies. He scoots three Mary Janes toward her – three yellow rectangles in each packet. She holds the money toward him. He hesitates, not wanting to touch her hand. She does not know how to move the finger of her right hand from the display counter or how to get the coins out of her left hand. Finally he reaches over and takes the pennies from her hand. His nails graze her damp palm.

Outside, Pecola feels the inexplicable shame ebb.

Dandelions. A dart of affection leaps out from her to them. But they do not look at her and do not send love back. She thinks, "They *are* ugly. They *are* weeds."

Preoccupied with that revelation, she trips on the sidewalk crack. Anger stirs and wakes in her; it opens its mouth, and like a hot-mouthed puppy, laps up the dredges of her shame.

Anger is better. There is a sense of being in anger. *698 words*

From: Toni Morrison. The Bluest Eye. *1970; London: Picador, 1990. 35–37.*

Annotations

2 buffeted: *G.: beschwingt*
2 dandelion: *G.: Löwenzahn, Pusteblume*
5 hunky: a derogatory term for unskilled workers from Eastern Europe
5 babushka: traditional Russian clothing
11 Mary Jane: a kind of candy
13 peal: *here:* a sudden strong feeling
16 blear-dropped: half closed and tired
19 honed on the doe-eyed Virgin Mary: always thinking of the image of the (white) Virgin Mary with her mild eyes
20 blunted: becoming less sensitive
21 feat: action which requires strength, effort
52 dredge: *here*: trace, mark

Lösungsvorschlag

HÖRVERSTEHEN

Transkript 1 Morning News

Hinweis: Aus lizenzrechtlichen Gründen ist die ungekürzte Original-Passage der NPR-Sendung abgedruckt. Die in der Abituraufgabe nicht berücksichtigten Passagen sind durch eine kleinere Schriftgröße kenntlich gemacht und für die Bearbeitung der Aufgaben nicht relevant.

Speaker 1: Good morning. I'm Steve Inskeep with the story of an overachiever. Moshe Kai Cavalin of California says he's nothing special, which is sort of true. Many people have published two books as he did, except he's done it by age 17. He earned a bachelor's degree from UCLA and is seeking a master's in cybersecurity. He's also working for NASA in his spare time. Not only that, California's legal driving age is 18, meaning that next year he can even drive by himself. It's MORNING EDITION.

Speaker 2: Good morning. I'm Steve Inskeep. It's like the old movie, "The Birds," except that instead of many attacking birds, there's one. An owl is attacking runners on a trail in Bethesda, Maryland. The trail is near Washington, favored by super-fit residents in the nation's capital. At least three were attacked and scratched by the owl. Rather than hunt the attacker, officials have posted a warning sign. Officials explain owls are territorial. And who's to say the area does not belong to the bird? You are listening to MORNING EDITION.

Speaker 3: Good morning, I'm Renee Montagne. And Big Ben is getting old. And at 156 years old, London's famous clock is slowing down, chiming a whole six seconds behind schedule. Fixing water erosion and cracks could silence its chimes for three years. Still, Big Ben's unauthorized Twitter account is keeping time, typing out B-O-N-Gs on the hour – bong, bong, bong, bong, bong, bong. It's MORNING EDITION.

Speaker 4: Good morning. I'm Steve Inskeep with a benefit of the information age – Melissa Gonzales can track her stolen car. Ever since somebody took the Colorado woman's SUV, she's been receiving clues to its location in the mail. She tells KMGH-TV she received a parking ticket, then a highway toll charge, and she received a photo radar ticket. We do not know the names of the four people photographed in the car. We do know they were driving 85 in a 45-mile-an-hour zone. It's MORNING EDITION.

From: © 2015 National Public Radio, Inc. NPR News report "Tickets, Toll Charges Sting For Stolen Car Owner" was originally broadcast on NPR's Morning Edition on October 21, 2015, and is used with the permission of NPR. Any unauthorized duplication is strictly prohibited.

Speaker 5: Good morning, I'm Renee Montagne. Voter turnout is a concern all over the country. But in one city, trudging to the polls for a mayoral election just got more rewarding. The online publication *Philadelphia Citizen* is sponsoring a kind of lottery, offering a $ 10,000 prize to one lucky voter. A polling place will be chosen at random and the prize money given to a random voter. As one organizer told the *Philadelphia Inquirer*, "desperate times require desperate measures". It's MORNING EDITION.

From: © 2015 National Public Radio, Inc. NPR News report "Philadelphia Publication To Give $10,000 To A Random Mayoral Race Voter" was originally broadcast on NPR's Morning Edition on October 23, 2015, and is used with the permission of NPR. Any unauthorized duplication is strictly prohibited.

Speaker 6: Good morning. I'm Steve Inskeep. This technique comes right out of a James Bond movie, though it no doubt happened by accident. A truck in Missouri spilled boxes of nails on the highway – 200 boxes – each box containing 2,000 nails. KOMU-TV reports that traffic on I-70 was stopped during the cleanup, and nobody caught the truck, of course, because who could pursue it after it dropped 400,000 nails? You're listening to MORNING EDITION.

From: © 2015 National Public Radio, Inc. NPR News report "Thousands Of Nails Stop Traffic On Missouri Highway" was originally broadcast on NPR's Morning Edition on October 27, 2015, and is used with the permission of NPR. Any unauthorized duplication is strictly prohibited.

TIPP

These text passages will help you find the correct answer:

1. "the story of an overachiever." (l. 1); "Many people have published two books as he did, except he's done it by age 17. He earned a bachelor's degree from UCLA and is seeking a master's in cyber security. He's also working for NASA in his spare time." (ll. 2–5)
2. "An owl is attacking runners on a trail in Bethesda, Maryland." (ll. 9/10); "Officials explain owls are territorial." (ll. 12/13)
3. "Big Ben is getting old. And at 156 years old, London's famous clock is slowing down, chiming a whole six seconds behind schedule. Fixing water erosion and cracks could silence its chimes for three years." (ll. 15–17)
4. "Melissa Gonzales can track her stolen car. Ever since somebody took the Colorado woman's SUV, she's been receiving clues to its location in the mail" (ll. 20–22); "she received a parking ticket, then a highway toll charge, and she received a photo radar ticket." (ll. 22–24)

5 "in one city, trudging to the polls for a mayoral election just got more rewarding." (ll. 27/28); "a kind of lottery, offering a $ 10,000 prize to one lucky voter. A polling place will be chosen at random and the prize money given to a random voter." (ll. 28–30)

6 "it no doubt happened by accident. A truck in Missouri spilled boxes of nails on the highway" (ll. 33/34); "traffic on I-70 was stopped during the cleanup" (l. 35)

Speaker	1	2	3	4	5	6
Headline	E	D	A	G	B	F

Transkript 2 Cereal Killer Café

Interviewer: Yesterday several hundred demonstrators held a protest, which turned into a riot against gentrification and middle-class hipsters moving into the neighbourhood. The world's man at the BBC in London is Leo Hornak. He filled me in on the protest.

Leo Hornak: Well, this group of self-described anarchists – several hundred of them marched through the streets of, err, Whitechapel, which is one of the oldest parts of the East End, traditionally a very poor area, and they targeted some of the classic symbols of gentrification. There were attempts to smash the windows of estate agents, rents going up, and also as you said this "Cereal killer café", which is a bit of a sort of symbol of what some people see as the hipsterfication of the East End and of London.

Interviewer: Yeah, has that café taken on any notoriety just because of what it does and what it serves?

Hornak: Well, I, I mean, I think that a lot of people maybe feel a little bit sorry for the people running this café. It's a small independent business. It does sell, err, novelty, err *(laughs),* breakfast cereals at a very, pretty high price. I think the going rate for some Coco Pops is about five and a half dollars, which obviously is just the Coco Pops plus some cold milk. And the reason this has attracted so much attention is that it's serving a crowd of young, quite affluent middle-class people [who] just maybe recently left university and this is a real area where they're attracted to and where they hang out – where there's clubs, bars and novelty kind of shops like this. Just looking at "Class War" – that's the group who organised this – this protest. Looking at their manifesto, they said, "We don't want luxury flats that no one can afford. We want genuinely affordable housing. We don't want pop-up gin bars and brioche buns. We want community."

Interviewer: So, what's been the response to demands like that?

Hornak: Well, it's really interesting, Marco, because it's divided people. I mean I live not that far from Whitechapel where this happened – you might say maybe I'm part of the problem – and it is an area which is traditionally the first place where new communities and immigrants arrive in London for hundreds of years. In the 19th century, at the time of Jack the Ripper, it was when Jewish immigrants from Eastern Europe arrived in London. And then, later on, it became the area where South Asian communities arrived and currently it's a mainly Bengali community. Now when you looked at the protestors who were throwing paint at the "Cereal Café" yesterday, most of them were themselves white and possibly middle class. They certainly weren't the community, the South-Asian community that is being forced out and most affected by gentrification in this area. It was only a few years ago that we had the London riots, which were much more widespread and maybe less overtly political. But it was the same sense that a certain sub-section of the poorest in London were being forgotten as a different section raced ahead.

From: Leo Hornak, Anti-hipster protest in London targets breakfast cereal cafe, 28 September 2015, http://www.pri.org/stories/2015-09-28/anti-hipster-protest-london-targets-breakfast-cereal-café (accessed: 10 February 2016).

TIPP

These text passages will help you find the correct answer:

1 "this group of self-described anarchists – several hundred of them marched through the streets of, err, Whitechapel […] and they targeted some of the classic symbols of gentrification. There were attempts to smash the windows" (ll. 5–8)

2 "it's serving a crowd of young, quite affluent middle-class people" (l. 19)

3 "Looking at their manifesto, they said, 'We don't want luxury flats that no one can afford. We want genuinely affordable housing.'" (ll. 22–24)

4 "it is an area which is traditionally the first place where new communities and immigrants arrive in London for hundreds of years." (ll. 29/30)

5 "Now when you looked at the protestors who were throwing paint at the 'Cereal Café' yesterday, most of them were themselves white and possibly middle class. They certainly weren't the community, the South-Asian community that is being forced out and most affected by gentrification in this area." (ll. 33–37)

6 "a protest, which turned into a riot against gentrification and middle-class hipsters moving into the neighbourhood" (ll. 1–3); "rents going up" (l. 9); "this 'Cereal killer café', which is a bit of a sort of symbol of what some people see as the hipsterfication of the East End and of London." (ll. 9–11); "traditionally a very poor area" (l. 7); "it's serving a crowd of young, quite affluent middle-class people […] this is a real area where they're attracted to and where they hang out – where there's clubs, bars and novelty kind of shops like this." (ll. 19–21)

1 When Leo Hornak talks about "self-described anarchists", he is referring to people who

c ✓ took part in violent demonstrations.

2 The Cereal Killer Café featured in the radio report

c ✓ attracts mostly people with money.

3 "Class War" wants

a ✓ low-cost flats.

4 Whitechapel, London

c ✓ used to be the location for newcomers.

5 The demonstrators mentioned in the programme

a ✓ are relatively well off.

6 The main focus of this programme is on

b ✓ urban change in London.

Transkript 3 Boredom

Sandi Mann: Boredom is excellent for many things, but one thing in particular that it's good for is to enable your creativity and I've done some research about all this actually that was published in 2014. We got people really bored. I got them to copy out phone numbers from a telephone book, which was not just boring and repetitive, but it's meaningless.

Interviewer: Oh, so they don't like that it's pointless?

Mann: Pointless and I think there's something about something not having meaning that makes us more bored. You know we like to have meaning in our lives. So, it was a pointless, meaningless task. They got really bored and then we gave them a test of creativity. We wanted to see how creative they were. So we gave them two polystyrene cups and said, "How many things can you think of – how many uses can you think of for these two cups?" The people who had the boring task to do actually came up with more – more things to do with these cups and they were more creative in the ideas they came up with than the people who weren't bored. And we thought that the reason for that is because when you're bored, your mind wanders, and when your mind wanders, you daydream, and when you daydream, you can come up with all sorts of fantastical ideas. Your mind can go on to flights of fancy, you can think laterally, because you're not constrained by your sub-conscious mind. So, what's good about boredom, it allows that creativity. That's the main thing, I think, for me.

Interviewer: So, boredom isn't necessarily the same as doing nothing. It's whether you wanted something to do and you haven't got something to do.

Mann: Boredom is a negative thing. It's a search for neural stimulation. So, once you've satisfied that search, then you are no longer bored, even though you may still not be doing anything. But your mind is active. So, if you're in a boring situation and you can't escape it and you're not allowed to have your mind wandering, then it's a very frustrating, negative feeling and it feels like boredom.

Interviewer: Sometimes people will count things, won't they?

Mann: Yes, I … oh my gosh, yeah I …

Interviewer: … and do anything to sort of change their mindset?

Mann: I had a paper that I published called "Counting window panes" and that was the strategy that a teacher used to cope in boring meetings. So, they counted the window panes. So yeah, when you have a strategy that is satisfying, then the experience becomes pleasant if you like – a kind of relaxation instead – and therefore technically would no longer be classified as boredom, but perhaps downtime instead.

Interviewer: At other times people are so bored that they vandalise things or do graffiti or do other anti-social things, because they're so bored and there's nothing to do. So how do you balance it?

Mann: Yes, so that's the downside. If you have too much boredom and especially chronic boredom with a lack of meaning. So, for those people they need to find meaning in their lives and that is very important because that's one of the problems of negative boredom, when you start doing negative things to cope with it. And this is the other thing about boredom. It's how you cope with it. There are negative ways and there are positive ways and we tend to do the negative things, like the anti-social behaviour, like eating, overeating. For example, I've got a piece of research coming out called "Bored people don't eat nuts" and what I've shown with this research is that if you get people bored and you give them a variety of snacks to eat, they won't go for the healthy stuff. They'll choose, they'll eat more of the unhealthy stuff, the fatty, sugary stuff. And the reason for that is that when we are bored we are seeking stimulation.

Interviewer: Oh, and everyone has done that – going to open the fridge cos you're just a bit bored.

Mann: It's that and it's also that we actually get a dopamine hit from sugary and fatty foods. Dopamine is the reward chemical – so it feels good.

Interviewer: And the psychological literature seems to divide boredom into two kinds.

Mann: There's a kind of negative and a positive side. I think there's this kind of misconception between boredom and relaxation, because I have a lot of people that say to me, "Well, I like doing nothing, you know, it's relaxing." That's not boredom. The thing about boredom is that it's a negative thing in that you are seeking stimulation. So, if you're in a situation where you're happy to have nothing to do and relaxing – that's the kind of positive boredom that I guess we're looking for, where we can just enjoy letting our minds go freely where they want to go.

From: Sandi Mann, Claudia Hammond, Why boredom could be good for you,
BBC *11 May 2016, http://www.bbc.co.uk/programmes/p03tsr5n (accessed: 29 November 2016).*

TIPP

These text passages will help you find the correct answer:

1 "Boredom is excellent for many things, but one thing in particular […] is to enable your creativity" (ll. 1/2); "So, what's good about boredom, it allows that creativity." (l. 19)

2 "We got people really bored. I got them to copy out phone numbers from a telephone book" (ll. 3/4)

3 "not just boring and repetitive, but it's meaningless." (ll. 4/5); "they don't like that it's pointless?" (l. 6); "Pointless and I think there's something about something not having meaning that makes us more bored. You know we like to have meaning in our lives. So, it was a pointless, meaningless task." (ll. 7–9)

4 "They got really bored and then we gave them a test of creativity. […] So we gave them two polystyrene cups and said, 'How many things can you think of – how many uses can you think of for these two cups?'" (ll. 9–12)

5 "The people who had the boring task to do actually came up with more – more things to do with these cups and they were more creative." (ll. 12–14)

6 "when you're bored, your mind wanders, and when your mind wanders, you daydream, and when you daydream, you can come up with all sorts of fantastical ideas. Your mind can go on to flights of fancy, you can think laterally, because you're not constrained by your sub-conscious mind." (ll. 15–18)

7 "So, if you're in a boring situation and you can't escape it and you're not allowed to have your mind wandering, then it's a very frustrating, negative feeling and it feels like boredom." (ll. 25–27)

8 "I had a paper that I published called 'Counting window panes' and that was the strategy that a teacher used to cope in boring meetings." (ll. 31/32)

9 "people are so bored that they vandalise things or do graffiti or do other anti-social things" (ll. 36/37); "that's the downside. If you have too much boredom and especially chronic boredom with a lack of meaning. […] one of the problems of negative boredom, when you start doing negative things to cope with it. […] There are negative ways and there are positive ways and we tend to do the negative things, like the anti-social behaviour." (ll. 39–45)

10 "we tend to do the negative things, like […] overeating. For example, I've got a piece of research coming out called 'Bored people don't eat nuts' […] if you get people bored and you give them a variety of snacks to eat, they won't go for the healthy stuff. They'll choose, they'll eat more of the unhealthy stuff, the fatty, sugary stuff." (ll. 44–49)

11 "a kind of negative and a positive side. […] there's this kind of misconception between boredom and relaxation, because I have a lot of people that say to me, 'Well, I like doing nothing, you know, it's relaxing.' That's not boredom." (ll. 56–58)

12 "you're happy to have nothing to do and relaxing – that's the kind of positive boredom that I guess we're looking for, where we can just enjoy letting our minds go freely where they want to go." (ll. 60–62)

1	Why might boredom be positive?	it makes creativity possible
2	What was the first thing people had to do in an experiment?	copy phone numbers from a telephone book
3	What was special about this activity?	it had no meaning / was meaningless / was pointless
4	What did people have to do in the second task?	complete a creativity test / think of as many different uses for two polystyrene cups as possible / come up with things to do with two polystyrene cups
5	What was the result of this experiment?	bored people had more ideas and were more creative
6	What happens when you daydream?	your mind wanders / you can have fantastical ideas / flights of fancy are possible / lateral thinking is possible / there are no constraints by your subconscious
7	When does boredom become a particularly unpleasant experience?	when you cannot escape a boring situation / when it is not possible to let your mind wander
8	What did a teacher do in meetings to overcome boredom?	he counted window panes
9	How does the psychologist explain behaviour like vandalizing?	result of too much boredom / result of chronic boredom / result of people lacking meaning in their lives / people do negative things to cope with negative boredom
10	Which eating habits of bored people are mentioned? Name two.	*Name two of the following:* bored people tend to overeat / bored people do not eat healthy food (like nuts) / bored people eat unhealthy/fatty/sugary food
11	What is boredom often confused with?	relaxation
12	What does "positive boredom" imply?	you are happy about having nothing to do / you are relaxing / you can enjoy letting your mind run free

TIPP

In this task you are required to write an article for the website of a project about popular fiction series. Do not forget to include a heading, an introduction, a well-structured and coherent main body as well as a conclusion. As your article mainly addresses students at an American high school, some colloquial expressions are possible. However, the general style or register should be rather formal, respectively neutral. Your text should contain the following aspects:

- Reihe hat ihren Ursprung in den USA, wurde dort allerdings abgesetzt
- erfreut sich großer Beliebtheit in Deutschland seit 1968
- generell ein Kinderbuch, aber auch für Erwachsene ansprechend
- Hauptfiguren: drei junge Hobbydetektive
- Handlungsort: imaginärer Ort in Kalifornien
- Gründe für den Erfolg:
  - ansprechend für verschiedene Generationen
  - authentische Helden verkörpern Ideale, ohne dabei perfekt zu sein
  - nostalgische Darstellung einer geordneten Welt
  - unverwechselbares Design der Cover
  - vielseitige Verfügbarkeit (Bücher, Hörspiele, Live-Shows)

***The Three ???*: How an American Detective Series for Children has been Capturing Germans of all Generations for more than 50 years**

Having started in 1968, the children's detective series *The Three Investigators*, which in German reads *The Three ???*, became an immediate success, and while the American original petered out in 1994, its German counterpart has been selling record numbers of books and CDs and has been filling venues all across Germany with live performances of the stories. So what makes the adventures of three young amateur detectives in an imaginary place in California so popular?

The formula for success could be narrowed down to the series offering exciting and slightly scary detective stories with a feel-good factor which are written for children but are still popular with the older generations. The three young heroes serve as an authentic embodiment of basic human characteristics, with one of the boys being the intellectual, the second his emotional counterpart and the third down-to-earth and pragmatic. While they present an ideal of teamwork and friendship, they retain individual weaknesses and are therefore perfect for identification. Furthermore, the well-ordered, somewhat nostalgic setting, to which only necessary technological innovations, but no swear words or excessively violent scenes have been added throughout the years, offers a simple and welcome escape from an otherwise complex and chaotic world.

The distinctive cover design and the fact that the stories are available as books, radio plays and live shows enabling different generations to listen to or watch the stories together adds to *The Three Investigators'* success. No wonder that in Germany the love of the series has been passed on from one generation to the next.

TEXTAUFGABE

Text I **Elizabeth George, "Introduction to *Crime from the Mind of a Woman*" (2002)**

1 **TIPP**

The command term *(dt. Operator)* "sum up" generally requires you to state the main points of a text in your own words. In this task, the summary's focus is on the reasons Elizabeth George gives for authors deciding to write crime fiction. Only write down what is essential. Your text should be well-structured and significantly shorter than the original. Do not copy from the excerpt and refrain from commenting on the text.
Your text should include the following reasons why writers turn to crime fiction:
- Crime fiction has been an integral component of our literary tradition for basically as long as writing itself exists.
- People have an inherent interest in any occurrence that is out of the ordinary.
- A crime gets characters into situations full of difficulties, drama and emotions, and thus serves as a perfect means to explore character traits.
- A crime serves as the story's structure, which can be kept simple or made more complex by the writer.

In the introduction to her crime stories collection *Crime from the Mind of a Woman*, which was published in 2002, Elizabeth George names several reasons why writers, and particularly female writers, find appeal in writing crime fiction.
According to George, many people are fascinated by crime stories due to the fact that crime is an anomaly, something outside the norm. What is more, this interest in something that is not part of our everyday life is age-old. Thus, crime writing plays an essential part in our literary tradition and there have practically always been crime stories.
George also states that placing characters in a situation where they are confronted with a crime – whether it be as victims, perpetrators or investigators – allows the author to explore facets of these characters that were previously unforeseen and unavailable for examination. The crime confronts them with a challenge that tests their ability to cope with difficult situations. This in turn results in drama and catharsis, which is a way to make the story more interesting to the reader.
Last but not least, a crime serves as a way to connect all the elements of the story. When it happens, its investigation and solution must take place within the duration of the book's plot. Thus, it gives the story a basic structure that can be developed according to the author's wishes, which means that he/she can decide whether to keep the tale more simple and straightforward or whether to embellish it with various elements of storytelling.

2 **TIPP**

In this task, the command term “analyse” requires you to take a closer look at the stylistic means used by the author and explain the resulting effects on the reader. It is essential that you work closely with the text at hand and support your points by giving evidence. Be as specific as possible in explaining what effect the different stylistic devices actually have on you as a reader.
Your analysis could include the following findings:

- The author uses rhetorical questions, which catch the readers’ interest and lead to their feeling involved in the argumentation.
- She repeats the key question (“Why crime?”) to stress her main concern.
- She uses further repetitions to allow the readers to follow easily.
- She makes use of enumerations and examples to illustrate her arguments.
- She applies figurative language, especially a metaphor of a skeleton, to make the readers visualise what she is trying to say.
- She uses expressive words to create emotion.

In explaining why writers turn to crime fiction, Elizabeth George uses several stylistic devices in order to strengthen her arguments.
Her use of multiple rhetorical questions containing the interrogative particle “why” (cf. ll. 4, 7–9, 24, 48) serves as a means to captivate and interest the readers in what she has to say. Rhetorical questions give the readers the impression that these are actually their own questions, which motivates them to carry on reading, as they want to find the answers to them. This is why rhetorical questions can mainly be found in the first paragraph. What is especially remarkable here is the fact that George even repeats the question “Why crime?” (ll. 4, 7) twice. She thus points out that this is the key question she wants to give answers to in what follows.
On top of that, George uses further examples of repetition as a way to connect the readers’ thoughts and make it easier for them to follow. These examples include the repetition of the phrase “Crime is mankind” (l. 15) as well as repeating the words “slow down”, “anomaly” and “interest” in successive sentences (cf. ll. 23–25).
Furthermore, there are many enumerations to be found throughout the text (cf. ll. 1–4, 4–7, 29, 31/32, 41–47). Instead of simply stating that several kinds of crime stories exist, that a number of different characters can be involved in the investigation, that everyone in a crime story is confronted with a challenge, or that the tale can be amplified by several elements of storytelling, Elizabeth George always lists various examples. By doing so, she illustrates her points and allows the readers to get a better idea of what she means.
To strengthen her arguments as to why crime fiction is so appealing, George also uses an abundance of figurative language. Phrases like “the intrusion of a crime into an otherwise peaceful landscape” (l. 28) – when explaining why a crime allows authors to explore their characters in detail – or “the unfortunates currently being extricated from mangled metal” (ll. 22/23) – when comparing the attractive power of a crime as

something out of the ordinary to that of a car accident on the freeway – increase the use of the readers' imagination.
Another means that is intended to create pictures in the readers' minds is used by George in describing "[w]hat a crime does in a piece of literature" (l. 35): the metaphor of the skeleton (cf. ll. 37–47). In a biological sense, the skeleton is what gives a body its structural integrity. In crime literature, this means that the crime itself gives the author a structure for the story he/she wants to tell. The writer then has two options regarding what to do with the skeleton. Either he/she uses only the bones and tells a story that is straightforward and without embellishment, or the skeleton is covered with muscles and other body parts – which represent different elements of storytelling, stylistic devices and motifs – to achieve a more complex story with several possibilities for interpretation. The metaphor of the skeleton enables the readers to visualise this concept and obtain a better understanding of what Elizabeth George is trying to say.
Finally, the author uses several expressive words, for example "devastated" (l. 14) or "gawk" (l. 24), which fuel the text's emotional effect on the readers.
To draw a conclusion, Elizabeth George's intention is to convince her readers of what she thinks are the reasons for writers turning to crime fiction. To reach this goal, she makes use of several stylistic devices which have the effect of capturing the readers' attention, creating emotions, illustrating points or emphasising arguments.

3 **TIPP**

This exercise is embedded in a situational context to which you should refer in some way. It requires you to write an essay in the course of your participation in an international summer school project that deals with crime fiction in schools. Your essay needs an introduction, a main part and a conclusion as well as a heading. As you have to discuss whether crime fiction should be dealt with in school or not, you are supposed to adduce arguments for and against the matter in question before you come to a logical conclusion that mirrors your personal opinion. Besides referring to Elizabeth George's text, you are also expected to mention materials studied in class. This could include the two short stories "A Scandal in Bohemia" and "The Tell-Tale Heart" as well as the television series *Sherlock*.
The following aspects could be mentioned in your essay:
- Possible arguments for incorporating crime fiction into the curriculum:
  - Crime stories are usually dramatic and exciting and therefore quite appealing to pupils.
  - Crime fiction is more accessible to younger readers, especially compared to classical literature, which often contains difficult language or unfamiliar topics.
  - Crime stories are representative of different literary periods.

- Possible arguments against incorporating crime fiction into the curriculum:
  - Some crime stories are not appropriate for pupils as they contain quite a large amount of violence.
  - Most curricula are already packed and adding crime fiction would mean even less time to read classical literature and deal with a story in detail.

Crime fiction in schools?

There is little to no debate as to whether plays like Shakespeare's *Romeo and Juliet* or classic novels such as Harper Lee's *To Kill a Mockingbird* should be an integral part of a school's literary curriculum. However, what about pieces such as the short stories "A Scandal in Bohemia" by A. C. Doyle or "The Tell-Tale Heart" by E. A. Poe? Should such crime stories also be dealt with in school? Opinions are deeply divided on this issue.

First of all, let me briefly explain how Elizabeth George, herself a writer of crime novels, summarises the advantages of crime stories. She states that a crime brings out the most in all characters involved, as they are tested in difficult situations, and attracts the attention of the reader because of our inherent curiosity about anything that is not ordinary. There is drama and action, and the plots are usually full of suspense. This is probably the most obvious reason why pupils generally tend to find crime stories interesting. On top of that, I could imagine that works of classical literature are not that accessible to many of them, as they often have problems with understanding the language or because the topics are foreign to them. Crime fiction, by contrast, is usually more approachable to young readers. Furthermore, crime stories are simply part of our literary tradition and thus should not be neglected.

For all these reasons, one could argue that crime fiction should be incorporated into the curriculum. Yet to what extent are these positive findings true in the case of concrete examples? Is the view of Elizabeth George correct when it comes to the two stories mentioned above?

Regarding "The Tell-Tale Heart", it must be said that this story would certainly complement every curriculum very well. It features quite a challenging symbol (the "vulture eye"), whose meaning one could speculate on for ages. What is more, the narrative perspective leaves the reader in the dark as to what exactly happens. Was the murder just a figment of the narrator's imagination, who shows clear signs of being mentally handicapped? Or if we happen to believe the narrator, what were the reasons for the crime? There is an air of mystery surrounding the story, and it serves as a prime example of how an alleged crime brings out extremes in a character. All in all, the story is fascinating, quite short and leaves a great deal of room for interpretation – good reasons for reading it in class.

Considering "A Scandal in Bohemia", however, it is doubtful whether this story meets the criteria mentioned by George. First of all, although the story does feature some dramatic twists and turns and therefore catches the reader by surprise from time to time, the plot is still comparatively simple. Besides, the reader is spoon-fed with information by a demigod-like protagonist, which leads to the fact that the "crime" could never scare or mesmerise the reader. As a consequence, there is the risk of this short story not being appealing to many pupils. However, it could perhaps be an option to include watching the BBC adaptation of the story, *A Scandal in Belgravia*. This film is part of the popular *Sherlock* series and therefore attracts a younger audience. In this case, reading "A Scandal in Bohemia" would be at least justifiable for comparative purposes.

As the examples show, George's positive appraisal does not apply equally to all crime stories.

Apart from that, I think there are also some more general reasons why crime fiction should not be added to the curriculum.

One argument against reading crime stories in the classroom is that they might overwhelm young, impressionable minds, as they sometimes contain quite a large amount of violence. For younger children especially, it may simply not be suitable to meet "mankind on the edge" (l. 15).

Furthermore, according to Elizabeth George, "a courtroom drama" (ll. 2/3) and other "tale[s] of suspense" (l. 1) also qualify as a crime story. It logically follows that *To Kill a Mockingbird* and *Romeo and Juliet* could also be considered crime stories in a broad sense. Both feature a crime (the forbidden marriage in *Romeo and Juliet* and the false accusations against Tom Robinson in *To Kill a Mockingbird*) and in both cases, this brings out the most in the characters – which, to quote George, "is the stuff of drama and catharsis" (l. 34). Just think of Romeo's final speech ("oh happy dagger") or the development of Jem Finch as a result of the unfair trial. In a nutshell: Why should the curricula in schools, which are usually too packed already, be charged with yet another literary genre when crime also features in the classics?

To sum up, I personally think there are some crime stories that are indeed suitable for being dealt with by pupils, whereas there are others that I would not want to read in class. In my view, the issue should not be whether or not to incorporate crime stories into the curriculum at all, but rather which ones to incorporate. In this regard, age is one of the factors that should not be ignored, as many crime stories tend to be more appropriate for older pupils. All in all, if the choice of stories is carefully considered, dealing with crime fiction in class can make sense. Nevertheless, the question remains whether it is absolutely necessary to make modifications to the curriculum as there is a sufficient amount of crime in classics anyway.

Text II Excerpt from Toni Morrison, *The Bluest Eye* (1970)

1 **TIPP**

The command term *(dt. Operator)* "summarize" asks you to state the main points of a text. For this task therefore, you need to find all the important aspects concerning Pecola's experience as depicted in the excerpt at hand: before, during and after buying candy. Only write down what is essential. Your text should be well-structured and significantly shorter than the original. Paraphrase the main points in your own words rather than copying from the excerpt. Furthermore, refrain from commenting on the text.
Your text could include the following aspects:

- Pecola, a young African-American girl, is on her way to the grocery store.
- Inside the store, the white shop owner treats her in a very unfriendly manner:
  - he does not really acknowledge her
  - he talks to her in a rude way
  - he tries to avoid touching her hand
- When Pecola leaves the store, she is embarrassed and sad.
- Outside, however, these feelings turn into anger.

The excerpt from the novel *The Bluest Eye*, which was written by Toni Morrison and published in 1970, deals with what the protagonist Pecola, a young African-American girl who lives in the American Midwest during the 1930s, experiences while going to the grocery store to buy candy.

While Pecola is still on her way to the store, she notices some dandelions at the bottom of a telephone pole. Whereas she herself thinks they are beautiful, she knows that other people call them weeds and that they often get rid of them. She remembers that people always care about the leaves but disregard the yellow heads, and wonders whether this might be because there are so many of them.

As soon as she arrives at the store, the young girl chooses which candies she wants, pulls her money out of her shoe – which is where she carries it around – and is ready to buy them. In the following, however, she is confronted with the unfriendly behaviour of the white shop owner, Mr. Yacobowski, which is expressed in his vacant, disapproving look, rude remarks and the attempt to avoid physical contact with her. Pecola, who is already familiar with reactions like this, attributes the man's behaviour to her skin colour.

When stepping out of the store, she feels ashamed and sad. Then, her eyes meet the dandelions once more. This time, though, she cannot see the beauty in them anymore and anger increasingly replaces the shame inside her.

2 **TIPP**

The command term "analyze" requires you to describe particular aspects or characteristics of a text in detail and support your points by giving evidence from the text. So, in this task, you are supposed to describe the white shop owner's behaviour towards Pecola, refer to significant text passages and explain how this behaviour changes the girl's self-esteem. Your text should be well-structured and contain an introduction as well as a conclusion.

The following findings could be mentioned in your text:

- shop owner's behaviour:
  - he does not really recognise Pecola, but just gives her an empty look
  - he is unfriendly and confronts her very rudely
  - he does not want to touch her hand while exchanging candy and money
- influence on Pecola:
  - her self-esteem is lowered
  - she feels less of a person

Self-esteem plays an important role in our lives, as it is often reflected in our behaviour. Apart from ourselves one of the biggest influences on our self-esteem are the people in our environment. To let people have an impact, we do not necessarily have to know them personally or be close to them – it is sufficient to simply bump into them on the street or meet them at a store, for example, just like Pecola meets Mr. Yacobowski in the novel *The Bluest Eye*.

In order to be able to see how Pecola's self-esteem changes, it is important to compare her behaviour at the beginning of the story with that at the end.

At the beginning of the story, the young girl comes across as a confident person who enjoys her life and sees the good in everything – a fact which is conveyed with the help of the dandelions. While everyone she knows detests them and calls them weeds, Pecola sees their beauty and does not care about what others think (cf. ll. 3–8). After leaving the store at the end of the story, however, she is disgusted by them and calls them ugly like everybody else (cf. ll. 49/50). This clearly shows that her attitude towards life has changed. While she was full of love for life and did not let the opinions of others influence her own at the beginning, she has adopted their negative view by the end. She feels worthless and inferior, and her "inexplicable shame" (l. 48) even turns into anger.

Thus, what Pecola experienced inside the store must have affected her behaviour and lowered her self-esteem. Since the shop owner Mr. Yacobowski is the only person she met there, it is glaringly obvious that it was he who played a significant role. However, what exactly did he do to cause such a drastic change?

The first interaction between the two characters that is noteworthy is the look Mr. Yacobowski gives the young girl after she enters the store. His gaze is portrayed as being pejorative and uninterested, as he looks at her but "does not see her, because for him there is nothing to see" (ll. 17/18). Additionally, Pecola describes this empty look as a "vacuum edged with distaste" (l. 31) – instead of showing interest in her as a person

and customer, he does not even seem to recognise her as a human being. Although Pecola has experienced being treated like this before (cf. ll. 27/28), it still affects her: she feels as if the white man – like all white people – is disgusted by her due to her skin colour and race (cf. ll. 28–31). Whereas she knows that the colour of her skin does not define who she is as a person, the shop owner's dehumanising behaviour still makes her feel out of place and insecure, which leads to a lowering of her self-esteem. In the interaction that follows, Pecola seems to be walking on eggshells, trying hard not to offend Mr. Yacobowski (cf. ll. 32–34). Feeling intimidated, she only points a finger at the candy she wants to buy. The shop owner, however, cannot identify which candy she is pointing to and confronts her in a very rude and condescending manner (cf. ll. 36, 39, 42), which amplifies the girl's insecurity even more.
When Mr. Yacobowski tries to avoid touching the girl's hand as best he can while giving her the candy and taking her money (cf. ll. 43–47), Pecola's self-esteem is finally deflated. Hence, she simply cannot help but feel ashamed when she leaves the store. Soon, however, this shame changes into anger (cf. ll. 48, 51–53).
To draw a conclusion, all these incidents show how Mr. Yacobowski's behaviour gradually leads to Pecola leaving the shop as a different person from when she entered it.

3 **TIPP**

This assignment is embedded in a situational context you should refer to in some way. It requires you to write an article for the online journal of a European school project. Your article needs an introduction, a main part and a persuasive conclusion as well as a headline. Furthermore, subheadings might be good to make the structure of the text more obvious to the reader. As you have to assess whether the image of the dandelion is an appropriate literary symbol for African-American protagonists in literature, you should explain the symbol's meaning first. Then, arguments for and against the matter in question are needed. Besides referring to the excerpt from Toni Morrison's novel *The Bluest Eye*, you are also expected to adduce examples from materials studied in class. This could include Harper Lee's novel *To Kill a Mockingbird.*

- Meaning of the symbol:
  - Many people have a stereotypical opinion of dandelions and reject them as weeds. → Many white people consider black people to be inferior and worthless.
  - First, Pecola thinks dandelions are pretty and strong, but then she, too, regards them as ugly weeds. → First, the girl has a positive view of herself and other African-American people, but then her opinion is negatively influenced by the discriminatory experience with the white shop owner.
- Possible arguments for the appropriateness of the symbol:
  - The white shop owner is impolite and condescending towards Pecola because, in his view, she does not deserve his attention.
  - The man's behaviour makes Pecola herself feel unwelcome and inferior.

- Black people are often discriminated against by the white majority (e. g. in *To Kill a Mockingbird*: Tom Robinson's discriminatory treatment and unfair trial, the fact that black people are regarded as only good for hard work in the fields).

– Possible arguments against the appropriateness of the symbol:
  - The symbol is too subjective (it expresses Pecola's specific point of view rather than a general perception).
  - Related to the first argument, the symbol is also too negative (e. g. in *To Kill a Mockingbird*: The Finches' unprejudiced attitude towards black people and their caring treatment of Calpurnia as an equal).

Flower Power – The power of dandelions

As part of the project on "The Power of Imagery in Literature", it is our main goal to first identify images used in different works of literature and then assess how well these images convey the intended meaning.
In her novel *The Bluest Eye*, Toni Morrison uses the dandelion as a literary symbol for the protagonist Pecola, a young African-American girl who lives in the American Midwest during the late 1930s, and for black people in general. However, is the dandelion really an appropriate image within Morrison's story? Could other African-American characters in literature also be symbolised by a dandelion? To answer this second question, Harper Lee's novel *To Kill a Mockingbird* will be taken as a reference.

A dandelion – what does that mean?

In *The Bluest Eye,* it is argued that many people have a rather stereotypical opinion of dandelions, regard them as weeds and want to get rid of them. Furthermore, if dandelions are plucked with the purpose of being used to make soup or wine, people are not interested in their yellow heads but only their leaves. If we assume that the plants stand for African Americans, this image symbolises the fact that many white people regard black people as inferior and worthless. Pecola initially considers dandelions to be beautiful and strong but later finds them ugly and useless. This illustrates that, at first, the black girl is a confident and happy person who views herself and other African-American people as being pretty, but is then influenced by the white shop owner's discriminatory behaviour while buying candy. She suffers from low self-esteem and accepts her fate of being seen as worthless, inferior and ugly by the white majority – although this makes her angry.

Are dandelions an appropriate choice?

In some respects, the image of the dandelion is an appropriate literary symbol for both Pecola and other black characters. Both in *The Bluest Eye* and *To Kill a Mockingbird*, for instance, there are African-American people who suffer discrimination due to their race. Many white people regard them as "weeds" because of the colour of their skin. In *The Bluest Eye*, the white shop owner considers the black girl to be unworthy of receiving his attention or polite treatment, so that eventually Pecola herself feels inferior and rejected. Similarly, in *To Kill a Mockingbird*, Tom Robinson is discriminated against by the white community of Maycomb and receives an unfair trial. The

white jury convicts him, which, in view of the fact that his lawyer Atticus refutes all evidence speaking against Tom Robinson, is clearly wrong and is highly likely to stem from the fact that he is black. Furthermore, in Pecola's description of the dandelions it is also said that people are usually only interested in their leaves and not their heads. In this regard, the image is again quite fitting for the situation depicted in *To Kill a Mockingbird,* where Maycomb's white society only shows interest in the bodies of the black people – as they work for them in the fields.
All in all, *The Bluest Eye* and *To Kill a Mockingbird* are two examples of stories in which many black people are marginalised by the white majority – just as dandelions are not wanted by many people.

To what extent are dandelions an inappropriate choice?
Nevertheless, dandelions are not necessarily an appropriate symbol for all African-American characters in literature. In *To Kill a Mockingbird,* this becomes very clear when comparing the attitude of the Finch family with those of the rest of Maycomb society. The Finches are not racist and get along very well with the black people around them. They have nothing to criticise about the black people, meaning that they do not regard them as "weeds" but rather as beautiful and equal, not to mention that they love their black housekeeper Calpurnia as if she was a family member. In contrast to Pecola in *The Bluest Eye*, Calpurnia does not get the feeling of being unwanted. Consequently, the image depicted in *The Bluest Eye* is quite subjective. It mirrors the way Pecola perceives the situation. However, as the symbol is rather negative, it is not appropriate as a general image for all African-American characters.
We can therefore conclude that the dandelion, as used by Toni Morrison in her novel *The Bluest Eye*, is a very appropriate literary symbol in this specific story and could also be transferred to some other African-American characters in literature. Nevertheless, it is not an image which can be used universally.

Niedersachsen Englisch ▪ Abiturprüfung 2019
Erhöhtes Anforderungsniveau

HÖRVERSTEHEN

You will hear each recording twice. After each listening you will have time to complete your answers.

Task 1: Young People and Their Education (5 BE)

You will hear five young people talking about their education. While listening, match the speakers 1 to 5 with the headings A to G. There are two more headings than you need.

Headings

A Choice of institution and consequences for family

B Choice of institution and student's peers

C Family expectations and career choice

D Family traditions and choice of institution

E Family traditions and reality of teaching

F School requirements and chances of good placement

G School requirements and student's dissatisfaction

Speaker	1	2	3	4	5
Heading					

Task 2: Buckingham Palace

(6 BE)

You will hear a news report about Buckingham Palace. While listening, tick (✓) the correct answer (a, b, c, or d). There is only one correct answer.

1 The refurbishment of Buckingham Palace requires
- **a** ☐ risky but important repair work.
- **b** ☐ the Queen to spend less money.
- **c** ☐ the agreement of Britain's legislation.
- **d** ☐ a large sum of money from private donations.

2 The palace is in a bad state because
- **a** ☐ not much has been done for decades.
- **b** ☐ there are too many visitors every year.
- **c** ☐ heavy rainfalls have damaged the roof.
- **d** ☐ mistakes were made during the construction.

3 The refurbishment work will be paid for by
- **a** ☐ selling specially-designed souvenirs.
- **b** ☐ putting up the entrance fee for visitors.
- **c** ☐ collecting money through sponsored events.
- **d** ☐ raising the monarch's income from the state.

4 Graham Smith points out that
- **a** ☐ the British monarchy should be abolished.
- **b** ☐ the majority of people opposes the project.
- **c** ☐ the Royals already get an annual monetary rise.
- **d** ☐ everyone is affected by reductions in state spending.

5 Duncan Wilson states that
- **a** ☐ the British monarchy needs to be preserved.
- **b** ☐ spending public money on the project is justified.
- **c** ☐ the disapproving Members of Parliament have a point.
- **d** ☐ many tourist sights in Great Britain are in need of repair.

6 At the end the tone of the news report is
- **a** ☐ critical.
- **b** ☐ neutral.
- **c** ☐ humorous.
- **d** ☐ enthusiastic.

Task 3: Huckleberry Finn

(14 BE)

You will hear a radio feature about Mark Twain's novel *The Adventures of Huckleberry Finn.* While listening, answer the questions. You need not write complete sentences. Unless otherwise specified, one aspect is enough.

1	What did Ernest Hemingway say about Mark Twain's novel? *(Name **one** aspect.)*	
2	What is/was the novel criticized for? a) today b) when it first came out	a) b)
3	What did Tom Reigstad and Mark Twain have in common?	
4	How did the Buffalo library get a part of Twain's manuscript?	
5	What did the *Buffalo Young Men's Association* do?	
6	What did Gluck do to get a part of Twain's manuscript?	
7	What happened shortly before Gluck died?	
8	Why wasn't the other part of the manuscript discovered earlier?	
9	What did Pam's sister wrongly assume?	
10	What did Reigstad want to find out after hearing about the discovery?	
11	What did some book dealers plan to do with the manuscript? *(Note down the **two** steps.)*	a) b)
12	How does the Buffalo library make sure that the manuscript is protected?	

SPRACHMITTLUNG

Aufgabenstellung

Your school is organizing an exchange with a high school in the USA. To help the American students prepare for their stay in Germany, your school is creating a website with information on different aspects of German customs and culture.
Using the information in the text, write an article for this website on the Germans' consumption of drinking water both in general and in restaurants.

Text

Michael Frank, „Leitungswasser hat in der deutschen Tischkultur keinen Stellenwert" (2016)

Ein Festmahl, ein Zechgelage ist eigentlich nur so gut, wie gut und reichlich seine wichtigste Ingredienz fließt, nämlich frisches, klares Wasser. Es stillt den Durst, es begleitet und umspielt Speisen und Getränke, es erschließt oft erst den genüsslichen Gehalt des Weiteren, denn ein feiner Tropfen gegen den Durst getrunken, das wäre erstens kein Genuss und zweitens groteske Verschwendung. Überdies schmeckt frisches, klares Wasser wunderbar.

In der deutschen Tischkultur hat es diesen Stellenwert nicht. Es ist kaum zwei Generationen her, dass man sich im privaten Rahmen wirklich Gedanken über Qualität und Geschmack von Wasser macht. Dass sich etwa Brauer für ihr Bier um die Qualität dieses Grundstoffes sorgen müssen, das kannte man. Einige wussten sogar noch, dass der Geschmack von Nudeln nicht zuletzt von der Beschaffenheit des Teigwassers abhängig ist. Aber Wasser als Geschmackserlebnis, das ist neu. Vielfach wird mit Wasser immer noch achtlos umgegangen, allenfalls zwischen „mit und ohne Kohlensäure" unterschieden und dabei Leitungswasser nachgerade verachtet. Die Zunft des Wassersommeliers ist noch exotisch, sie hat mit Missionstätigkeit zu tun.

Rigidere Alkoholbestimmungen im Verkehr und eine Rückbesinnung auf alles, was gesund und „pur" ist, haben dem Wasser im Alltagsgebrauch dennoch eine ganz neue Rolle beschert. 1970 trank jeder Bundesbürger pro Kopf und Jahr statistisch etwa 14,5 Liter Mineralwasser, heute sind es 175 Liter. Haben die Leute vorher Leitungswasser getrunken? Eher nicht, sonst hatte sich die Vorliebe doch halten müssen, indem man auch in Restaurant, Gasthaus oder Imbiss leichthin Leitungswasser bekäme. Seinetwegen muss man es in mancher Gaststube beinahe auf einen Streit ankommen lassen.

Bestellt man zum Essen ein Glas Wasser, macht man sich sofort verdächtig, ein ekelhafter Geizhals zu sein. Der Wirt nimmt an, man wolle das Glas Leitungswasser gratis. Denn Mineralwasser aus der Flasche – oder heute Tafelwasser aus dem Zapfhahn – ist die Ware, die einem Gastronomen in Deutschland die mit Abstand höchste Gewinnmarge bringt. Der Generalfehler der Leitungswasserdebatte ist aber, dass sie meist unter der Rubrik Sparsamkeit abgehandelt wird, also als Frage des Geldes. Dass der Geschmack, aber auch Umweltbewusstsein das Hauptmotiv hartnäckiger Nachfrage nach Leitungswasser sein kann, glaubt fast niemand.

Leitungswasser war bis vor relativ kurzer Zeit tatsächlich so eine Sache. Der auch in kulinarischen Dingen äußerst engagierte Historiker Hans Ottomeyer, lange Chef des Deutschen Historischen Museums in Berlin, erinnert daran, dass Leitungswasser noch bis in die Achtziger meist „fast bis zur Ungenießbarkeit" mit Chlor versetzt war. [...]

Selters, Urmarke des deutschen Mineralwassers, war lange Zeit ein gesuchtes Luxusgut, weil gesundheitlich absolut unbedenklich und damit die Ausnahme. Einst durften etwa in München Färber, Gerber und Kürschner an Brautagen nicht arbeiten. Da man aus den Zuflüssen der Isar schöpfte, wollte man keine giftigen Säuren und Laugen aus deren Abwasser im Bier haben. Im 19. Jahrhundert erkannte man städtische Gewässer als Brutstätten der Cholera und anderer teuflischer Gefahren. „Wasser macht Läuse im Bauch", haben noch die Großeltern nur halb im Scherz gewarnt. Das sitzt tief.

In vielen Nachbarländern ist es schon lange Brauch, dass für den Gast als Erstes eine Karaffe Wasser auf den Tisch kommt. Dies wohlgemerkt in Gegenden, deren Wasserqualität weit unter der deutschen liegt. In Frankreich, berichtet der Wassersommelier Armin Schönenberger, hat schon seit den Sechzigerjahren jeder Gast das gesetzliche Anrecht auf einen Krug Gratiswasser. [...]

Wenn Höchstpreislokale Mineralwassersorten von bis zu 100 Euro die Flasche anbieten, hat das mehr mit Verpackungsfirlefanz zu tun als mit Qualität. Auch mit Wasser wird geprotzt heutzutage. Und da kommen ernsthaft Menschen und insistieren auf Wasser aus der Leitung?

Armin Schönenberger, der Wassersommelier, sieht das so: „Wasser ist ein Menschenrecht. Jeder Gast kann meiner Meinung nach überall Leitungswasser verlangen. Der Wirt kann das nicht verweigern, aber er hat nun mal das Hausrecht. Er kann bestimmen, zu welchem Preis er diese Leistung gewährt." Alles, was ein Wirt seinen Gästen bietet, soll seinen Preis haben. Auch Leitungswasser muss serviert werden und braucht ein ansprechendes Glas. Es auszuschenken ist Leistung. Leitungswasser darf im Lokal also etwas kosten.

640 Wörter

Quelle: Michael Frank, „Leitungswasser hat in der deutschen Tischkultur keinen Stellenwert", in: Süddeutsche Zeitung, *30. 12. 2016*

Anmerkungen

15 Sommelier: Experte, der Restaurantgäste bei der Auswahl von Wein berät
50 Firlefanz: Überflüssiges oder wertloses Zeug

Lösungsvorschlag

HÖRVERSTEHEN

Transkript 1 Young People and Their Education

Speaker 1: My parents immigrated to the US from India to pursue a better life than their parents and to give me a better life than them, specifically sending me to an elite private school with a pricey tuition. This was so important that they accepted the yearly five-figure payment even if it wasn't always easy. I can't remember the last time we've gone on a vacation as a family.

From: Nila Venkat: My pricey education, https://yr.media/news/my-pricey-education/, © Youth Radio

Speaker 2: I went to a big, public high school. It wasn't the best learning environment for me. I was stressed out by all the homework, work sheets and tests. Rather than encouraging me to think for myself, my grades seemed to be determined by how well I could memorise facts and dates. I felt like a robot.

From: Marie Sosa: What I didn't learn in high school, https://yr.media/news/what-i-didnt-learn-in-high-school/ © Youth Radio

Speaker 3: I come from a family of high achievers. Both my parents attended Ivy League universities but for college I chose a different path. For much of high school, I put everything into school work. I didn't think too much about girls, looks or popularity. My outlook changed when my sister chose a small liberal arts college over an Ivy. I was shocked but over time I saw how happy she was at her school. It made me reconsider how I viewed college, how my choice didn't have to be based on rankings or legacy.

From: Benjamin Rossi: Turning away from the IVY League, https://yr.media/news/turning-away-from-the-ivy-league-2/, © Youth Radio

Speaker 4: For three years I attended a private middle school. Our books were always new, the food always organic and my teachers had one-on-one check-ins with us every week. But something was missing. I would talk with my friends at lunch, all of them white and middle class like me, and note how we all had the same opinions and things to say. By eighth grade it was getting really old. Throughout middle school people talked about public schools the same way you'd talk about city sewers but I was fascinated. I wanted to meet people who were different than me, and have friends who I could actually learn from.

From: Natalie Bettendorf: The benefits of a public education, https://yr.media/news/the-benefits-of-a-public-education/, © Youth Radio

Speaker 5: My 18-year-old sister is studying for medical school. My 14-year-old brother already designs programs with my dad, a software engineer. My aunt a doctor, my uncle an engineer. And me? I'm interested in public affairs. My mom regularly asks me in the car, "Do you know what you want to be when you grow up?" I used to answer, "a lawyer, a journalist, a politician" but we got into arguments so often that now I just tell her I don't really know yet. I know my parents want the best for me and I keep their suggestions in mind. In Indian culture, careers in STEM are seen as good, high-paying jobs. The rest? Not so much. The thought of their son in a liberal arts profession is a difficult pill for them to swallow.

From: Arnav Gupta: Going against my family's career goals, https://yr.media/news/going-against-my-familys-career-goals/, © Youth Radio

TIPP

These text passages will help you find the correct answer:

1 "sending me to an elite private school with a pricey tuition. […] they accepted the yearly five-figure payment even if it wasn't always easy. I can't remember the last time we've gone on a vacation as a family." (ll. 2–5)

2 "I was stressed out by all the homework, work sheets and tests. […] I felt like a robot." (ll. 7–9)

3 "I come from a family of high achievers. Both my parents attended Ivy League universities but for college I chose a different path. […] my choice didn't have to be based on rankings or legacy." (ll. 10–16)

4 "For three years I attended a private middle school. […] I would talk with my friends at lunch, all of them white and middle class like me […]. Throughout middle school people talked about public schools the same way you'd talk about city sewers but I was fascinated. I wanted to meet people who were different than me" (ll. 17–23)

5 "I know my parents want the best for me and I keep their suggestions in mind. […] The thought of their son in a liberal arts profession is a difficult pill for them to swallow." (ll. 30–33)

Speaker	1	2	3	4	5
Heading	A	G	D	B	C

Transkript 2 Buckingham Palace

Reporter: Here in Britain it's been announced that Queen Elizabeth's official London residence, Buckingham Palace, is to have refurbishment, which will cost around $ 450 million. The work, which will go before Parliament for approval, will involve the replacement of the palace's wiring, heating and plumbing. Officials say the repairs are needed to avoid catastrophic problems but critics of the royal family have questioned whether the spending can be justified during a time of austerity. Here's our royal correspondent, Sarah Campbell.

Sarah Campbell: The official London residence of the Queen, a building which palace officials describe today as part of the nation's DNA is now in a dangerous state of disrepair. It contains more than 100 miles of electric cabling and 20 miles of heating pipes, along with six and a half thousand plug sockets and 5,000 light fittings. Little has been replaced since the 1950s, leaving the palace at risk of fire or flood damage on a catastrophic scale according to an independent assessment. The plan is to spread the refurbishments over 10 years. The tax payer will fund the work through a 66 % increase in the annual treasury payments to the Queen, known as the Sovereign Grant. Graham Smith is from the anti-monarchy group, Republic.

Graham Smith: I think it's pretty appalling that the palace have gone yet again to the taxpayer to ask for more money. Everybody else is suffering huge cuts: public services, you know, welfare, benefits and so on. Thirty-eight per cent increase on royal funding over the last five years and yet they're demanding even more.

Sarah Campbell: Some MPs have also questioned the amount of public money to be used, however Duncan Wilson from Heritage England, which will be involved in approving the works, says the palace is a special case.

Duncan Wilson: If any building deserves the title 'iconic', and representing the UK to the world outside, it must be Buckingham Palace, so surely we need to protect it for future generations and do that properly.

Sarah Campbell: The Queen is completely supportive of the plan, say palace officials, and although she won't have to move out when the builders move in, she is prepared to move rooms to accommodate them. With 775 to choose from, Her Majesty should be able to avoid the noise.

TIPP

These text passages will help you find the correct answer:

1. "The work, which will go before Parliament for approval, […]" (l. 3)
2. "Little has been replaced since the 1950s, leaving the palace at risk of fire or flood damage on a catastrophic scale according to an independent assessment." (ll. 11–13)
3. "The tax payer will fund the work through a 66 % increase in the annual treasury payments to the Queen, known as the Sovereign Grant." (ll. 14–16)
4. "Everybody else is suffering huge cuts: public services, you know, welfare, benefits and so on." (ll. 18/19)
5. "If any building deserves the title 'iconic' […], it must be Buckingham Palace, so surely we need to protect it for future generations and do that properly." (ll. 24–26)
6. "With 775 to choose from, Her Majesty should be able to avoid the noise." (ll. 29/30)

1 The refurbishment of Buckingham Palace requires

c ✓ the agreement of Britain's legislation.

2 The palace is in a bad state because

a ✓ not much has been done for decades.

3 The refurbishment work will be paid for by

d ✓ raising the monarch's income from the state.

4 Graham Smith points out that

d ✓ everyone is affected by reductions in state spending.

5 Duncan Wilson states that

b ✓ spending public money on the project is justified.

6 At the end the tone of the news report is

c ✓ humorous.

Transkript 3 Huckleberry Finn

Rachel Gillman: […] *The Adventures of Huckleberry Finn* tells the story of the young white Huck Finn and his black friend Jim and the things they got up to on the Mississippi River.

Tom Reigstad: The American novelist Ernest Hemingway proclaimed that it's the best American novel ever written, that nothing will ever be written like it and that all American literature came from that book. The novel, while mildly controversial when it was first published, has become increasingly controversial.

Rachel Gillman: Controversial because the racial stereotypes and language used in the book seem shocking to a modern audience. But at the time it was published, it was seen as vulgar and challenging to social norms. Tom Reigstad is a professor of English at Buffalo University. […]

Tom Reigstad: My first job out of college was at the *Buffalo Courier-Express,* a thriving Buffalo newspaper, a daily newspaper that Twain had worked for years earlier and I started reading some of Twain's original writings […] and in 1979, I wrote a feature story where I researched the handwritten manuscript of *Adventures of Huckleberry Finn* that was housed in the Buffalo Library. The only known part of that handwritten manuscript to that date was the second half of the novel. […]

Rachel Gillman: Tom found out that the manuscript had been donated to the library in the late 19th century by a Buffalo lawyer called James Gluck. His granddaughter is Pam Lindholm. […]

Pam Lindholm: My grandfather'd started or he was one of the people that'd started *The Buffalo Young Men's Association* and that's what they did: they collected signatures and poems and whatnot and he thought it would be good to collect manuscripts and

I'm sure a few others did too but he was one of the first that thought that that was a good idea. […]

Rachel Gillman: Pam's grandfather had written to Mark Twain and asked the author if he would mind sending any original manuscripts of his books that he had kept.

Pam Lindholm: Mark Twain sent him the manuscript. He said, "I can only find half of it. I can only find the second half but I'll send it to you." So he did. Well, a couple of years later Mark Twain wrote my grandfather and said, "I've found the second half and I'll send it along." […]

Rachel Gillman: But the two parts of the manuscript didn't get reunited. Shortly after receiving the other half from Twain, James Gluck died. The manuscript was left in a trunk and it was passed down through the generations of the Gluck family. Nobody rifled through the papers inside the trunk and nothing more was heard about the missing pages, until Pam Lindholm received a phone call from her sister, a librarian, in February 1990.

Pam Lindholm: So, she called and she said, "Guess what I found?" And I said, "Heavens, what?" And she said, "I found the original handwritten manuscript of *Huck Finn.*" And at that time, she thought it was the whole thing because it was very fat. […]

Rachel Gillman: The sisters decided to call the auction house Sotheby's. […] News began to leak out about the remarkable discovery. […]

Tom Reigstad: […] The news went viral. The next day, there was a big story in *The New York Times.* The news went international because it was such a, you know, stunning find.

Rachel Gillman: And how did you feel at that moment?

Tom Reigstad: I just, you know, was shocked and amazed. It was such terrific news and I couldn't wait to take a look at the manuscript and see what changes Twain had made, the way he would, you know, cross things out, and add words. It's just as if you're looking over Twain's shoulder when he's in the midst of the composing process. […]

Rachel Gillman: […] Gluck's family, the Buffalo Public Library and The Mark Twain Project, an archive of some of Twain's works, fought a legal battle over the manuscript. […]

Tom Reigstad: Publicly, Sotheby's planned to auction off the newly discovered portion of *The Adventures of Huckleberry Finn* manuscript for between $ 500 and $ 750,000. Secretly, there was some movement by a consortium of rare book dealers across the country, who got wind of this and they had agreed with Sotheby's to purchase the manuscript for a million and a half dollars and then divide it up. […] Thankfully, that didn't happen.

Rachel Gillman: Pam and her sister settled for a much smaller amount of money to ensure it went to the Buffalo Public Library. The complete century-old manuscript is safely housed there to this day in a temperature-controlled vault where thousands of tourists come to visit it. […]

https://www.bbc.co.uk/sounds/play/p04svth5

TIPP

These text passages will help you find the correct answer:

1 "The American novelist Ernest Hemingway proclaimed that it's the best American novel ever written, that nothing will ever be written like it and that all American literature came from that book." (ll. 4–6)

2 "Controversial because the racial stereotypes and language used in the book seem shocking to a modern audience. But at the time it was published, it was seen as vulgar and challenging to social norms." (ll. 8–10)

3 "My first job out of college was at the *Buffalo Courier-Express,* a thriving Buffalo newspaper, a daily newspaper that Twain had worked for years earlier" (ll. 12/13)

4 "Tom found out that the manuscript had been donated to the library in the late 19th century by a Buffalo lawyer called James Gluck." (ll. 18/19)

5 "My grandfather'd started or he was one of the people that'd started *The Buffalo Young Men's Association* and that's what they did: they collected signatures and poems and whatnot and he thought it would be good to collect manuscripts" (ll. 21–23)

6 "Pam's grandfather had written to Mark Twain and asked the author if he would mind sending any original manuscripts of his books that he had kept." (ll. 26/27)

7 "Shortly after receiving the other half from Twain, James Gluck died." (ll. 32/33)

8 "The manuscript was left in a trunk and it was passed down through the generations of the Gluck family. Nobody rifled through the papers inside the trunk" (ll. 33–35)

9 "she said, 'I found the original handwritten manuscript of *Huck Finn.*' And at that time, she thought it was the whole thing because it was very fat." (ll. 39/40)

10 "I couldn't wait to take a look at the manuscript and see what changes Twain had made, the way he would, you know, cross things out, and add words. It's just as if you're looking over Twain's shoulder when he's in the midst of the composing process." (ll. 49–52)

11 "Secretly, there was some movement by a consortium of rare book dealers across the country, who got wind of this and they had agreed with Sotheby's to purchase the manuscript for a million and a half dollars and then divide it up." (ll. 58–60)

12 "The complete century-old manuscript is safely housed there to this day in a temperature-controlled vault" (ll. 63/64)

1	What did Ernest Hemingway say about Mark Twain's novel? *(Name **one** aspect.)*	(it's the) best American novel (ever written) / nothing will ever be written like it / all American literature came from it
2	What is/was the novel criticized for? a) today b) when it first came out	 a) racial stereotypes/language / racism b) vulgar / challenging to social norms
3	What did Tom Reigstad and Mark Twain have in common?	(they) worked for the same (daily) newspaper / (they both) worked in Buffalo
4	How did the Buffalo library get a part of Twain's manuscript?	(it) was donated (to the library) / (James) Gluck donated it
5	What did the *Buffalo Young Men's Association* do?	(they) collected signatures/poems/manuscripts
6	What did Gluck do to get a part of Twain's manuscript?	(he) wrote to the author (and asked for manuscripts)
7	What happened shortly before Gluck died?	Twain sent Gluck the other half of the manuscript / (he) got the other half of the manuscript from Twain
8	Why wasn't the other part of the manuscript discovered earlier?	(it) was left in a trunk / nobody looked through the papers
9	What did Pam's sister wrongly assume?	(that) she had found the whole manuscript
10	What did Reigstad want to find out after hearing about the discovery?	what changes Twain had made / which words Twain had crossed out/added / (about) Twain's composing process
11	What did some book dealers plan to do with the manuscript? *(Note down the **two** steps.)*	a) purchase the manuscript (for a million and a half dollars) b) divide it up
12	How does the Buffalo library make sure that the manuscript is protected?	(it is) housed in a temperature-controlled vault/room

SPRACHMITTLUNG

TIPP

Your task is to create an article for a website with information for high school students. Usually, this allows for quite colloquial language, but given the topic of the article you have to deal with, a mainly neutral language register is required. Don't forget the heading which does not have to be the same as in the German article and round off your text with a short conclusion. Keep in mind your readership, who consist of American high school students. So, you ought to mention differences between Germany and the USA. A possible structure for your text could be:

- Allgemeines zum Wasserkonsum in Deutschland
- Leitungswasser versus (in Flaschen abgefülltes) Mineralwasser
- besondere Regeln in Restaurants

Tap water versus bottled (mineral) water

Coming from a country where customers are served a carafe of free water as a matter of course at any decent restaurant, you may be interested to learn about the Germans' habits concerning drinking water at home and when eating out.

Although it seems that water did not play any significant role in German drinking culture for a long time, its consumption has been rising constantly over the last few decades. Due to a crackdown on drunk driving coupled with a general inclination towards a healthy lifestyle and the realisation that water has its own distinctive taste, people are tending to drink more of it.

A distrust of the quality of tap water, which in the past often tasted of chlorine or was even endangering people's health, still lingers and explains a widespread preference of bottled water over tap water.

In restaurants, being served tap water cannot be taken for granted. Customers ordering it might be eyed with suspicion. It is often thought that they are trying to avoid paying for their drinks. Few will believe that a persistent request for tap water can stem from motives like sustainability or better taste. Obviously, restaurants can charge for tap water as they are offering a service, but that is not nearly as profitable as selling mineral water. At some high-priced restaurants people sometimes even show off by drinking it at 100 euros a bottle.

So, you see, things are different here!

Niedersachsen Englisch ▪ Abiturprüfung 2021
Erhöhtes Anforderungsniveau

HÖRVERSTEHEN

You will hear each recording twice. After each listening you will have time to complete your answers.

Task 1: Street Trees (7 BE)

You will hear a podcast on trees in Detroit.
While listening, answer the questions. You need not write complete sentences. Unless otherwise specified, name one aspect.

1	What are the advantages of street trees according to the presenter? *(Name two.)*	• • • make streets look nicer
2	What did a study say about the effect of planting eleven more trees per block?	
3	What was the paradoxical situation in Detroit between 2011 and 2014?	
4	What was the aim of Christine Carmichael's campaign?	
5	According to Christine Carmichael, what were some people in disadvantaged neighborhoods worried about?	
6	What would change these people's attitude towards street trees?	

Task 2: Border

(6 BE)

You will hear a radio report about life on the Mexican-American border with the cities of El Paso on the American side, and Juarez on the Mexican side. While listening, tick (✓) the correct answer (a, b, c, or d). There is only one correct answer.

1 According to the female presenter, how do young locals see the border?

- **a** ☐ as a sad reality
- **b** ☐ as separating families
- **c** ☐ as having little importance
- **d** ☐ as separating different cultures

2 How does Antonio Villasenor-Baca perceive the border?

- **a** ☐ as a protective measure
- **b** ☐ as a necessary measure
- **c** ☐ as an annoying measure
- **d** ☐ as a threatening measure

3 Why are some children from Juarez able to attend an American school?

- **a** ☐ The school is run privately.
- **b** ☐ The American school is in Mexico.
- **c** ☐ They take part in a special program.
- **d** ☐ They have an American and a Mexican passport.

4 What is said about the connection of the two border cities?

- **a** ☐ They are twin cities.
- **b** ☐ They are interdependent.
- **c** ☐ Their police forces cooperate closely.
- **d** ☐ El Paso dominates Juarez financially.

5 Why can Kenia Guerrero cross the border faster?

- **a** ☐ She holds a Green Card.
- **b** ☐ She uses the commercial lane.
- **c** ☐ She only has a small backpack.
- **d** ☐ She has bought a special document.

6 What has made crossing the border more difficult for Kenia?

- **a** ☐ a change in politics
- **b** ☐ rising drug trafficking
- **c** ☐ increased illegal migration
- **d** ☐ the introduction of body scans

Task 3: Ship

(12 BE)

You will hear an interview with Sam King, one of the passengers of the *Empire Windrush*, a ship that took about 500 people from Jamaica to Great Britain in 1948. While listening, fill in the missing information. You need not write complete sentences. Unless otherwise specified, name one aspect.

1	Why the economic situation in Jamaica was so serious in 1948	
2	What Sam King's father wanted his son to do	
3	Why Sam King had spent time away from Jamaica	
4	What Sam King realized when back in Jamaica	
5	What Sam King says about the fare for the passage *(Name **one** aspect.)*	
6	What the journey of the *Windrush* led to	
7	Why some middle-aged passengers found it hard to leave Jamaica	
8	What some travellers did when learning a woman was on board illegally	
9	Why Sam considered the food on board bad *(Name **one** reason.)*	
10	How people spent their time on board *(Name **two** activities.)*	• •
11	What some younger passengers worried about	

SPRACHMITTLUNG

Aufgabenstellung

Your US exchange partner has to give a presentation in class about a German tradition and decides to talk about travelling journeymen, as he/she saw one in your hometown last summer. He/She asks you for some help.
Using the information in the text, write an email in which you present the tradition of travelling journeymen and the situation now.

Text

Andrea Döring, „Mit Stock und Hut auf Wanderschaft gehen" (2018)

Hut, Stock und ein Bündel – der freundliche junge Mann mit den langen Rasta-Locken ist unschwer als Wandergeselle zu erkennen. An einer Raststätte an der A61 in Rheinland-Pfalz fragt er nach einer Mitfahrgelegenheit. Bis Worms passen die Pläne zusammen, und das kleine Bündel, auch Charlottenburger genannt, hat locker Platz im Kofferraum. Konstantin Schäfer stammt aus Saarlouis und ist Zimmermann. Gerade kommt der 24-Jährige von einer Feier in der Eifel. Jetzt ist er auf dem Weg zu seinem bislang letzten Arbeitgeber im südhessischen Heppenheim. Der soll ihm in seinem Wanderbuch noch ein Zeugnis ausstellen.

Das Wanderbuch, der knotige Stock, auch Stenz genannt, und das Bündel gehören zur Grundausstattung jedes Wandergesellen dazu. Stolz trägt Schäfer den traditionellen schwarzen Hut, einen Ohrring, ein weißes Hemd, darüber eine Weste mit acht Perlmuttknöpfen, ein Jackett und weite Schlaghosen. Seine Kluft ist schwarz. Das weist ihn als Zimmermann aus, denn jedes Gewerk hat seine eigene Farbe.

Wer Meister werden wollte, musste vom Spätmittelalter bis zur beginnenden Industrialisierung auf Wanderschaft gehen. Arbeits- und Lebenserfahrung sollten die jungen Männer sammeln. In ungefähr 35 Handwerken ist das bis heute möglich: Bäcker, Betonbauer, Bootsbauer, Goldschmiede, Köche, Landwirte, Maurer und Schneider gehören etwa dazu.

„Es ist wunderbar, wenn junge Menschen Erfahrungen sammeln. In der Bäckerei habe ich Wandersleute allerdings noch nie gesehen", erzählt Peter Görtz, Inhaber einer großen Bäckerei-Kette in Ludwigshafen und Umgebung. „Ich würde sofort 20 nehmen."

Maternus Burauen von der IG Bau und erster Sekretär der Conföderation Europäischer Gesellenzünfte (CCEG) schätzt, dass derzeit etwa 450 bis 550 Gesellen auf der Walz sind. Eine offizielle Statistik gibt es nicht. Aktuell seien schätzungsweise zehn bis zwanzig Prozent der Wandersleute Frauen. […]

Seit 2014 gehört die Walz in Deutschland zum immateriellen Kulturerbe der UNESCO. Wer sich auf sie begeben will, muss einige Regeln beachten: Er muss in einem Handwerk einen Gesellenbrief erlangt haben, unverheiratet sowie schuldenfrei sein. Die Wanderschaft dauert zwei oder drei Jahre – und einen Tag. In dieser Zeit darf man sich seinem Heimatort bis auf 50 Kilometer nicht nähern. Ursprünglich war dies als Marktkontrolle für die Meister gedacht – ihre Gesellen sollten woanders ihr Glück finden und ihnen keine Konkurrenz machen.

„Ich hatte Fernweh", sagt Schäfer. Seit fast zwei Jahren ist er schon unterwegs. Durch Holland, Belgien, Frankreich, Österreich, die Schweiz und Israel führte ihn bereits sein Weg. „Viele unterschiedliche Arbeitstechniken habe ich kennengelernt, aber wichtiger als die handwerkliche ist die Erfahrung mit Menschen und die Selbsterkenntnis", sagt er.

„Beim Österreichischen Hospiz in Jerusalem habe ich am Eingangsportal Schusslöcher zugespachtelt", berichtet er. Welche Arbeitgeber Schäfer nach seinem Besuch in Heppenheim findet, ist offen. Der Geselle will nach Norwegen. „Die zahlen gut", hofft er. Der Lohn richtet sich nach den ortsüblichen Tarifen. Üblich ist oft auch Kost und Logis.

In Worms am Dom ist die gemeinsame Fahrt zu Ende, es bleibt noch der Weg bis Heppenheim. Dort hat sich Schäfers zwischenzeitlicher Arbeitgeber und früherer Altgeselle Jerome Schmitt bereits mit 25 Jahren selbstständig gemacht. „Ich habe ihn unter meine Fittiche genommen, habe ihm beigebracht, wie das Leben auf der Landstraße funktioniert, wie man Arbeit findet, als ich vor zwei Jahren selber noch unterwegs war", berichtet Schmitt. „Wer auf Wanderschaft geht, hat schon ein gewisses handwerkliches Know-how. Man lernt mehr im Bereich des Menschlichen", erzählt er. „Wichtig ist das vor allem bei problematischen Kunden. Man ist pragmatisch und zielorientiert, wirft nicht so schnell die Flinte ins Korn", sagt er zum Wert der alten Traditionen. „Man gibt sein Wort, man lässt sich festnageln."

Festnageln ist dabei im buchstäblichen Sinne gemeint. „Man wird auch heute noch mit dem Ohrläppchen an einen Balken genagelt. Dann bekommt man Ringe an die Ohren. Ursprünglich waren die dazu da, die Beerdigung zu bezahlen, wenn man unterwegs stirbt", sagt Schmitt. Im Zeitalter von Piercings und Tattoos wirkt das aber gar nicht mehr so archaisch. Und ganz modern erscheint auch die Idee der Walz, an verschiedenen Orten zu leben und zu arbeiten. *638 Wörter*

Foto: picture alliance/Andrea Döring/dpa | Andrea Döring
Text: Andrea Döring: Mit Stock und Hut auf Wanderschaft gehen, DPA vom 28. 05. 2018

Anmerkungen

16 Gewerk – Handwerk
28 Walz – Wanderschaft eines Handwerksgesellen

TEXTAUFGABE

Von den zwei Aufgaben ist eine auszuwählen und zu bearbeiten.

Aufgabe I: Aufgabenstellung

1 Sum up the excerpt. (30 %)

2 Examine the atmosphere created in the text. (30 %)

3 You are taking part in an international project entitled "Facing Life's Crossroads," dealing with the choices young people are confronted with. You have to hand in an article for the project website in which you discuss the following statement by the writer Roy T. Bennett: "You are not the victim of the world, but rather the master of your own destiny. It is your choices and decisions that determine your destiny."
Write the article, also referring to the text at hand and materials studied in class, such as the novel *Never Let Me Go* and the story "Two Kinds." (40 %)

Text I — Excerpt from Sophie Mackintosh, *Blue Ticket* (2020)

Calla is a 14-year-old teenager living in a dystopian society. She has just reached puberty and therefore has to go to "the lottery," which determines whether she will have children or not.

The lottery station was a lot like the clinic: two storeys of pale brick, a flat roof. When we pulled up, the emissary outside was smoking a cigarette, but he threw it into the road when he saw us. Congratulations, he said to me. He led us inside to where the others waited.

The floorboards were wooden, varnished aggressively. Countless feet had scuffed that floor. It pooled the reflections of all the lights – spotlights from the ceiling, a lamp on the desk where a man in a dark suit sat on an orange plastic chair, watching us, legs crossed. He could have been a doctor, but he wore no white coat, no white plastic gloves. There were four other girls in their own dresses sitting in a row on a wooden bench, flowers both real and fake pinned to chests. They were not the girls from my school. One wore velvet, two wore tulle, and the other wore satin like me. I took a shine to the girl in satin. Same species.

We lined up, waiting to pull our tickets from the machine, the way you would take your number at the butcher's counter. The music popular that year played from speakers on the ceiling. Just gravity enough. Just ceremony enough. Not necessarily such an important thing, after all.

My name was called first. They watched me as I walked the length of the room, towards the machine inside its cloaked box. I put my hand in it. I was apprehensive but ready for my life to be decided. I closed my eyes and thought about my father with the wine bottle to his eye. The machine was silent as it discharged a sliver of hard paper into my hand. It was a deep cobalt. Congratulations, the possible doctor in the dark suit said to me.

The other girls followed, each taking their own ticket from the machine in turn. Almost a full house! he exclaimed at the end, reading a piece of paper spat out from the machine. We huddled and compared tickets. They were all blue, except for one, which was white. The girl with the white ticket was escorted into a separate room by the doctor and another emissary. We watched the three of them walk through an unlit doorway. When the doctor came back he clapped his hands twice. You have been spared, he said with a terrible benevolence. […]

The bathroom of the lottery house was filled with yellow light, the veins of my thin neck standing out underneath it. I was a plucked chicken with badly applied eye-shadow, but the locket was around my throat now. There was a long, low mirror above the sink, a wicker chair in the corner and two bathroom stalls painted peach. In the mirror I watched the other girls leaning against the wall. Toes flexing. Eyes raised to the ceiling, moving to the door when the girl with the white ticket came in to join us, then back to the ceiling. There was a dying flower arrangement at the corner of the sink, gaps of oasis showing through pink carnations. The music came through in here too, speakers in the ceiling or underneath the sink.

At first I kept looking at the girl who had drawn the white ticket, the other girl in satin, though hers was pale blue and dirty at the hem where it dragged. Her eyes were red. I had the urge to take her arm and run with her somewhere, out to the woodland where I used to smoke with the other girls in my class between lessons, beyond the broken barbed wire of the school perimeter where the teachers could not see us. But I did not touch her; I made myself stop looking.

Inside the cubicle I spent some time reading the names and dates scratched on the door. With the safety pin that held on my fake peony corsage I engraved *Calla, Blue Ticket,* a smiley face and the date underneath. The swell of relief, smooth and natural as a muscle. I would never have children. And I was glad. I had been a child myself, not so long ago. I did not want to put any other puny creature through that. […]

An emissary handed us each a bottle of water, a compass and a sandwich from the table, wrapped in a napkin. We did not get to pick the filling. The bottle given to the white-ticket girl was larger than ours, I noticed, and she received two sandwiches. It was happening immediately, the diverging of our paths, no time to spare.

Go, the doctor said to us. To the place of your choice. Walk into it. Anywhere but here. Congratulations.

I met my father's gaze. I had a city in mind. He looked back at me and nodded his head.

We walked out together into the cool night. The adults stayed in the light, for coffee and refreshments, to debrief with the doctor. We might see our parents again, we might not. Some of the girls halted at once when we got outside. They didn't know where to go. New and bewildered as the fawns I saw at the edges of the trees, in the dusk. The girl with the white ticket, though, she walked directly into the woods, the lights of our torches bouncing off the satin until she was gone into the dark. We were not so different.

I put the compass in the palm of my hand. North or south, east or west. The flicker of the needle, the splintered light of the moon on its glass casing. I knew I could do this […]. My life was out there, ahead of me. I had to run to it, now that the shape was cast.

967 words

From: Sophie Mackintosh. Blue Ticket. *New York: Doubleday, 2020. 9–12.*

Annotations

2 Calla and her father

20 Earlier in the story, her father holds an empty wine bottle to his eye like a telescope with which he can see into the future.

21 cobalt – *here:* the colour blue

32 Girls and women keep their white or blue ticket in a locket (a small piece of jewellery that opens to show a small picture or object).

Aufgabe II: Aufgabenstellung

1 Outline what makes the Joker an appealing character according to Rob Bricken. (30 %)

2 Compare the Joker and Richard III – in Shakespeare's play and Loncraine's movie – as embodiments of villains. (30 %)

3 Polygon, a website focusing on games and movies, has invited readers to send in articles to be published as part of their online content, commenting on the statement "It is the evil characters that fascinate us most."
Write the article, referring to the text at hand, the play *King Richard III,* and its movie adaptation by Richard Loncraine. (40 %)

Text II Rob Bricken, "How Joker Became an Unlikely Icon of Anarchy" (2019)

He's murdered thousands of people. He's tortured, poisoned, and maimed even more. [...] He dresses like a clown. And he's the most popular supervillain in the world.

Actually, DC Comics' Joker is more than that: He's one of the four most recognizable comic book characters in the world, along with Spider-Man, Superman, and Batman. He's a character so well-known that his own self-titled movie – Joker, starring Joaquin Phoenix, opening October 4 – doesn't even need a cameo from his superhero archnemesis to sell tickets.

The Joker's fame makes him the most popular fictional mass murderer in the world. Because the Joker has fans, far beyond his role as Batman's greatest foe and foil.

His hatred of the principles of society often shades him as an anti-establishment figure. Whatever horrible things the character has done, there is a core of the Joker that could appeal to anyone who feels let down by society or disenfranchised. He is the supervillain that inspires anyone who, justly or otherwise, wants to see the world burn. Unfortunately, that inspiration can reach into the real world, too. [...]

Regardless of whatever loose change Two-Face carries around in his pockets, Batman and Joker will always be the two sides of the same coin. They're both obsessed with their missions, but while Batman's goal is to enforce order and to save people, the Joker's desire is to wreak havoc, and his primary tool to achieve that end is murder. Batman believes in the sanctity of life so much he refuses to kill his villains, no matter how dangerous they are.

The Joker will kill for any reason: He's murdered countless policemen to avoid arrest, and when he's caught, he murders his way out of Arkham Asylum to escape. He kills for the fun of it, like when he handed out poisoned cotton candy to Boy Scouts in *The Dark Knight Returns*. [...]

His crimes make the Joker a villain, but that's not what makes the character appealing. Heroes are traditionally represented by light and color, while most villains operate, thematically and literally, in the darkness of night. However, since Batman is a hero who co-opts the dark, the Joker takes on heroic visual signifiers to serve as a contrast. His purple suit and clownish face are designed to draw attention. He announces his murders ahead of time, as in his first comic appearance. In 2011, he escaped Arkham by leaving his own cut-off face stuck on the wall, just to remind people how crazy he is. And whatever heinous acts he does, he does it all with a laugh. Batman is serious and grim, but the Joker is the one having *fun*.

Few comic villains have done more horrible things than the Joker, but there's still a real allure to the character's utter disregard for any conventions of society – especially when it's directed at what seems like a worthy target. He once killed a corrupt Gotham City mayor in Ed Brubaker and Greg Rucka's *Gotham Central* comics, and in Grant Morrison's *Batman R.I.P.*, he was largely responsible for the defeat of the Black Glove criminal organization while Batman was undergoing some mental issues himself. Hell, sometimes the Joker even defeats other villains just because they're in his way, or to be a jerk, or because he got bored. […]

But part of the appeal of this new Joker was his nihilistic take on society. Sure, he was obsessed with Batman, as per usual, but also proving … well, I'll quote him from the film:

> You see, [people's] morals, their code, it's a bad joke. Dropped at the first sign of trouble. They're only as good as the world allows them to be. I'll show you. When the chips are down, these ... these civilized people, they'll eat each other. See, I'm not a monster. I'm just ahead of the curve.

This worldview has also come to be seen as disturbingly sympathetic by those who ignore his body count. In 2015, a theory stating that the Joker was the real hero of *The Dark Knight* got thousands of upvotes and a great deal of media coverage. Googling "the joker is right" brings you hundreds of millions of blogs, vlogs, and this infinitely depressing related search term: "childhood is when you idolize batman, adulthood is when you realize that the joker makes more sense."

The problem here is that the Joker is a lot of things. If you've ever thought "the world seems like it's gone crazy" – I do, at least four times a day – then congratulations, you and I agree with the Joker about something. But there are those disturbed people who feel the Joker is right about everything – how society is dysfunctional and morality a lie, so there's no reason to adhere to either of them. This can be a very attractive idea to someone who feels society has failed them, because it also justifies their revenge. Despite the horrible acts of violence he commits in *The Dark Knight*, the Joker has fans – and when mass murderers have fans, bad things happen. There's a long list of real people who have either emulated or directly invoked the Joker after 2008. While some of these instances are as benign as donning Joker cosplay while trying to steal movie posters, others are far more sinister, resulting in disfigurement, arson, and murder.

These tragedies have not undercut the Joker's appeal. Quite the contrary, in fact; Todd Phillips' Joker is not only an origin story for a new incarnation of the character (named Arthur Fleck), but one that posits his descent into homicidal madness is at least partially due to society's failings. According to early reviews, Arthur's early killings are seen as an attack on the one-percent[12], inspiring others who are similarly disenfranchised to do the same. That's one of the most sympathetic origins the supervillain has ever had, not least because it feels so timely. *990 words*

Rob Bricken: How Joker became an unlikely icon of anarchy – From fighting Batman, to fighting The Man, Polygon *vom 02. 10. 2019, https://www.polygon.com/comics/2019/10/2/20895027/joker-anarchy-dc-comics-batman-history-movie*

Annotations

3 DC Comics – a comic book publisher
6 cameo – *here:* brief appearance in a movie
7 arch-nemesis – *here:* arch-enemy
9 foil – a character that contrasts with, and therefore emphasizes, the qualities of another character
15 Two-Face – another villain in the Batman comic book series
22 Arkham Asylum – fictional psychiatric hospital and prison for the criminals in the Batman stories
30 reference to *Batman: Detective Comics Vol. 1: Faces of Death*, published in 2011
37 Gotham City – fictional city and home of Batman
49 body count – number of people killed
63 cosplay – *here:* costume to represent a specific movie character
66 Todd Phillips – director of the 2019 movie *Joker*
69 one-percent – reference to the richest one percent of people

Lösungsvorschlag

HÖRVERSTEHEN

Transkript 1 **Street Trees**

Jason G. Goldman: This is Scientific American, Sixty Seconds Science. I am Jason Goldman. Trees in cities do measurable good for biodiversity and for human health. They scrub pollution from the air. They provide habitat for wildlife. They make streets look nicer. And they even reduce stress and have been linked to reductions in crime.
Back in 2015 a group of Toronto-based researchers discovered that planting just eleven more trees per city block could reduce heart-related conditions by the same amount as if everybody living on that block became a year and a half younger.
But in Detroit between 2011 and 2014 a quarter of eligible homeowners turned down an offer from a local nonprofit for free street trees. Ironic, considering Detroit's nickname was once the City of Trees.

Christine Carmichael: It was actually over 1,800 trees that were rejected out of an eligible 7,425. So it was a big enough issue at that point where it warranted further investigation.

Jason G. Goldman: Forestry researcher Christine Carmichael, who did the research at Michigan State and has since moved to the University of Vermont.
The nonprofit created an education campaign to get more residents to accept the free trees. The assumption being that if people had all the facts, they'd be more likely to take the trees. But when Carmichael talked to residents, she found that they understood the benefits of trees. Their unease was about trust.

Christine Carmichael: Basically what I found was that opposition in Detroit to tree planting among some of these residents resulted primarily from negative past experiences with street trees, particularly in low-income neighborhoods that were grappling with blight from vacant properties, which created an additional burden of care for their neighborhood.

Jason G. Goldman: In the last half-century or so, more than half a million Detroit trees died from disease and neglect. It was primarily low-income African American communities who were forced to deal with the consequences and the hazards, like falling limbs, posed by dead trees.
In speaking with residents, Carmichael found that they would be more willing to accept free trees if they could be more involved in the decision-making process. Locals wanted input on tree size and whether they produced flowers. They also very reasonably wanted to avoid trees that could drop rotting fruits or sap on cars and sidewalks.

Jason G. Goldman: Do-Gooders Should Survey Communities First, Scientific American *vom 22. 01. 2019, https://www.scientificamerican.com/podcast/episode/do-gooders-should-survey-communities-first/,*

TIPP

These text passages will help you find the correct answer:

1 "Trees in cities do measurable good for biodiversity and for human health. They scrub pollution from the air. They provide habitat for wildlife. They make streets look nicer. And they even reduce stress and have been linked to reductions in crime." (ll. 2–5)

2 "Back in 2015 a group of Toronto-based researchers discovered that planting just eleven more trees per city block could reduce heart-related conditions by the same amount as if everybody living on that block became a year and a half younger." (ll. 6–8)

3 "But in Detroit between 2011 and 2014 a quarter of eligible homeowners turned down an offer from a local nonprofit for free street trees. Ironic, considering Detroit's nickname was once the City of Trees." (ll. 9–11)

4 "The nonprofit created an education campaign to get more residents to accept the free trees." (ll. 17/18)

5 "opposition in Detroit to tree planting […] resulted primarily from negative past experiences with street trees, particularly in low-income neighborhoods that were grappling with blight from vacant properties, which created an additional burden of care for their neighborhood." (ll. 21–25); "It was primarily low-income African American communities who were forced to deal with the consequences and the hazards, like falling limbs, posed by dead trees." (ll. 27–29)

6 "In speaking with residents, Carmichael found that they would be more willing to accept free trees if they could be more involved in the decision-making process. […] They also very reasonably wanted to avoid trees that could drop rotting fruits or sap on cars and sidewalks." (ll. 30–34)

1	What are the advantages of street trees according to the presenter? *(Name two.)*	*two of the following:* • good for biodiversity • good for human health • scrub pollution from the air • provide habitat for wildlife • reduce stress • reduce crime • *make streets look nicer*
2	What did a study say about the effect of planting eleven more trees per block?	reduce heart-related conditions (as if people became one-and-a-half years younger)
3	What was the paradoxical situation in Detroit between 2011 and 2014?	homeowners didn't want free trees although Detroit is called city of trees
4	What was the aim of Christine Carmichael's campaign?	get more residents to accept free trees

5	According to Christine Carmichael, what were some people in disadvantaged neighborhoods worried about?	(that the trees) create (an additional) burden of care / (that the trees) mean extra work
6	What would change these people's attitude towards street trees?	be (more) involved in decision-making process (about which trees are planted) / avoid planting certain trees

Transkript 2 Border

Hinweis: Aus lizenzrechtlichen Gründen ist die ungekürzte Original-Passage der NPR-Sendung abgedruckt. Die in der Abituraufgabe nicht berücksichtigten Passagen sind durch eine kleinere Schriftgröße kenntlich gemacht und für die Bearbeitung der Aufgaben nicht relevant.

Ailsa Chang, *Host:* The conversation on family separation is at a high pitch right now. Youth Radio's team covering the border spoke with young people from El Paso, Texas, and Juarez, Mexico, who grew up never seeing the border as a dividing line. Billy Cruz reports.

Billy Cruz, *Byline:* Along the dry, rocky desert of El Paso, past all the food chains and shopping malls, a brown fence stretches for miles. Is this giant fence that we are looking at right here – is that the border?

Antonio Villasenor-Baca: Yeah. So this freeway right here, like, going, like, in two different directions is I-10. And then you go down, and then there's the actual border. And then you're in Juarez.

Cruz: Antonio Villasenor-Baca is 22. He was born here in El Paso, a huge borderplex that spans the Rio Grande River. But he has an uncle in Juarez. And growing up, Antonio's dad would take him back and forth a lot.

Villasenor-Baca: You know, like, you want to go out and party, you go to Juarez. You have family in Juarez, but you live in El Paso, or vice versa. It really seems like just a huge hassle to, like, go through all of this stuff at the border.

Cruz: For young people like Antonio, life on the border isn't just about the momentous crossings we read about in the news. Commuting between two countries is a part of everyday life. There are even kids with dual citizenship who live in Juarez with their parents and cross the border to go to school.

Villasenor-Baca: It's really weird because growing up as a kid, there's just other kids in your school. And it's not until you get older that you start seeing, well, it's the kids who speak Spanish who are the – doing the daily commute. And it's when the terms like American and Mexican and Mexican-American start coming into place.

Cruz: Many people and goods flow between El Paso and Juarez every day. The culture and economies of both cities rely on each other. Twenty-three-year-old Kenia Guerrero is part of that flow. She grew up in Juarez but just finished college in El Paso. And she crosses the border every day to help out at her parents' cowboy boot shop.

Kenia Guerrero: Yeah, so we are at the Santa Fe Bridge. This is in the central part of El Paso. As you can see, like, cars are coming in from Juarez. It usually takes about half an hour to three hours to cross to El Paso.

Cruz: To make her commute easier, Kenia got something called a SENTRI pass, which cuts down the time it takes to cross. Thousands of people in the El Paso-Juarez region pay the fees and go through the background checks to get one. Kenia says she feels equally at home in Juarez and here in El Paso.

Guerrero: My first 15 years, I didn't know about borders. Like, I live in Juarez, but I would buy my clothes here and would buy certain food items here. It was pretty normal. And now it's not like that anymore because you're sometimes afraid.

Cruz: Now Kenia has to be extra careful whenever she crosses because she says agents have gotten stricter since President Trump took office. If she's caught with a prohibited item like even an apple she packed for lunch and forgot to throw away, Kenia could lose her fastpass. Recently she had a close call.

Guerrero: Had a crushed candy in my cup holder. And the agent asked me, is that cocaine? And I got nervous not because it was cocaine but because it's just a question. Like, how can he think that I'm bringing cocaine? I just told him something along the lines, no, but if you want to try it, you can.

Cruz: The agent passed on the candy and eventually let her cross. As security and media attention at the border increases, Kenia and Antonio are just trying to hold on to their sense of hometown normalcy.

Villasenor-Barca: Yeah, it's a border, and anywhere else in the country will say it as such. But for us, it's just two cities that's divided by a fence.

Cruz: For the time being at least, Antonio and Kenia will keep crossing that fence because for the people who live and work here, these two cities El Paso and Juarez really do feel like one. For NPR News, I'm Billy Cruz in El Paso, Texas.

Chang: That story was produced by Youth Radio.

(SOUNDBITE OF MASSIVE ATTACK'S "MONTAGE")

Billy Cruz: Young People Adapt To A Changing Life At The Texas-Mexico Border, NPR 20. 07. 2018, https://www.npr.org/2018/07/20/630076251/young-people-adapt-to-a-changing-life-at-the-texas-mexico-border

TIPP

These text passages will help you find the correct answer:

1. "Youth Radio's team covering the border spoke with young people from El Paso, Texas, and Juarez, Mexico, who grew up never seeing the border as a dividing line." (ll. 1–3)
2. "It really seems like just a huge hassle to, like, go through all of this stuff at the border." (ll. 14/15)
3. "There are even kids with dual citizenship who live in Juarez with their parents and cross the border to go to school." (ll. 18/19)

4 “Many people and goods flow between El Paso and Juarez every day. The culture and economies of both cities rely on each other.” (ll. 24/25)

5 “To make her commute easier, Kenia got something called a SENTRI pass, which cuts down the time it takes to cross.” (ll. 31/32)

6 “Now Kenia has to be extra careful whenever she crosses because she says agents have gotten stricter since President Trump took office. If she’s caught with a prohibited item […], Kenia could lose her fastpass.” (ll. 38–41)

1 According to the female presenter, how do young locals see the border?

c [✓] as having little importance

2 How does Antonio Villasenor-Baca perceive the border?

c [✓] as an annoying measure

3 Why are some children from Juarez able to attend an American school?

d [✓] They have an American and a Mexican passport.

4 What is said about the connection of the two border cities?

b [✓] They are interdependent.

5 Why can Kenia Guerrero cross the border faster?

d [✓] She has bought a special document.

6 What has made crossing the border more difficult for Kenia?

a [✓] a change in politics

Transkript 3 Ship

Alan Johnston, *Host*: It is 1948 in Jamaica and the island is in bad shape. It’s still recovering from a hurricane a few years earlier and Sam King remembers the economy being in a desperate state.

Sam King: Things again were very bad because the coconuts were destroyed in ‘44. It takes five to six years for the coconuts to rebuild. The whole structure of farming was undermined. I didn’t see any future. Of course, my father was very glad I was there because I’m the eldest son and like him, eventually I would take over the farm to pick pimento and to plant banana and all that and all that. But I had no intention of planting bananas.

Alan Johnston: Back then, Sam was just 22 years old, but he’d already seen the outside world. He’d volunteered during WWII and served in the Royal Air Force in Britain. With the coming of peace, he’d returned to the hills of Eastern Jamaica. But he knew he wouldn’t stay. And within months, he spotted a chance to get away.

Sam King: It was in the daily Jamaican newspaper that this troop ship would call to Jamaica in about two weeks’ time. And the passage was 28 pounds 10 shillings.

Let's get that straight: The average man didn't have 28 pounds 10 shillings. It was equivalent to about three cows.

Alan Johnston: So you are sitting, reading the newspaper. And what goes through your mind?

Sam King: I'm going back to England.

Alan Johnston: Eventually nearly 500 passengers boarded the ship, bound for England and a new life. They would turn out to be pioneers. Their journey marked the start of a new wave of migration. In the decade to come, a quarter of a million West Indians would follow in the wake of the Windrush. Sam remembers the mood that evening when she slips slowly out of Kingston harbour.

Sam King: People were waving, things were happening on the docks. Now for about half of us, we had no intention of coming back to our colony. We were looking forward, we were looking towards a new home. But there were some men in their 40s who had wife and children. They were looking back at the yard, they were waving, they – but we, chiefly the young ones, we were not looking back, we were looking forward.

Alan Johnston: Several stowaways had managed to smuggle themselves on board, one was a woman and out of kindness, Sam and some of the other passengers clubbed together and paid to buy her a ticket, enabling her to make the voyage legally. But conditions on the troop ship in those first years after the war were far from luxurious.

Sam King: Sad to say, you have mashed potato in tins from New Zealand two years, they put it on the table, mix it up with water. Now if you didn't eat it then, in the evening they mix it with cabbage and if you didn't eat it then, in the morning they fried it and called it bubble and squeak. I would eat it sometimes before, when I was resident in Britain. Men were playing dominoes and things, but we had the decks, were chiefly blankets and a few bunks. But the women were in cabins. So we just mill around and in the evenings they have boxing competitions and things like that and dance and all things. But the main thing is, it was to mentally get yourself ready to land.

Alan Johnston: And the other young guys who, unlike you, hadn't seen Britain before, were they asking lots of questions?

Sam King: Time and again they would come, "Sam, what, will I have a job?" They were more concerned about jobs. I said, "Settle down." In the evening after supper about 6.30, I would go on the lower deck to you know about ten of them I said, "Look. Food is rationed in England, you can't grasp that, but work is all over the place, so work is not the problem."

From: BBC World Service (26. 06. 2011). Witness History, The Voyage of the Empire Windrush, https://www.bbc.co.uk/programmes/p00h8xkq

TIPP

These text passages will help you find the correct answer:

1 "It is 1948 in Jamaica and the island is in bad shape. It's still recovering from a hurricane a few years earlier" (ll. 1/2); "the coconuts were destroyed in '44. [...] The whole structure of farming was undermined." (ll. 4–6)

2 "my father was very glad I was there because I'm the eldest son and like him, eventually I would take over the farm to pick pimento and to plant banana" (ll. 6–8)

3 "Back then, Sam was just 22 years old, but he'd already seen the outside world. He'd volunteered during WWII and served in the Royal Air Force in Britain." (ll. 10/11)

4 "he'd returned to the hills of Eastern Jamaica. But he knew he wouldn't stay." (ll. 12/13)

5 "the passage was 28 pounds 10 shillings. [...] The average man didn't have 28 pounds 10 shillings. It was equivalent to about three cows." (ll. 15–17)

6 "Their journey marked the start of a new wave of migration. In the decade to come, a quarter of a million West Indians would follow in the wake of the Windrush." (ll. 22–24)

7 "there were some men in their 40s who had wife and children. They were looking back at the yard, they were waving" (ll. 28–30)

8 "Several stowaways had managed to smuggle themselves on board, one was a woman and out of kindness, Sam and some of the other passengers clubbed together and paid to buy her a ticket, enabling her to make the voyage legally." (ll. 32–34)

9 "Sad to say, you have mashed potato in tins from New Zealand two years, they put it on the table, mix it up with water. Now if you didn't eat it then, in the evening they mix it with cabbage and if you didn't eat it then, in the morning they fried it and called it bubble and squeak." (ll. 37–40)

10 "Men were playing dominoes and things [...] we just mill around and in the evenings they have boxing competitions and things like that and dance and all things. But the main thing is, it was to mentally get yourself ready to land." (ll. 41–45)

11 "Time and again they would come, 'Sam, what, will I have a job?' They were more concerned about jobs." (ll. 48/49)

1	Why the economic situation in Jamaica was so serious in 1948	(recovering from a) recent hurricane / a hurricane a few years earlier / coconuts were destroyed (in 1944) / whole structure of farming was undermined
2	What Sam King's father wanted his son to do	(to) take over the farm / (to) pick pimentos / (to) plant bananas

3	Why Sam King had spent time away from Jamaica	volunteered during WW II / served in Royal Air Force in Britain
4	What Sam King realized when back in Jamaica	(he knew) he wouldn't stay
5	What Sam King says about the fare for the passage *(Name **one** aspect.)*	28 pounds, 10 shillings / the average man didn't have 28 pounds, 10 shillings / too expensive for average people / equivalent to about three cows
6	What the journey of the *Windrush* led to	a new wave of migration / a quarter of a million West-Indians emigrating
7	Why some middle-aged passengers found it hard to leave Jamaica	had (to leave their) wives and children / had to leave their families behind
8	What some travellers did when learning a woman was on board illegally	(they) clubbed together and paid to buy her a ticket / (they) bought her a ticket
9	Why Sam considered the food on board bad *(Name **one** reason.)*	old, tinned food / same food served again and again
10	How people spent their time on board *(Name **two** activities.)*	*two of the following:* • playing dominoes • milling around • boxing competitions • dances / dancing • mentally getting (themselves) ready to land
11	What some younger passengers worried about	finding a job

TIPP

Before you start writing, pay close attention to the assignment. It tells you for whom you have to summarise the information (an American exchange partner) and in what form (a personal email). This will determine the style you should use: write in correct, formal language because your friend needs the information for a presentation at school. However, do not forget to use a more colloquial style when you address your friend and his/her situation. When it comes to content, you should only sum up the pieces of information that are relevant for your friend's presentation: so leave out the concrete personal examples mentioned in the article. Instead, focus on what makes the tradition of travelling journeymen special, where it comes from and why and how it is still practised today.

You should include the following aspects:

- appearance of travelling journeymen:
  - equipment: bindle, hiking pole, logbook
  - traditional clothing: hat, waistcoat, jacket, flared trousers, shirt
  - colour of clothes different depending on craft
  - earring (traditional and current custom of being "nailed down"; original use: payment for funeral costs)
- rules for travelling journeymen:
  - completed apprenticeship, unmarried, no debts, travel for two or three years and one day
  - staying away at least 50 km from hometown
- history of the tradition:
  - dates back to Middle Ages
  - obligatory to become masters until the beginnings of industrialisation
- present situation:
  - 450–550 journeying craftspeople, ten to 20 per cent women
  - custom recognised by UNESCO since 2004
  - many also work abroad
  - normal pay, often free board and lodging
- reasons for travelling:
  - improve skills and learn new techniques
  - gain new experiences, learn about the world and oneself

Hello Cheryl,

introduction

Thanks for your email. That's an interesting subject for your presentation. I'd be glad to help you with some information I found in a German newspaper.

appearance of travelling journeymen

As you might remember from last summer, travelling journeymen can easily be recognised by their traditional clothing, consisting of a hat, a waistcoat, a jacket, flared trousers and a shirt. The colour of these depends on the journeymen's craft. They carry a bindle, a pole and a logbook to record their journey. Another interesting feature is the earring they all wear. Originally, the rings were meant to pay for their funeral in case they died on the trip. They are also reminders of the tradition of nailing the journeymen's earlobes to a post. This custom is still being practised as a symbol of the craftsmen's reliability.

rules for travelling journeymen

There are more strict rules to observe: the journeymen must have finished their apprenticeship and must be unmarried, free of debt and prepared to travel for two to three years and one day. They must also keep a distance of at least 50 km from their hometown to avoid competing with their masters.

history of the tradition

The tradition of travelling began in the late Middle Ages. Until the beginning of the Industrial Age, travelling in this way was obligatory for anyone who wanted to become a master of their craft.

present situation

Currently, there are about 450 to 550 journeying craftspeople, ten to 20 per cent of whom are women. They are paid at the standard rate for their trade, with board and lodging often being free. In 2004, the UNESCO recognised the custom's cultural value by giving it world heritage status.

reasons for travelling

There are several reasons for its ongoing popularity: the journeymen, who often travel abroad these days, can improve their learned trade by acquiring new techniques. Moreover, they meet many people, gain experiences and learn skills, such as perseverance and pragmatism. All of this can prove helpful when dealing with customers, especially with difficult ones.

ending (fitting to text form)

I hope you'll find this information useful. Please tell me how your presentation went.

Love,
Lily

TEXTAUFGABE

Text I **Excerpt from Sophie Mackintosh, *Blue Ticket* (2020)**

1 **TIPP**

The command term "sum up" requires you to state the main points of a text. Thus, you have to write a text which is significantly shorter than the original. Moreover, you mustn't quote from the text but should use your own words. Also remember to use the simple present. Begin your summary by mentioning the title of the story, the author and the year of publication. Then outline what happens in the excerpt. In this case, it is best to proceed chronologically and arrange the events in the same order as they appear in the text.

The following aspects should be included in your solution:
- the narrator arrives at the lottery station with her father
- lines up in front of a ticket machine together with four other girls
- narrator draws a blue ticket, meaning she won't have children → feels relieved
- girl with a white ticket is taken to a different room → returns looking as if she has been crying
- finally, the girls are given refreshments and a compass
- they set out on their own, while their parents stay behind at the lottery station

The text provided is from the story *Blue Ticket*, which was written by Sophie Mackintosh and published in 2020.

introduction: title, author, year

In the excerpt in hand, the main character Calla arrives at a place called the "lottery station" together with her father. First, she is led into a waiting room, where she carefully observes the other four girls who are also waiting there along with a man in a dark suit. Then they all queue in front of a machine, which eventually produces a ticket for every girl. The protagonist gets a blue ticket and is relieved about this, as this means that she does not have to have children. The same is true for the rest of the girls – except for a girl who gets a white ticket and is ushered into a different room afterwards. When she returns a bit later she looks as if she has been crying. The protagonist first wants to comfort the girl with the white ticket, but then decides against it. In the end, the girls are handed some refreshments and a compass and are free to walk anywhere they want to, but without their parents, who stay behind at the lottery station.

main part: events in chronological order

2 **TIPP**

In this task, you have to analyse the atmosphere created in the excerpt. You should write about what the atmosphere is like and how this effect is achieved. The command term "examine" requires you to work closely with the text and back up your findings by means of direct or indirect quotations. The following aspects could be mentioned in your solution:

atmosphere can generally be described as uncanny:
- overall situation of a "lottery" deciding the girls' fates
- rather negative description of the "lottery station":
  - bleak building
  - uncomfortable, loveless furniture
  - floors that have been "varnished aggressively" and worn out by "countless feet" → aseptic ambience, repetition of what happens at the station
  - no decoration except from withering flowers → sense of foreboding
- description of people inside the lottery station:
  - queue up as if "at the butcher's", "plucked chicken" → motif of violence
  - man in suit: superficially friendly, but "terrible benevolence"
  - girls released into the night and the surrounding dark forests → imagery of darkness
  - sombre atmosphere lightened up by the protagonist's determination to find her way in life
- limited point of view of first-person narrator Calla: violence at the core of the story is only hinted at, not told explicitly → unsettling effect

introduction: thesis: uncanny atmosphere

When reading the excerpt from *Blue Ticket*, the reader cannot help but feel uneasy, which is due to the uncanny and threatening atmosphere created. But how is this effect achieved?

main part: situation of lottery deciding girls' fates

Quite often, an "uncanny" (as opposed to straight-out scary) ambience arises, when the setting appears somehow familiar, like something you know from your everyday life – yet at the same time, there are things that seem out-of-place and unsettling. This also applies to the overall situation of the "lottery" in *Blue Ticket*: Expressions such as "lottery" (l. 1) or "full house" (l. 24) are normally used in the context of card games or gambling. Many people enjoy playing games as a leisure-time activity and do it for fun. By contrast, what is at stake in the "lottery" in this story is a life-altering question indeed, namely whether or not the girls will have children. Like in a lottery or card game, their fate is determined solely by random luck or bad luck – they do not have any control over their lives.

What further adds to the uncanny atmosphere are the negatively connotated expressions with which the setting of the "lottery station" is described. The building itself is compared to a hospital (cf. l. 1) and described as being made of "pale brick" (l. 1), which from the beginning makes it sound like a bleak place. The furniture inside appears uncomfortable and loveless, consisting of only a hard "wooden bench" (ll. 9/10) and an "orange plastic chair" (l. 7). The floors are described as having been "varnished aggressively" (l. 5), which – together with the glary lights (cf. ll. 6/7, 30) – conveys a rather aseptic ambience. The fact that the floorboards are already worn thin by "[c]ountless feet" (l. 5) suggests that what happens at this place has repeated itself many times before. The only ornamental element in the building which could serve to embellish the place is a "dying flower arrangement at the corner of the sink" (ll. 36/37) in the bathroom. Flowers often serve to symbolise the beauty and abundance of life, yet in this case, all life has been sucked out of them – they are not taken care of and are left to wither.

description of "lottery station":

bleak building

uncomfortable, loveless furniture

worn-out floors and glaring lights

withering flowers

This conveys a sense of foreboding, which can also be observed in the description of people inside the "lottery station". When the girls line up to get their tickets, this is compared to a queue "at the butcher's counter" (l. 14). The example of the "butcher" takes up the theme of dead matter and moreover hints at violence taking place. This becomes even clearer when the narrator later describes herself as a "plucked chicken" (l. 31). The man in the dark suit, or "doctor", as the narrator calls him, appears friendly on the surface, e. g. when he congratulates the narrator on her blue ticket (cf. ll. 21/22). When he later tells the girls with the blue tickets that they have been "spared", it becomes obvious that there is something violent going on beneath the surface and that his seeming benevolence is indeed "terrible" (l. 29).

description of people:

comparison to queue at the butcher's

man in suit: friendliness only superficial

Finally, another aspect that adds to the uncanny atmosphere is the narrative perspective. The story is told from the point of view of the first-person narrator Calla. The reader is limited to her perception of events, such as when the girl with the white ticket is taken away and later returns, looking as if she has been crying. Like the protagonist, the reader can only guess what might have been done to her in-between. The fact that what happens in this core scene is left out and not told explicitly makes the story all the more unsettling.

narrative perspective: limited point of view of Calla; main event omitted

In the end, the girls are released into the "cool night" (l. 58) and the girl with the white ticket walks "directly into the woods" (l. 62). This imagery of darkness again adds to the overall sombre atmosphere. However, the narrator's determination that she "knew [she] could do this" and that her "life was out there, ahead of [her]" (ll. 66/67) makes the story end on a slightly more positive and hopeful note.

ending: sombre atmosphere lightened by narrator's determination

In summary, the atmosphere in the excerpt can be described as uncanny, an effect which is achieved through the overall situation of a "lottery" deciding the girls' fates, the choice of words in the description of the building and the characters, and the limited point of view of the narrator which leaves the reader to imagine the violence taking place at the station. This is only lifted at the very end due to the protagonist's determination to make the best of the situation. **conclusion**

3 **TIPP**

In this task you have to write an article discussing the question as to whether or not young people can determine their own futures. In the introduction you should refer to the given quotation by the writer Roy T. Bennett and briefly explain it. In your main part, you have to give arguments supporting Bennett's view and arguments opposing it. Moreover, you must refer to the text *Blue Ticket* and to materials studied in class. Finally, you should arrive at a conclusion to what degree you either agree or disagree with Bennett's view. It is probably best to take some notes and sort them before beginning to write to make sure that your text is structured coherently. Don't forget to give your article a proper heading and to use a more formal language register.
The following aspects could be included in your solution:

- introduction:
  Bennett's quotation that "you are not the victim of the world, but rather the master of your own destiny" → young people can determine their own futures
- arguments supporting Bennett's view:
  - declining influence of parents and society → greater freedom of young people to make their own choices
  - "Two Kinds": Jing-Mei manages to emancipate herself from expectations of her mother and culture
  - *Blue Ticket:* Calla determined to make her way in life despite "lottery"
- arguments opposing Bennett's view:
  - *Blue Ticket:* girls' lives determined by mere luck and by society (which invented system of the "lottery")
  - *Never Let Me Go:* fates of clones determined by their status in society
  - marginalised groups in real world: opportunities in life often limited by stereotypes and structural discrimination
- conclusion:
  neither "victims" nor "masters" → chances in life influenced by social structures, but agency to make the best of our situation and change the system from within

Victims of the world or masters of our own destiny?

heading

As young people, we are facing some of life's most important crossroads – the questions of where we want to work, where and with whom we want to live, whether we want to have a family or not, and so on. The writer Roy T. Bennett argues that it is up to us to choose the path for our own future. According to him, "you are not the victim of the world, but rather the master of your own destiny." But is his optimism really justified? And what can works of literature teach us about this question?

introduction: reference to quote by Bennett

At first sight, one is inclined to agree with Bennett. Compared to past centuries or decades, young people nowadays have more possibilities of making their own choices in life. In former times, it was your parents or strict social norms who determined the choice of your partner or profession, for example. Today, most young people decide for themselves how they want to earn their living and who they want to spend their life with. Of course, this varies depending on the cultural context, but the overall tendency seems to prevail.

main part: arguments supporting Bennett's view declining influence of parents and society

Take the protagonist of the short story "Two Kinds", for example. Jing-Mei is an American girl with a Chinese cultural background. Her mother has the best intentions for her and wants her daughter to be a child prodigy. At first, Jing-Mei tries to meet the expectations of her mother and comply with the cultural norm of being the obedient daughter. However, when she realises that she is bound to fail and feels increasingly unhappy, she rebels against her mother's plans. Eventually, Jing-Mei emancipates herself from both the parental and cultural influence and finds her inner peace. This shows that, while it may not always be easy, it is indeed possible to take life into one's own hands and become the masters of our destiny.

reference to "Two Kinds": emancipation from parental and cultural influence

Another case in point is the text *Blue Ticket*. In the story, a lottery decides whether a girl will have children or not, without the girls having any control over it. In spite of this, the protagonist, Calla, is determined to be able to choose her own path in life, which would likewise support Bennett's argument.

reference to *Blue Ticket:* determination to shape own life

However, the same story can be used to counter Bennett's optimism. On closer inspection, it becomes clear that Calla only feels like the "mistress of her destiny", because she didn't want to have children anyway and was lucky enough to get a blue ticket, meaning that she won't have to get pregnant. Thus, she can continue her life as planned and feels free to go where she wants to go and do what she wants to do. For the girl in the story who draws a white ticket and is forced to have a child, the situation looks quite different: her life has been changed in a very far-reaching manner, without her having any say in it. In this story, it is not the characters who determine their future,

arguments opposing Bennett's view reference to *Blue Ticket*

fate decided by luck and society

but mere luck and – in the last instance – society, which designed the cruel system of the "lottery" in the first place.

reference to *Never Let Me Go:* fate determined by society

The strong impact of society on people's lives is also the topic of the novel *Never Let Me Go*. The protagonists are clones who have been created for the sole purpose of donating their organs to "ordinary" humans. Thus, their fate is determined from the start. Two of the protagonists, Tommy and Kathy, fall in love and try to reach a "deferral", which would allow them to spend some more time together. They go to extreme risks to formally request a deferral only to find out in the end that such a thing has never existed in the first place. Thus, their hope of having some agency over their own lives ultimately turns out to be an illusion. They could be described as "victims of the world".

real world: impact of structural discrimination and stereotypes

Of course, the criticism of society in dystopian texts such as *Blue Ticket* and *Never Let Me Go* is somewhat exaggerated. Still, there is a grain of truth to it: In the "real" world, society often severely narrows which paths we can choose. If you are a member of a marginalised group (a person of colour or a member of the LGBTIQ community, for example), your opportunities in life are frequently limited by structural discrimination and unconscious stereotypes. You may work hard for a career and have the best qualification, and still not get the job just because of the colour of your skin or your sexual identity. And it is mere luck which situation you are born into, whether you can start your course in life from a relatively privileged or disadvantaged position. This makes it hard to agree full-heartedly with Bennett's view that we are in complete control of our futures.

conclusion

In summary, Bennett is too optimistic in arguing that we are all the "masters of our destiny", because not everyone is given the same chances in life to do what they want to do. And yet, we do have agency in making the best of our situation, and we can try to change the system from within and create a more just society that grants equal opportunities to everyone. Life can metaphorically deal us bad cards, but it is up to us to play them well and perhaps change the rules of the game.

Text II Rob Bricken, "How Joker Became an Unlikely Icon of Anarchy" (2019)

1 **TIPP**

The command term "outline" requires you to state the main points of a text, omitting minor details. Moreover, you are to focus on a particular aspect of the text, namely the question as to what makes the Joker an appealing character. Go through the article again and underline the passages that are relevant to the task. Then paraphrase them in your own words – do not quote from the text. Don't forget to write an introductory sentence in which you name the title and author of the article, the date of publication and the topic.

reasons for Joker's appeal:

- role of misfit who has moved beyond social norms → makes him attractive for people who likewise feel deserted by society and secretly wish to take revenge
- targeting of other villains makes his deeds appear justified
- differs from other villains in his appearance and attitude: flashy colours (instead of dark clothes), mad joy (instead of earnest attitude)

introduction: source and topic

In "How Joker Became an Unlikely Icon of Anarchy" published online in 2019, Rob Bricken explains why the Joker is such an appealing character.

main part: reasons for Joker's appeal

Firstly, Bricken argues, the Joker strikes a chord with the audience because he is a misfit, an underdog in society. The Joker moves completely outside social norms and seeks to create chaos by killing other people. This makes him an attractive figure for people who likewise feel deserted by society and share the secret wish to take revenge. A second aspect that makes him so appealing is that he sometimes targets other villains. In these cases, the viewers might feel that his victims do not deserve any better and consider his deeds to be justified. Thirdly, the Joker differs from other evil characters because of his unique appearance and attitude: While a lot of other villains wear dark clothes, the Joker wears flashy colours and a clown face. He is not as earnest as the other characters but seems to experience a mad joy in what he does.

2 **TIPP**

The command term "compare" asks you to look for similarities and differences between two things. In this case, it is your task to compare the Joker as portrayed in the text with the character of Richard III in Shakespeare's play and in the film version. It is advisable to take some notes before starting to write.

Remember to back up your argument with quotes from Bricken's article and references to *Richard III*.

- similarities:
  - both Richard and the Joker stand out because of their outward appearance
  - both are outsiders who feel they have been failed by society
  - both lack moral scruples and do not even refrain from killing
- differences:
  - Richard uses helpers, while the Joker commits his murders himself
  - Richard kills to achieve a particular goal (to become king), while the Joker merely has a vague desire to create chaos

introduction: reference to task, thesis

At first sight, one could think that a 20th-century comic book character and the protagonist of a Shakespeare play can't have very much in common. And yet, the Joker and Richard III lend themselves perfectly for a comparison. Both can be seen as embodiments of a villain and have quite a few similarities.

similarities: outward appearance

The first thing to mention is that neither the Joker nor Richard III can blend in physically. It stands out that they stand out – Richard with his hunched back and the Joker with his clownish appearance.

role as outsiders

Moreover, both Richard and the Joker are social outsiders. As a man of war, Richard feels unsuited for a society at peace. Although he is a member of the royal family, he appears out of place in elegant society and does not seem to be particularly attractive to women either. This is the reason he himself gives for why he has ultimately turned evil: In the famous opening soliloquy he states that he is determined to "prove a villain" since he "cannot prove a lover". Quite similarly, the Joker is presented as an "anti-establishment figure" (ll. 10/11), someone who does not fit in. At least in Todd Phillips' film version, it is moreover suggested that – as in the case of Richard – his "descent into homicidal madness is at least partially due to society's failings" (ll. 67/68).

lack of moral scruples

Another thing which makes Richard and Joker comparable is their lack of moral scruples, which does not even make them refrain from murder. The Joker shows an "utter disregard for any conventions of society" (l. 35) and will sometimes kill just "for the fun of it" (l. 23). According to the text, "whatever heinous acts he does, he does it all with a laugh" (l. 32). Richard likewise enjoys crossing moral boundaries. For example, he takes a cruel pleasure in winning over Lady Anne, whose husband and father he had killed before. In the film version, he even seems to dance for joy when leaving the morgue after his encounter with Lady Anne. Moreover, he often spreads lies and false accusations, manipulates and deceives other people and chuckles at the thought of his victims being killed.

That being said, there are also a lot of differences beneath the surface. The first, most obvious point is that Richard uses assassins to "do the dirty work". For example, he hires a henchman called Tyrrell to kill his brother Clarence and the princes in the Tower. Only in the very first scenes of the film version, when he is at war, is he seen killing others directly. The Joker, by contrast, is a straight-forward murderer.

differences: using helpers vs. committing murders oneself

What is more, Richard wants to achieve a very particular goal with his murderous scheme, which is to claim the throne. Thus, his victims are primarily people who stand in the way of his ambition. His brother and nephews, for instance, have to die because they are before him in the line of succession. The Joker, by contrast, "will kill for any reason" (l. 21) and without any other aim than to "wreak havoc" (l. 18). Hence, his victims range from police officers (cf. l. 21) to Boy Scouts (cf. l. 23) to other villains (cf. ll. 36–41).

killing to achieve a particular goal vs. to create chaos

Summing up, it can be said that although they have been devised at completely different times, the characters of Richard III and the Joker have many things in common, although they also differ in several aspects.

conclusion

3 **TIPP**

For this task, you have to write an article. This means, your text should have a heading and a well-structured main part. Your target group are readers of a webpage on games and movies – thus, your style should probably not be too formal, but not entirely colloquial either. In your text, you have to comment on the statement that it is the evil characters which fascinate us most, i. e., you have to give your own opinion on it. You can either agree with the statement, disagree or take a stance somewhere in-between. The important thing is to support your opinion by means of arguments and examples. Moreover, the task requires you to refer to the given text about the Joker as well as to the play and the film *Richard III*.
In the following sample solution, it is argued that the given statement is by and large true, although it has to be qualified to a certain extent. The following aspects are mentioned:

- watching villains as a way to give vent to our own anarchic feelings, yet in a harmless way → brief escape from real life, thrill of the forbidden
- identification with "social-outcast-turned-into-powerful-avenger" → appeal to people who similarly feel let down by society
- psychological interest in multi-dimensional characters; fictional villains as a possibility to learn more about the minds of real-life murderers
- fascination with cleverness of the villains' schemes
- conclusion: particular appeal of evil characters, but primarily if they are psychologically complex or their crimes are particularly sophisticated

The thrill of the forbidden – why villains fascinate us

heading

Both in literature and film, villains have always enjoyed great popularity. From Shakespeare's Richard III to DC Marvel's "super-villain" Joker – audiences throughout the centuries have been fascinated by killer figures. In fact, there seems to be quite a bit of truth in the saying that it is the evil characters – rather than the shining heroes – which fascinate us most. But why is this so? And is this true in each and every case? A brief look at the two above-mentioned fictional examples will provide some answers.

introduction:
reference to statement, thesis

Although we may or may not admit it, quite a few people somehow feel drawn to evil characters because they allow us a glimpse into the darker sides of our own personality. This is not to argue (as the Joker does) that there is a killer in all of us – that would probably be taking it too far. Yet many of us secretly admire villains for their audacity to do what they want without caring for the consequences or what other people think about them. In this way, they allow us to give vent to our own anarchic feelings – yet in a socially acceptable manner and without causing any harm in real life.

main part: arguments supporting the statement
giving vent to own anarchic impulses

The Joker, for example, does whatever he wants, just for the fun of it. He kills and settles scores at whim – and gets away with it. By watching the Joker, we can imagine just for two hours what it would be like to completely ignore all social conventions. A lot of people enjoy such a brief escape from their everyday lives and experience a secret thrill. And perhaps, for a few people, cheering for the Joker may not even feel like a "forbidden" pleasure. As the Joker sometimes kills other villains, they consider his deeds to be somehow justified, and root for him without a guilty conscience.

escapism / thrill of the forbidden

The examples of the Joker and of Richard III also point at another possible reason why we are often spellbound by evil characters. In both cases, it is hinted that the protagonists become evil because they feel rejected by society. This feeling of being an outsider is something a lot of people can relate to or even sympathise with to a certain extent. The Joker's development into a powerful avenger moreover makes him attractive for those viewers who similarly feel like failures and dream of getting back at society. By identifying with the Joker, they can play out their secret fantasies. Disturbingly, in some cases, this identification has gone so far as to reach a point where viewers have imitated the Joker's deeds in real life.

identification with outsider figure

Yet villains don't just speak to our emotions and subconscious drives. Sometimes we may also be fascinated on a more intellectual level.

psychological interest in complex characters / learning about real-life murderers

A lot of us take a general psychological interest in complex characters that have more than one dimension to them. Often, we watch fictional villains in the hope of learning more about the minds of real-life murderers and understanding their motivations. For example, in the film version of *Richard III*, the whole setting reminds us of the Nazi era in Germany. This makes us reflect on the question as to whether there are parallels between Richard III and other dictators in history, and what might be the reasons for their evilness and complete lack of empathy.

fascination with artistry of crime

On an intellectual level, we may also marvel at the cleverness and sophistication of a villain's intrigues. For example, in his soliloquies, Richard III gives us an insight into his murderous plans, such as when he talks about how he wants to get rid of his two brothers Clarence and King Edward to claim the throne. In consequence, we are curious to see whether his schemes will actually work out. In the film version he often speaks directly to the camera, thereby putting the viewers into the role of "partners in crime".

conclusion

In brief, evil characters seem to exert a particular appeal because they take us to a dark place, yet leave us in the comfort zone of our sofas at the same time. Often, they engage both our more primitive impulses as well as our brains. However, most people would probably feel repulsed or become bored merely watching a "bad guy" set out on a killing spree. As the examples of Richard and the Joker have shown, there has to be a certain psychological depth to the characters or their crimes have to be particularly artful in order for them to truly captivate the audience.

Niedersachsen Englisch ▪ Abiturprüfung 2022
Erhöhtes Anforderungsniveau

HÖRVERSTEHEN

You will hear each recording twice. After each listening you will have time to complete your answers.

Task 1: Book reviews (5 BE)

Preparation time: 40 seconds

You will hear the beginnings of five book reviews.
Choose from the list (A–G) which description best applies to which book review (1–5). For each book review there is only one correct answer. There are two more descriptions than you need.

	Descriptions
A	Dealing with characters' secrets
B	Describing a character's dreams
C	Tracing a character's self-exploration
D	Inspired by very different historical events
E	Presenting the lives of prominent individuals
F	Telling the story of formerly overlooked people
G	Based on historical events and connected to current issues

Book review	1	2	3	4	5
Description					

Now listen to the recording again.

Task 2: Baroness Trumpington (14 BE)

Preparation time: 1:30 minutes

You will hear a radio report about Lady Jean Trumpington (born Jean Campbell-Harris, 1922–2018, a British politician).
While listening, fill in the missing information. You need not write complete sentences. Unless otherwise specified, name one aspect.

1	Why did Lady Trumpington's departure from politics attract so much attention?	
2	Why does the host of a TV show mention the invention of television?	
3	Which incident made Lady Trumpington widely known?	
4	What is said about her education?	
5	In which two different fields of work was she active during World War II?	• •
6	Why did she return to Great Britain?	
7	What did she change in her life during her time in Cambridge?	
8	Why did she choose the title "Baroness Trumpington"?	
9	What was special about her holding her governmental position at the end of the 1980s?	
10	What did she do in Downing Street that helped her keep her position?	
11	What was her duty as Baroness in Waiting?	

12	Which interest will she continue to pursue after retiring?	

Now think of the text as a whole. Tick (✓) the correct answer (a, b or c). There is only one correct answer.

13 In the radio report, Lady Trumpington's personality is presented as being …

a ☐ charitable and caring.
b ☐ cautious and level-headed.
c ☐ self-confident and unconventional.

Now listen to the recording again.

Task 3: Sea otters (6 BE)

Preparation time: 1:30 minutes

You will hear a radio report about research on sea otters in Canada.
While listening, tick (✓) the correct answer (a, b or c). There is only one correct answer.

1 The research focusses on the

a ☐ effects of sea otter populations on the local economy.
b ☐ behavioural patterns of sea otters living close to humans.
c ☐ consequences of climate change for sea otter populations.

2 There was more seafood in the area after the Europeans had arrived because

a ☐ sea otters were exterminated.
b ☐ Europeans relied mainly on farming.
c ☐ the native population was moved inland.

3 The scientists have chosen Vancouver Island for their research project because

a ☐ university facilities are readily available.
b ☐ a particular species of sea otters lives there.
c ☐ the place is suitable for comparative field studies.

4 The sea otters affect the ecosystem because

a ☐ they tend to destroy habitats of other species.
b ☐ their feeding behaviour fosters the growth of fish.
c ☐ they help to reduce the impact of invasive species.

5 Ecologist Edward Gregr addresses the issue that

a ☐ visits to the area need to be regulated.
b ☐ not everyone in the area profits in the same way.
c ☐ too many sea otters threaten the fragile ecosystem.

6 Native Canadians living in isolated communities perceive the growing population of sea otters as

a ☐ a potential threat.
b ☐ a minor nuisance.
c ☐ a welcome source of income.

Now listen to the recording again.

SPRACHMITTLUNG

Aufgabenstellung

You are taking part in a German-American youth project in which the participants share information about changing traditions. You have decided to focus on the role of porcelain in Germany.
Based on the interview below, write an article for the project website in which you describe the current situation of manufacturing and using porcelain in Germany and the developments responsible for it.

Text „Zurück zur Tischkultur“ – Interview von Sophie Hilgenstock

Herr Holler, ist das nur so ein Gefühl, oder erlebt Porzellan tatsächlich gerade eine Renaissance?
Nein, anhand der Zahlen können wir leider nicht erkennen, dass es eine Renaissance gibt. In diesem Jahr hatten die deutschen Porzellanhersteller im Vergleich zum Vorjahr einen Umsatzrückgang von 5,1 Prozent. Ähnlich sah es im letzten Jahr aus. Daher ist es schwierig zu behaupten, Porzellan erlebe eine Renaissance. Lediglich im Projektgeschäft, also im professionellen Bereich, ist die Nachfrage zuletzt gestiegen. In Gaststätten, Seniorenwohnanlagen und Krankenhäusern wird neuerdings wieder mehr Wert

auf gutes Geschirr gelegt, dort konnten die deutschen Porzellanhersteller in den vergangenen Jahren große Erfolge feiern.

Wie sieht es in Privathaushalten aus? Spätestens zu Weihnachten ist gutes Geschirr doch der Renner.
Das ist richtig. Je näher Weihnachten rückt, umso besser läuft das Geschäft. Viele Kunden haben es dabei vor allem auf die Weihnachtskollektionen abgesehen, die viele Hersteller im Angebot haben. Gemeint ist Porzellan mit Weihnachtsdekor, also mit Tannenbäumen, Glocken und Nikoläusen. Diese Porzellanlinien funktionieren gut, speziell bei Familien mit Kindern.

Woran liegt es, dass Porzellan ansonsten aus der Mode ist?
Das hat mehrere Gründe. Der wohl wichtigste Faktor ist, dass jüngere Generationen weniger Wert auf hochwertiges Porzellan und Essen am gedeckten Tisch legen. Die sonntägliche Kaffeetafel, Familienfeiern zu Hause, Gäste zum Abendessen – die Anlässe, das gute Geschirr aus dem Schrank zu holen, sind aus der Mode gekommen. Wer greift heute noch zur Kaffeekanne aus Porzellan? Man stellt seinen Becher direkt unter den Kaffeeautomaten oder läuft mit Thermobecher aus dem Haus. Das ist ein Kulturwandel, den man nur in Teilen auffangen kann – etwa, indem die Geschirrhersteller Coffee-to-go-Becher aus Porzellan herstellen, die man immer wieder verwenden kann. Aber den Trend halten wir nicht auf.

Einst war die Porzellanmarke identitätsstiftend. Gilt Porzellan heute noch als Statussymbol?
Nicht mehr so wie früher. Es ist nicht mehr die Regel, dass jede Familie ein gutes Geschirr besitzt oder auf eine bestimmte Marke schwört. Porzellan gehört auch nicht mehr typischerweise zur Aussteuer. Es gibt zwar noch Hochzeitspaare, die zur Trauung ein bestimmtes Service bekommen, aber die sind aus unserer Sicht viel zu selten geworden – die meisten wünschen sich Geld für die Hochzeitsreise. Schaut man sich an, wofür junge Menschen heute Geld ausgeben, liegen die Prioritäten ganz klar woanders: Es ist kein Problem, sich für 800 Euro ein Handy zu kaufen, bei hochwertigem Porzellan sieht es oft anders aus.

Wie wollen Sie das ändern?
Mit modernem Design, guter Qualität und pfiffigen Ideen. Das Ziel muss es sein, sich von den Billigimporten aus Asien abzuheben. Außerdem müssen wir Online als Vertriebsweg ausbauen. Uns sterben zunehmend die Fachhändler weg – gab es früher in jeder Kleinstadt ein klassisches Haushaltswarengeschäft, machen heute etwa 40 Fachgeschäfte pro Jahr in den Innenstädten dicht. Aber Porzellan will man anfassen, bevor man es kauft. Der Onlinehandel ist damit eine Herausforderung.

Deutschland war einmal Porzellanland. Was ist schiefgelaufen?
Deutschland ist in Europa weiterhin der größte Standort der Porzellanherstellung, und ich bin sicher, das wird auch so bleiben. Die Herausforderungen allerdings werden nicht kleiner. Der Endverbraucher greift oft lieber zur Dumpingware aus China – also zu Porzellan, das weit unter Herstellungskosten auf den Markt geschwemmt wird. Inzwischen gibt es deshalb auf chinesische Importware Strafzölle. Aber damit sind die

Probleme nicht vom Tisch: Die politischen Rahmenbedingungen für die deutschen Porzellanhersteller sind schwierig. Sie haben europaweit die höchsten Energiekosten und die höchste Abgabenlast. […]

Wie schaffen es altehrwürdige Häuser wie Meissen, KPM oder Fürstenberg, sich am Markt zu halten?

In den letzten Jahren sind mit Russland oder dem Vorderen Orient wichtige Exportmärkte weggebrochen. Je mehr Krisen und Kriege die Welt erschüttern, umso schwieriger wird es auch für die Produzenten von kunsthandwerklich hergestelltem Porzellan. Nichtsdestoweniger gibt es weiterhin ein großes Interesse an individuellen, hochwertigen Produkten – von Porzellanfiguren über handbemalte Vasen bis hin zu aufwendig gestalteten Tellern. Wer heute noch am Markt ist, hat bewiesen, dass er sich trotz schwierigster Rahmenbedingungen mit seinen Produkten durchsetzen kann – von daher sehe ich nicht schwarz. *645 Wörter*

Quelle: Hergt, K. und Hilgenstock, S. (2018, 10. Dezember). „Zurück zur Tischkultur: Ein Besuch in der Manufaktur Fürstenberg“. Leipziger Volkszeitung. *https://www.lvz.de/Nachrichten/Panorama/Zurueck-zur-Tischkultur-Ein-Besuch-in-der- Porzellanmanufaktur-Fuerstenberg.*

Anmerkungen

1 Christoph René Holler – Hauptgeschäftsführer des Bundesverbands Keramische Industrie
21 Kaffeetafel – ein festlich gedeckter Tisch für Kaffee und Kuchen am Nachmittag
32 Aussteuer – Ausstattung für den künftigen Haushalt, die eine Braut traditionell von ihrer Familie zur Hochzeit geschenkt bekam
32 KPM – Königliche Porzellan-Manufaktur Berlin

TEXTAUFGABE

Von den zwei Aufgaben ist eine auszuwählen und zu bearbeiten.

Aufgabe I: Aufgabenstellung

1 Outline the autobiographical information given by Joseph Azam. (30 %)

2 Examine the significance the author's names have for him. (30 %)

3 You are taking part in a workshop titled "Displacement and Identity in Literature." You have to hand in an article about the struggles of integration, discussing the statement "It is not easy to be stranded between two worlds, the sad truth is that we can never be completely comfortable in either world" by the novelist Sharon Kay Penman.
Write the article, also referring to the text at hand and materials studied in class, such as the short stories by Lahiri, Levy, Pandit, and Shahraz. (40 %)

Text I — Excerpt from Joseph Azam, "Last, First, Middle" (2018)

The writer Joseph Azam and his family fled Afghanistan in the early 1980s when he was still a baby.

Growing up, my name – Mohammad – caused me to dread the fall. While some kids fretted about months of monotony, my angst was focused squarely on the first moments of the school year when roll would be taken out loud for the first time. By the first grade, I had come up with a routine designed to ensure that my teacher wouldn't even utter the name Mohammad. […]

I had a lot of friends from immigrant families with strange sounding names and most of them went even further than I did in trying to fortify their American-ness. Instead of going by their given names, many of them took on noms de guerre like Michael, or Danny, or Jessica in the struggle to fit in. I never had the courage or the permission to go that far myself. I had abandoned Mohammad, but I never asked to be called Joseph or Joe, in part because it felt dishonest but mostly because I was worried about my parents somehow finding out and seeing it as a rejection of who we were. Ironically enough, years later they would do it for me. […]

When it came time to enroll me in [high] school, my father made a choice that short-circuited my unrest, at least for a time. As we stood there at the registrar's counter, he very casually, and without so much as turning to me, registered me as Joseph Azam. To this day I don't know what went into his decision. Perhaps he and my mother had noticed my mushrooming anxiety, and perhaps they realized it had something to do with how I thought I was going to fare in this new place. In any case, my father's decision liberated me from the immigrant self-gaze that had consumed me for so long, but it also felt like a death.

So much of what I had been through with my parents over the years – Kabul, India, Germany, our early days in New York – seemed to fall instantly out of focus as the name Yousuf faded. Being known as Joseph or Joe outside of my family brought with it the ordinariness and anonymity that I had so desperately wanted at age six, but at fifteen it brought me discomfort and waves of guilt at home.

[…] I wondered whether it stung my parents that on top of the many things they lost and left behind in Kabul, a decade and a half later they felt compelled to surrender my name as well. More than anything, I brooded over what my grandfather would have thought of the way in which I had treated his exquisite gift to me.

I'll never know exactly how or to what extent going through high school under an alias colored my experience, or whether or not it somehow helped clear a path for me – to college back in New York, to graduate school, to law school, to a career in corporate America. What it did do was leave me with an entirely new dilemma over what was worse: being identifiably foreign or secretly false. It was a question I tortured myself with throughout high school and one that was thrown into relief not long after I graduated at a U.S. Citizenship and Immigration Services Center just south of Los Angeles.

My parents had become naturalized U.S. citizens when I was very young but hadn't gotten around to filling out the paperwork for me to claim my derivative citizenship until we had moved to California. I was eighteen years old by the time my application was up for review, which meant I had to go in for a citizenship interview as part of the process. I remember breezing through my interview and sitting in a drab corridor in the immigration center as I waited to submit my passport application that same day. The fluorescent lights above my head had lulled me into a trance when my eyes suddenly fixated on the first fields of the still blank application: Name (Last, First, Middle); Place of Birth; Address; List All Other Names You Have Used.

No sooner had I realized the choice that lay in front of me than my number was called; I found myself standing with my father at a counter once again being asked to register my name. This time the decision was mine alone to make, he made sure of that. At a loss for what to do and with an impatient clerk scowling at my empty form I panicked and dropped the stack of documents that I had been toting around all morning.

Realizing that she had frazzled me, even if she was unsure of why, the clerk behind the counter told me to take my time gathering myself and cleaning up my mess. She had no idea how many years I had spent trying to do just that.

As I knelt down to pull together the papers that had fallen around my feet, I was confronted by the dissonance that I had lived with for so many years. I picked up the green card with the photo of Yousuf, the wide-eyed asylum seeker. I picked up the California driver's license with the awkward photo of Joseph, the gangly teenager who had just barely passed his driving test. I picked up my parents' citizenship certificates. I picked up duplicate after duplicate I had brought of my various citizenship forms that outlined in detail the places we had lived. I picked up my passport application and I picked up my pen.

What I did next is simply what felt most honest. Instead of choosing between my names, I chose all of them.

Joseph Mohammad Yousuf Azam. It was disjointed, redundant perhaps, but it made whole again the hopes of my grandfather and added to them my own. It didn't fit in the space provided on the form that day but it fit the moment and it fit me.

This was my American name. *991 words*

From: Joseph Azam. "Last, First, Middle." The Displaced: Refugee Writers on Refugee Lives. *Ed. Viet Thanh Nguyen. New York: Abrams, 2018. 29–33.*

Annotations

4/5 Azam asked his teachers to address him by his middle-name Yousuf only.
8 nom de guerre – *German: Deckname*
29/30 His grandfather in Kabul named the new-born baby Mohammad Yousuf.
32 alias – a fake name used to conceal one's identity
33/34 corporate America – the world of large American businesses
40 derivative citizenship – a type of citizenship for children born abroad whose parents are U.S. citizens
54 to frazzle s. o. – to make s. o. nervous

Hilfsmittel

Ein- und zweisprachiges Wörterbuch der Zielsprache

Aufgabe II: Aufgabenstellung

1 Sum up the excerpt. (30 %)

2 Compare the scientist Capaldi with Victor Frankenstein from Mary Shelley's novel. (30 %)

3 As a contribution to its monthly topic "Science Meets Literature," your online book club has asked its members to contribute a blog entry, commenting on the following statement by software programmer Justin Rosenberg:

> "[A]s the frontiers are pushed further and further, the unintended consequences of how science and technology are used could affect who we are as humans, the viability of our planet, and how society evolves."

Write the blog entry, also referring to the text at hand and materials studied in class, such as Mary Shelley's novel *Frankenstein*. (40 %)

Text II Excerpt from Kazuo Ishiguro, *Klara and the Sun* (2021)

The novel is set in a dystopian future, in which it has not only become common for wealthy people to buy human-like androids, so-called 'Artificial Friends' (or AFs), as companions for their teenage children, but also to have their children genetically modified in order to enhance their intellectual abilities. Due to this procedure, 15-year-old Josie has become seriously ill. She, her parents and her AF Klara are at the studio of Mr Capaldi, who is creating a 'portrait' of Josie at her mother's request. While walking through his studio, Klara has discovered that this 'portrait' is actually a life-size replica of Josie's body.

I stepped out onto the balcony, now making no effort to conceal myself or to soften my footsteps. Leaning over the steel rail, I saw the Mother had sat down where earlier Josie had been sitting – on the metal chair in front of the charts. Mr Capaldi came across the floor till he was directly below me, and I could see the top of his bald head, but not his expression. He then continued to walk slowly towards the Mother, as if slowness were a mark of his kindness, and stopped beside the tripod-stand lamp.

'I can see you're having misgivings,' he said in a new, soft voice. 'Let me tell you. I've seen this kind of thing happen many times before. And it's the ones who stick with it, keep faith, who win out.'

'Damn right I'm having misgivings.'

'You mustn't let <u>Paul</u> sway you. Remember. You've thought this through and he hasn't. Paul is confused.'

'It's not Paul. To hell with Paul. It's that … that portrait up there.'

As she said this, she glanced up in my direction and saw me. She stared past the dazzle of the ceiling lights, then Mr Capaldi also turned and looked up at me. Then he looked at the Mother questioningly. The Mother continued to gaze at me, her hand now raised to her forehead.

'Okay, Klara,' she said finally. 'Come on down.'

As I descended the metal steps, I was interested to see that instead of anger, the Mother showed anxiety. I crossed the floor but stopped while still several strides away. It was Mr Capaldi who spoke first.

'What do you think, Klara? Am I doing a good job?'

'She resembles Josie quite accurately.'

'Then I guess that's a yes. By the way, Klara, how did you get on with the survey?'

'I completed it, Mr Capaldi.'

'Then I'm grateful for your cooperation. And you stored the data safely?'

'Yes, Mr Capaldi. My responses are stored.'

There was a silence, while the Mother continued to stare at me from her chair and Mr Capaldi from beside his tripod light. I realized they were waiting for me to say something further, so I continued: 'It's a pity Josie and the Father have left. Mr Capaldi's work on the portrait may be temporarily impeded.'

'It's okay,' he said. 'Not a serious setback.'

'I need to hear,' the Mother said. 'I need to hear, Klara, what you think. About what you saw.'

'I apologize for examining the portrait without permission. But in the circumstances, I felt it best to do so.'

'Okay,' the Mother said, and again I saw she was fearful rather than angry. 'Now tell us what you thought. Or rather, tell us what you think you saw up there.'

'I'd suspected for some time that Mr Capaldi's portrait wasn't a picture or a sculpture, but an AF. I went in to confirm my speculation. Mr Capaldi has done an accurate job of catching Josie's outward appearance. Though perhaps the hips should be a little narrower.'

'Thank you,' Mr Capaldi said. 'I'll bear that in mind. It's still a work in progress.'

[…]

'Klara,' the Mother said. 'We came here today, the main reason. It wasn't so Josie could sit more. We came here because of you.'

'I understand,' I said. 'I understood about the survey. It was to test how well I've come to know Josie. How well I understand how she makes her decisions and why she has her feelings. I think the results will show I'm well able to train the Josie upstairs. But I say again, it's wrong to give up hope.'

'You still don't quite understand,' Mr Capaldi said. Although he was standing there before me, his voice seemed to come from the edges of my vision, because all I could see still were the Mother's eyes. 'Let me explain to her, Chrissie. It'll be easier coming from me. Klara, we're not asking you to train the new Josie. We're asking you to *become* her. That Josie you saw up there, as you noticed, is empty. If the day comes – I hope it doesn't, but if it does – we want you to inhabit that Josie up there with everything you've learned.'

'You wish me to inhabit her?'

'Chrissie chose you carefully with that in mind. She believed you to be the one best equipped to learn Josie. Not just superficially, but deeply, entirely. Learn her till there's no difference between the first Josie and the second.' [...]

'So you see what's being asked of you, Klara,' Mr Capaldi said. 'You're not being required simply to mimic Josie's outward behavior. You're being asked to continue her for Chrissie. And for everyone who loves Josie.'

'But is that going to be possible?' the Mother said. 'Could she really continue Josie for me?'

'Yes, she can,' Mr Capaldi said. 'And now Klara's completed the survey up there, I'll be able to give you scientific proof of it. Proof she's already well on her way to accessing quite comprehensively all of Josie's impulses and desires. The trouble is, Chrissie, you're like me. We're both of us sentimental. We can't help it. Our generation still carry the old feelings. A part of us refuses to let go. The part that wants to keep believing there's something unreachable inside each of us. Something that's unique and won't transfer. But there's nothing like that, we know that now. *You* know that. For people our age it's a hard one to let go. We *have* to let it go, Chrissie. There's nothing there. Nothing inside Josie that's beyond the Klaras of this world to continue. The second Josie won't be a copy. She'll be the exact same and you'll have every right to love her just as you love Josie now. It's not faith you need. Only rationality. I had to do it, it was tough but now it works for me just fine. And it will for you.' *994 words*

From: Kazuo Ishiguro. Klara and the Sun. *London: Faber & Faber, 2021. 205–210.*

Annotations
11 Paul – Josie's father

Hilfsmittel
Ein- und zweisprachiges Wörterbuch der Zielsprache

Lösungsvorschlag

HÖRVERSTEHEN

Transkript 1 Book reviews

1 Welcome to Book Club and a novel that's set in the aftermath of the First World War but crackles with contemporary relevance. James Meek's novel *The People's Act of Love* is set in the wastes of Siberia in 1919. And in a way, it is a Russian novel, because its action springs from the turmoil of that country in its dark history.

2 Hello and welcome to Book Club from Swansea. Sheers's book is a psychological thriller that mixes suspense – Michael, the central character, tries to conceal an awful event out of fear – with a story of the relationship between two men who both have something to hide.

3 Hello. If you look at *The New York Times* for October 4th, 1951, you will see two headlines jostling together on the front page, one reporting that "Giants win over the Brooklyn Dodgers in a famous baseball game", the other saying, "Soviets explode atomic bomb". Well, when Don DeLillo looked at those headlines in the early nineties, 40 years on, the prickle of excitement started him on a journey of the imagination that led to *Underworld*.

4 Hello and welcome to Book Club and a biographical feast. We're talking this month about the story of two interlocked families, and at the head of them, the two most glamorous figures of the late Victorian stage, Sir Henry Irving and Ellen Terry. They're the joint subjects of one of our most admired literary biographers, Michael Holroyd, now in his eighties, who's our guest today.

5 Hello and welcome to Book Club. This month's book is funny and breezy, but don't be misled by that. *Rachel's Holiday* is also a journey into darkness with Rachel discovering the depths of her drug addiction and its threat to her whole life. Her holiday is, in fact, a trip into rehab, away from the high life she's been enjoying in New York to a clinic in Dublin, the Cloisters, where she imagines that she'll get away from it all, but instead discovers more about herself than she expected.

based on: bbc.co.uk/sounds/play/m000dxtp; bbc.co.uk/sounds/play/m0007b4t; bbc.co.uk/sounds/play/b07sxttn; bbc.co.uk/sounds/play/b072htqw; bbc.co.uk/sounds/play/m000fw1j

TIPP

You do not have a lot of time to read through the task, so concentrate on highlighting the keywords which sum up the main idea of each description. Also mark words you think are essential for comprehension. You will have a very short break before and in between sets to look them up, but do not overestimate the time frame. The listening comprehension in your exam takes its complexity not only from the level of sophistication of the audio files, but also from the speed with which you have to solve the tasks.

- **1 – G:** The key phrases in the description are "historical events" as well as "connected to current issues" (= "contemporary relevance", l. 2), which is the main difference when compared to description **D**, which only speaks of "historical events". It also differs from **D** in that it does not deal with "very different historical events" but rather focuses on a specific historical period of a specific country.
- **2 – A:** The key word here is "secret", which is indirectly mentioned several times: The review talks about the protagonist "tr[ying] to conceal" (l. 6) something and about two men "hav[ing] something to hide" (ll. 7/8).
- **3 – D:** The fact that the review talks about "headlines jostling" (l. 10) points towards "very different historical events", as mentioned in **D**. If you don't know the word "jostling", the headlines give you an even stronger clue: One is about a baseball game (cf. ll. 10/11), the other about the explosion of an atomic bomb (cf. ll. 11/12), which do not have anything in common.
- **4 – E:** Finding the correct solution can be tricky here, because you might mistake the word "interlocked" (l. 16) for "overlooked". In this case, you might be tempted to choose **F** ("story of overlooked people") as an answer. It is, however, stated that the book deals with "the two most glamorous figures of the late Victorian stage" (ll. 16/17), which then leaves **E** ("prominent individuals") as the correct solution.
- **5 – C:** This review hints at the correct description quite often. It is about "self-exploration", which is expressed in phrases like "journey into darkness" (l. 21), with the protagonist "discovering the depths of her drug addiction" (ll. 21/22) and "discover[ing] more about herself than she expected" (l. 25).

Book review	1	2	3	4	5
Description	G	A	D	E	C

Transkript 2 Baroness Trumpington

Edward Stourton: It should surely not come as a shock when a nonagenarian decides to retire. But Lady Trumpington's decision to leave the House of Lords when she reaches 95 this month made a splash. Perhaps that's because she's been part of the place for so long. No one can quite imagine the scene without her.

TV host: It would be ungallant of me to tell you Her Ladyship's age. So let's just say she was born before this programme started. And before BBC One started. And before television started. Please welcome Baroness Trumpington.

Stourton: She began among pearls and ermine, and she's ending her long career in similar territory. On the way, she's lived our history and known most of the people who made it. But she only really became famous in her late eighties when she was caught by the cameras making a V-sign at one of her fellow peers, as the comedian Jack Whitehall reminded her on "Have I Got News for You?".

Jack Whitehall: Did you regret swearing at him or …?

Baroness Trumpington: No, because I regretted what he said, which was that people of my age were starting to look very, very, very old. Well, wouldn't you do that if you …?

Jack Whitehall: Yeah, I can see …

Stourton: Jean Campbell-Harris was born in 1922. Her father was a former major in the Bengal Lancers with the right connections. Her mother was the heir to a Chicago paint fortune. Her formal education was limited, as was often the way for women then. And she says she's never taken an exam. But finishing school in Paris gave her good French and German. The war began when she was 16.

Old news report: Down on the farm, the land girls are doing their bit and a bit more.

Stourton: Like thousands of other young women, Jean Campbell-Harris was sent to work as a land girl, filling the gap left when the countryside's young men went to fight. In 1940, she took her language skills to the secret codebreaking centre of Bletchley Park. She was a cipher clerk. Jean worked on Madison Avenue in the post-war Mad Men days, and it was in the United States that she met her very English husband, Alan Barker, a historian, then working at the Ivy League University, Yale. His career brought him back to a teaching post at Eton and then to the headmaster's job at the Leys, a private school in Cambridge. *[excerpt from song]* And it was during her years as a headmaster's wife that Jean Barker, as she then was, really turned her attention to politics.

Georgina Morley: She became a councillor in Cambridge and then ultimately mayor of Cambridge, and I think she rather loved being mayor.

Stourton: Cambridge local politics was a long way from life in Mayfair and Manhattan, and her early political career was hard graft. She tried and failed to become an MP. The political scene was dominated by another powerful woman, Margaret Thatcher. In 1980, Jean Barker was given a peerage by the new Tory government. She already had contacts in the House of Lords, including the Tory peer, Viscount Astor, whose mother had been Jean's friend and fellow clerk at Bletchley.

Viscount Astor: Jean took to the House of Lords like a duck to water, as it were, because she could actually kind of deflate someone who was being pompous, for example.

Stourton: There remained the little matter of deciding on a title. Her reputation for a robust speaking style was already established, so she rejected Baroness Barker. She explained her final decision to the prominent eighties Tory John Gummer, now Lord Deben.

Lord Deben: So, she said I had to choose the village nearest to me. And there were two possibilities. One was Trumpington and the other was Six Mile Bottom. She thought that was not a good idea. So, Trumpington it was.

Stourton: Lady Trumpington's husband Alan died after a stroke in 1988, leaving her a widow in her mid-sixties. She was serving as a minister at Agriculture at the time, the first ever woman minister there, and threw herself into her work. She survived at the ministry when John Major succeeded Margaret Thatcher until …

Georgina Morley: At one point she was called into Downing Street. And John Major, it turned out, had decided that the time had come for her to retire from the front bench, and she was not expecting this. And she told me afterwards, shamelessly, that she cried. Whereupon the Prime Minister patted her on the shoulder and said, "There, there, all right then, well, never mind, we'll leave you as you are." So, she stayed on.

Stourton: By 1992, she was the oldest ever serving woman minister, and during John Major's second term, she became a Baroness in Waiting, representing the Queen on formal occasions until the Tories lost power in 1997. Lady Trumpington isn't giving up all her passions. Her enthusiasm for horse racing, for example, is as fierce as ever. But her son, Adam, says that by giving up the Lords, she's giving up more than a job.

Adam Barker: The Lords became her family.

based on: bbc.co.uk/sounds/play/b098bqr1

TIPP

This task requires an in-depth knowledge of vocabulary, the ability to distinguish between several native speakers talking, and the skill to understand various accents of British English. You also have to cope with inferior sound quality in bits of historic audio documents. However, do not worry too much, as you can rely on the order of the questions following the chronology of the recording and you mostly need to note down only one aspect out of several mentioned.

1 There are several reasons why "Lady Trumpington's decision to leave the House of Lords" (l. 2), or in other words "politics", attracted attention or "made a splash" (l. 3): "she's been part of the place for so long" (ll. 3/4), "no one can quite imagine the scene without her" (l. 4), and also "she reaches 95 this month" (ll. 2/3).

2 By mentioning the invention of television the host reveals Lady Trumpington's age in an indirect and humorous way ("It would be ungallant of me to tell you Her Ladyship's age." l. 5): "So let's just say she was born before this programme started. And before BBC One started. And before television started." (ll. 5–7)

3 You do not need to know that the "V-sign" is a rude gesture (when the palm is facing towards the person making the sign) – it is enough to recognise the host mentioning that "she only really became famous in her late eighties when she was caught by the cameras making a V-sign at one of her fellow peers" (ll. 10/11). In the next sentence it becomes clear that she was swearing at him (cf. l. 13).

4 The show continues with milestones in Baroness Trumpington's life. Be careful, however, because this task only asks for Trumpington's education. You only need to note down one aspect from lines 20 to 22:

"formal education was limited […] she's never taken an exam […] finishing school in Paris […] good French and German."

5 Listen closely here: The short clipping from a wartime news report serves as a distractor and the term "land girl(s)" (ll. 23, 25) is mentioned quite fast, meaning that she worked on a farm during the war. Her second job as a "cipher clerk" (l. 27) is not only hard to understand, but also no longer common and you need to know "clerk" as another word for "secretary" or "office worker". Bletchley Park was a facility of the British Intelligence Service to decode secret German messages in World War II. If you know that, you can also give "intelligence work" or "code breaking" as an answer.

6 Here, you need to deduct the answer from what is said about Trumpington's husband, whom she met in the United States (cf. ll. 28/29) and who was "a historian, then working at […] Yale. His career brought him back to […] Eton and then to […] a private school in Cambridge" (ll. 29–31), so Jean Barker, as she was now called, became "a headmaster's wife" (l. 32) in England. And here, the Baroness "turned her attention to politics" (l. 33) by becoming councillor and mayor (cf. l. 34) there.

7 In order to answer this question correctly, you must not lose track of the audio. It ends with the story of Trumpington's husband who got a job in Cambridge.

8 Listen particularly closely after the key word "title" (l. 44). As Trumpington "rejected [the title of] Baroness Barker" (l. 45), she then had "to choose the village nearest to [her]" (l. 48) and as she refused to be called "Six Mile Bottom", she chose the other village called "Trumpington" (cf. ll. 49/50).

9 Pay attention when the year 1988 is mentioned (cf. l. 51), which points towards the question of "her governmental position at the end of the 1980s". The audio says that "[s]he was serving as a minister of Agriculture at the time, the first ever woman minister there" (ll. 52/53) and that she still was "at the ministry when John Major succeeded Margaret Thatcher" (l. 54).

10 Here, "Downing Street" is the key word. Pay attention to what Lady Trumpington did when she was asked to resign by John Major, then Prime Minister: "she cried" (ll. 57/58), which led to "the Prime Minister patt[ing] her on the shoulder" and leaving her in office (cf. ll. 58–60).

11 The moment the audio mentions "Baroness in Waiting" (l. 62), it is explained that she was "representing the Queen on formal occasions" (ll. 62/63).

12 This information is also given very fast and rather at the end of the audio when your concentration might be decreasing. It is stated that the Baroness has a passion for horse racing (cf. l. 64), so you can deduce that this is what she will continue to follow after retiring.

13 Here you need to understand the general character of Baroness Trumpington. By having a look at your answers in tasks 1 to 12, there is nothing that hints towards "charitable and caring" (**a**). If that were the case, the audio would have given some examples. The same goes for "cautious and level-headed" (**b**).

A person who became a politician without formal education (cf. ll. 20–22, 32–35), went to the United States on her own (cf. ll. 27/28), gave inappropriate hand signs towards a colleague (cf. ll. 10–16), and was still active in her 90s (cf. ll. 1–4) can be nothing more than "self-confident and unconventional" (**c**).

1	Why did Lady Trumpington's departure from politics attract so much attention?	she had been there for so long / she retired at the age of 95 / hard to imagine House of Lords without her
2	Why does the host of a TV show mention the invention of television?	to show/allude to Lady Trumpington's (advanced) age / because Lady Trumpington had been born before TV was invented / to introduce a guest in a humorous way
3	Which incident made Lady Trumpington widely known?	making V-sign / swearing (at a fellow peer) / making a rude gesture
4	What is said about her education?	limited formal education / has never taken an exam / (went to) finishing school (in Paris) / (fairly) typical of women's education at the time / good command of German and French
5	In which two different fields of work was she active during World War II?	• farming / agriculture / (work as) land girl • code breaking / intelligence / office work / (work as) cipher clerk
6	Why did she return to Great Britain?	followed her (English) husband / because of her husband's job
7	What did she change in her life during her time in Cambridge?	started her political career / turned her attention to politics / became councillor/mayor
8	Why did she choose the title "Baroness Trumpington"?	(name of/refers to) nearest village / did not like other options (Barker/Six Mile Bottom)
9	What was special about her holding her governmental position at the end of the 1980s?	first (ever) female Minister at Agriculture / first (ever) woman holding that position / stayed in office when the Prime Minister changed
10	What did she do in Downing Street that helped her keep her position?	she cried / she made the Prime Minister feel sorry for her
11	What was her duty as Baroness in Waiting?	representing the Queen on formal occasions

12	Which interest will she continue to pursue after retiring?	horse racing

13 In the radio report, Lady Trumpington's personality is presented as being …

c ☑ self-confident and unconventional.

Transkript 3 Sea otters

Ari Shapiro *(host)*: Let's talk about sea otters. They float on the water, cuddle their little babies. Same time, they're voracious eaters that gobble up shellfish. And that has brought them into conflict with people who rely on shellfish for their livelihoods. NPR's Nell Greenfield-Boyce reports that scientists have now assessed the economic impact of restoring sea otters to their historic homes.

Nell Greenfield-Boyce *(byline)*: Sea otters are pretty big. They can weigh 60 pounds or more. To survive in the cold waters of the Northern Pacific, they need to eat a lot.

Jane Watson: And so a sea otter is going to eat about a quarter of its body mass, its body weight, in food each day.

Greenfield-Boyce: Jane Watson is a researcher with Vancouver Island University in Canada. She says historically sea otters coexisted with Indigenous people. But when the Europeans arrived, hunters with the fur trade wiped the otters out.

Watson: All of a sudden, all of the prey that otters eat no longer had their principal predator eating them anymore.

Greenfield-Boyce: Clams, crabs, sea urchins – their populations took off, and people got used to the abundance. Well, a few decades ago, sea otters were reintroduced to the west coast of Vancouver Island. Edward Gregr is an ecologist at the University of British Columbia. He says further down the coast from where the otters now live, there's another spot where the otters haven't yet moved in.

Edward Gregr: And so we thought, this is, you know, this is a perfect natural experiment to compare what the ecosystem looks like with and without sea otters.

Greenfield-Boyce: In the journal *Science*, they say otters do eat up clams and crabs worth millions of dollars. They also devour sea urchins, and that allows kelp to flourish. The kelp supports fish species that are worth a lot of money. What's more, tourists will pay to watch the otters frolic. Gregr says, all in all, the financial benefits of otters are more than seven times greater than the losses. But, he says ...

Gregr: We want to make sure we don't lose sight of the caveats around that, mainly the fact that, you know, these costs and benefits are not going to be distributed equally across fisheries or communities.

Greenfield-Boyce: Tourism, for example, isn't necessarily a realistic or attractive option for people who live in remote areas where access to food is a real issue. Barbara Wilson is a member of the Haida Nation who's studied Indigenous people's feelings about the sea otters.

Barbara Wilson: The impact for us is fairly critical.

Greenfield-Boyce: She says Canadian law currently protects the otters. The otters have a right to eat, but so do people. Nell Greenfield-Boyce, NPR News.

TIPP

This task can be difficult insofar as the vocabulary is rather sophisticated or technical and the correct answer is often hidden behind complex expressions. Take your time before the first listening round to look up keywords to which you should pay attention while listening to the text.

1 The scientists are doing research on the impact sea otters have on the local economy (cf. **a**): in lines 2 and 3 the host mentions "gobbl[ing] up shellfish […] brought [the otters] into conflict with people who rely on shellfish for their livelihoods" and in lines 4 and 5 he says that "scientists have now assessed the economic impact of restoring sea otters to their historic homes".

2 The audio mentions that otters were "wiped out" (another word for being "exterminated", cf. **a**) by the Europeans (cf. l. 12). Next, the podcast explains that "all of the prey that otters eat no longer had their principal predator eating them anymore" (ll. 13/14), which eventually led to an "abundance" (l. 16) of seafood in the area.

3 A scientist explains why Vancouver Island is the perfect place for a "natural experiment to compare what the ecosystem looks like with and without sea otters" (ll. 20/21). A key word which helps you find the correct answer is "comparative" (cf. **c**), which is the adjective of the verb "compare" that is mentioned in the audio.

4 Here you need to find out that in places where there are sea otters the fish population increases. The following sentence explains why: "[The otters] also devour sea urchins, and that allows kelp to flourish. The kelp supports fish species that are worth a lot of money" (ll. 23/24), which means that "their feeding behaviour fosters the growth of fish" (**b**). The other options ("destroying habitats", **a**, and "help to reduce the impact of invasive species", **c**) are not mentioned in the text.

5 The solution can be found in lines 28 and 29: "these costs and benefits are not going to be distributed equally across fisheries or communities." A potential threat to the ecosystem (cf. **c**) is not mentioned in the audio and although one might be tempted to tick **a** because of tourists visiting the area (cf. l. 25), this is not called an issue at all.

6 The correct solution lies in the quote by Barbara Wilson, who is a representative of the Haida and expresses "Indigenous people's feelings about the sea otters" (ll. 32/33). She explicitly states that "The impact [of the growing population of sea otters] for us is fairly critical" (l. 34). This is too severe a way of talking about that issue to call it "a minor nuisance" (**b**), while "a welcome source of income" (**c**) is not mentioned at all.

1 The research focusses on the …

a ☑ effects of sea otter populations on the local economy.

2 There was more seafood in the area after the Europeans had arrived because …

a ☑ sea otters were exterminated.

3 The scientists have chosen Vancouver Island for their research project because …

c ☑ the place is suitable for comparative field studies.

4 The sea otters affect the ecosystem because …

b ☑ their feeding behaviour fosters the growth of fish.

5 Ecologist Edward Gregr addresses the issue that …

b ☑ not everyone in the area profits in the same way.

6 Native Canadians living in isolated communities perceive the growing population of sea otters as …

a ☑ a potential threat.

SPRACHMITTLUNG

TIPP

In this task, you have to pay attention to the text form (an article always needs a headline) and the style or register. You should use formal language, but as the addressees are participants of a youth project, some more colloquial expressions are allowed.

You should include the following aspects:

- **introductory paragraph:** summary of the current situation of the German porcelain industry:
  - difficult situation, decline in sales in recent years (cf. ll. 3–5)
  - however, Germany is still Europe's biggest manufacturer (cf. l. 46)
- **reasons for difficulties:**
  - changing eating traditions ("to-go" culture instead of fixed family dinners) (cf. ll. 19–24)
  - porcelain no longer a status symbol or a typical wedding present (cf. ll. 28–34)
  - young people often have other spending priorities (holidays, smartphones, etc.) (cf. ll. 34–36)
  - competition from cheap products from Asia (cf. ll. 40, 48/49)

- many shop closures of homeware stores, online trade is not really taking off (cf. ll. 40–43)
- German manufacturers have to pay high energy costs and other expenses (cf. ll. 52/53)
- difficult political circumstances: crises challenging for luxury goods, such as porcelain, markets in some countries lost for political reasons (cf. ll. 56–58)

– **still, partly hopeful outlook on the future:**
  - professional branches (restaurants, hospitals, retirement homes) still have a demand for high-quality products (cf. ll. 6–10)
  - Christmas collections are also sought after (cf. ll. 13–17)
  - strategy for the future: focus on quality (cf. ll. 38/39, 59–61) and adapting to new modern ways (cf. ll. 25/26, 39/40)

The times are a-changing: Is German porcelain on the way out?	**headline**
Germany has a history of high-quality porcelain production and the country still is the biggest manufacturer in Europe. Yet in recent years, there has been a steady decline in sales.	**introductory paragraph**
The reasons for this are manifold: Due to changing eating habits, such as takeaway meals often replacing fixed family dinners, using high-quality cups and plates is no longer as important as it used to be. Consequently, porcelain has lost its attractiveness as a status symbol or a typical wedding present. Generally, young people nowadays often have other spending priorities.	**reasons for difficulties:** changing traditions
Another challenge lies in the sale venues: Quite a significant number of homeware shops have closed all over Germany and online selling has not really taken off yet. When it comes to the porcelain market, customers usually want to lay their hands on a product before they buy it.	shop closures and difficulties of online trade
Moreover, manufacturers have to compete with cheap products from China. This is especially difficult because of the high costs that make production in Germany expensive.	competition from China
Furthermore, in times of crises, people tend to buy fewer "unnecessary" luxury items. Another consequence of recent political developments is that some of the main German export markets in Russia and the Middle East have become more difficult to access.	difficult political circumstances
Still, the future of German porcelain production does not look entirely grim: Restaurants, hospitals and retirement homes are showing an increasing demand for high-quality crockery. Christmas collections are also exceptionally sought after. So, by keeping their standards high and at the same time adapting to some of the challenges of modern times, the German porcelain industry could well prove that change can be an opportunity rather than a threat.	**hopeful outlook on the future**

TEXTAUFGABE

Text I Excerpt from Joseph Azam, "Last, First, Middle" (2018)

1 **TIPP**

The command term "outline" rarely comes alone, but is often combined with a focus topic, i. e., a certain aspect of the text you have to concentrate on. In this task you are asked to only outline the autobiographical information Joseph Azam gives about himself. You can underline the information about the author's life with a pen to make sure you only include relevant aspects in your solution. Your text should be significantly shorter than the input text. Do not cite from the text, but use your own words.

Important autobiographical information about the author:
- born in Kabul, Afghanistan
- his family fled Kabul in the early 1980s, and via India and Germany arrived in the US
- he attended primary school and was later enrolled in high school by his father
- took the citizenship test in California and decided to combine all of his previous first names (Joseph Mohammad Yousef)
- graduated college and law school and eventually made a career in the American business sector

In his autobiographical text "Last, First, Middle" published in 2018, Joseph Azam relates the journey of his life as an immigrant to the US.

introduction: title, author, year

The author was born in Kabul, Afghanistan, but his family fled the country in the early 1980s when he was still very young. From Kabul, they travelled to India and Germany, before they eventually arrived in the US. Azam attended primary school and his father later enrolled him in high school. All throughout his childhood years, the author had problems identifying with his name. When he applied for American citizenship at age 18, he decided to combine all of his previous first names into one and call himself Joseph Mohammad Yousef Azam. After graduating from high school, Azam went on to attend college and completed law school successfully. At the moment of writing in 2018, he is looking back on a career he has eked out for himself in the American business sector. On top of that, he seems to be a successful writer.

main part: autobiographical information

2 **TIPP**

In this task you need to examine the significance the author's names have for him. First, go through the text again and identify the first names the author uses during the different stages of his life. Then look out for detailed information on how the author feels about each name. Underline the relevant passages and make notes next to the text using your own words. Begin your text with a brief introduction in which you mention the topic of your analysis. In your main part, you could dedicate one section to each of the author's different first names and what they mean to the author. Don't forget to support your findings with evidence from the text.

You could include the following aspects:

- "Mohammad": marks the author as a foreigner, yet also reminds him of his family roots in Afghanistan
- "Yousuf": the name which he likes to be called in primary school; compromise: does not sound as foreign as Mohammad, but still testifies to his roots
- "Joseph": Americanized version of "Yousuf", helps him blend in, but also gives him pangs of guilt for betraying his heritage
- "Joseph Mohammad Yousuf": reconciliation of all parts of his identity

introduction

Being torn between your native country and your newly chosen home is an experience many immigrants share, not just in the US, but everywhere in the world. For the author, this inner conflict has always been most keenly felt when it comes to his name, which therefore carries a strong emotional significance for him.

main part:
"Mohammad Yousuf":
connects him to his roots

"Mohammad": marks him as a foreigner

"Yousuf" as a compromise

As a baby, Azam is given the first names "Mohammad Yousuf" by his grandfather. For the author, this name brings with it both positive and negative feelings: On the one hand, it represents an "exquisite gift" (l. 30) for him, as it reminds him of "the hopes of [his] grandfather" (l. 68) and the family's roots in Afghanistan. On the other hand, as a child, particularly the name Mohammad is also associated with "angst" (l. 2): In their new home in the US, it makes him "identifiably foreign" (l. 35) and he is afraid that it will turn him into an outsider, which is why he keeps this name a secret at primary school by ensuring that his "teacher wouldn't even utter the name Mohammad" (ll. 4/5). However, despite this rejection of his name, the author does not want to adopt an entirely American name either – unlike many of his immigrant friends, who had taken on "noms de guerre like Michael, or Danny, or Jessica in the struggle to fit in" (l. 9). Instead, he settles on a compromise by asking his teachers to call him by his second name, "Yousuf". To him, this name sounds less obviously "foreign" than Mohammad, but does not wipe out his origins altogether.

Later in life, the author's father enrolls his son at high school under the name "Joseph" Azam, an Americanized version of "Yousuf". For the author, this feels ironical (cf. l. 13) because he himself would not have dared take on an American name for fear of disappointing his parents (cf. ll. 11/12).

"Joseph/Joe":

Yet the name Joseph again comes with mixed feelings and does not feel entirely right. On the one hand, having the decision to adopt this name taken from him by his father is a relief for Azam, as it "liberated [him] from the immigrant self-gaze that had consumed [him] for so long" (l. 20) and finally allows him to blend in: "Being known as Joseph or Joe outside of my family brought with it the ordinariness and anonymity that I had so desperately wanted at age six" (l. 25). At the same time, however, dropping "Yousef" for "Joseph" also feels "like a death" (l. 21) and gives him pangs of a guilty conscience for betraying his heritage: "I brooded over what my grandfather would have thought of the way in which I had treated his exquisite gift to me" (ll. 29/30).

allows him to blend in

feels like a betrayal of his origins

The author's inner conflict is resolved when, at age 18, he applies for US citizenship and has to fill in a form with his name. This time, his father does not complete the form for him, but leaves it up to his son to choose a name himself (cf. ll. 49–51). In this pivotal moment, the author combines all the names that had caused him struggles in the past to blend into one name, which allows for his history to be integrated and reflected: "Instead of choosing between my names, I chose all of them. Joseph Mohammad Yousuf Azam." (ll. 65–67). That this represents an act of empowerment and self-determination becomes evident when the author reports that the whole name did not fit in the blank space in the form, which basically could have left him with the option of feeling compelled to drop one part of his name – either "Mohammad" or "Yousuf" or "Joseph". However, he does not see it as his duty to do justice to the form and the blank space it provides. Rather, America has to accept his full "American name" (l. 70).

"Joseph Mohammad Yousuf": reconciles the different parts of his identity

3 **TIPP**

There are different elements which have to be taken into consideration when tackling this assignment. First, you need to present your results in the form of an article. So apart from the general structure of an essay (introduction – well-structured main part – conclusion), which should be stuck to here as well, your text must also include a headline. As your article is for a workshop, your language should not be too informal. Secondly, you have to pay attention to the command term. A discussion asks you to present both arguments for and against a thesis. Thirdly, the task requires you to back up the points you are making with evidence from the text at hand and materials studied in class, such as the short stories "She Shall Not Be Moved", "The Escape", "The Third and Final Continent" and "Loose Change".

The following arguments are mentioned in the sample solution:

- **introduction with explanation of Penman's quote:**
  immigrant experience marked by inner conflict (being torn between culture of origin and culture of new home)
- **arguments supporting Penman's view:**
  - immigrants often have to face hostile reactions in their new home (e. g. Somali woman in "She Shall Not Be Moved" discriminated against due to her skin colour)
  - complete assimilation and denying one's cultural heritage can lead to feelings of guilt and emptiness (e. g. author of "Last, First, Middle" after being enrolled as "Joseph" at high school)
- **arguments against Penman's view:**
  - it is possible to reconcile one's different experiences and adopt a multicultural identity (e. g. author at the end of "Last, First, Middle")
  - sometimes inner conflicts may just be a temporary phase (e. g. protagonists in "The Escape" and "The Third and Final Continent" ultimately feel comfortable in their new homes and at peace with their identities)
- **conclusion:** Penman's quote is too generalising

Home is where the heart is – so are immigrants automatically heart-broken?

heading

Immigration has always been a feature of human societies, and currently, with the climate crisis and conflicts around the planet, more people than ever are on the move to find a better place to live. A lot of immigrants feel torn between their culture of origin and that of the new environment they have moved to. The novelist Sharon Kay Penman, an immigrant herself, argues that this inner conflict is at the core of the immigrant experience, and that immigrants "can never be completely comfortable in either world". But is she right? Do you constantly feel heart-broken if your heart has more than one home?

introduction: reference to quote

main part: arguments supporting Penman's view

There are quite a lot of examples that furnish us with arguments in support of Penman's statement.

discrimination can make it hard to feel at home in the new country; reference to "She Shall not Be Moved"

First of all, a lot of immigrants have to deal with hostile reactions in the country they move to, which makes it hard for them to feel fully at home there. If you look at the short story "She Shall Not Be Moved", in which a Somali woman is verbally abused on a public bus, with no one jumping to her rescue, Penman's statement rings true. This woman can probably never feel completely comfortable in her new home, as there will always be people who discriminate against her because of her skin colour. Even the narrator of the story, who has a family history of migration herself, does not do anything to defuse the situation, at least not until it is safe to support her because the perpetrators have got off the bus.

denial of origins can lead to feelings of guilt and emptiness

reference to "Last, First, Middle"

Many immigrants also have the feeling that they have to leave their culture of origin behind in order to be accepted in their new surroundings. In many cases, denying one's roots and cutting all ties to the past leads to feelings of guilt and emptiness. In the autobiographical story by Joseph Azam, for example, the author is enrolled in high school by his father. While the author's original first names are Mohammad Yousuf, his father just puts "Joseph" on the form, which leaves the author with the "dilemma over what was worse: being identifiably foreign or secretly false." (ll. 34/35). At one point, he even explicitly states that constantly having to choose one side, or in his case one first name, is like torture (cf. l. 35). The evidence seems crystal-clear: You cannot get more uncomfortable than that.

arguments against Penman's view

arriving at a multicultural identity is possible; reference to "Last, First, Middle"

However, upon closer inspection, Azam's story could also serve as an argument against Penman's quote. Importantly, at the end of the story, the author chooses to combine all of his first names into one and call himself "Joseph Mohammad Yousuf", in defiance of the space which is allocated to him on the form sheet. And it is not just a name he chooses, it is a multicultural identity that reconciles everything that makes him who he is: his Afghan roots, his past as a refugee and his American identity. So we should be very careful to differentiate between the beginning of a story and a story's end.

reference to "The Escape"

This also holds true for the short story "The Escape". After the death of his beloved wife, the protagonist, Samir, suddenly feels out of place in England and is overcome with a nostalgic desire to travel to his country of origin, Pakistan. Yet upon arriving there, he finds that it no longer feels like his homeland. While talking to an Asian British man called Ibrahim on the plane back to the UK, Samir comes to realise that he actually considers England to be his home. The brief insecurity about his identity did not have to do just with his status as an immigrant. Rather, it was caused by the loss of his beloved wife. When Samir finally decides to reside in an old people's home with his new friend Ibrahim, and can connect to peers again, his broken heart is mended and he feels comfortable in England again.

In a similar way, the characters in the short story "The Third and Final Continent" ultimately feel happy and comfortable in their new home, America. While the Indian protagonist from the beginning finds it easy to settle in the US, his wife initially has more difficulties reconciling her Indian identity with the American way of life. Arriving late as a consequence of an arranged marriage, she first sticks to her traditional dress code, for example, and does not change her diet either. Yet in the end, both feel entirely comfortable as American citizens, while cherishing both the American and Indian parts of their identity.

reference to "The Third and Final Continent"

To sum up, as the stories mentioned above have shown, Penman's statement that immigrants can "never feel comfortable in either world" is too generalising. Being an immigrant can, but need not necessarily mean that you feel torn between two cultures. Sometimes, the inner conflict Penman describes may also be just a stage on the journey towards arriving at a multicultural identity.

conclusion

Text II — Excerpt from Kazuo Ishiguro, *Klara and the Sun* (2021)

1 **TIPP**

In this task you are required to summarise the main information about the excerpt so that someone who has not read it would know what it is about. Your solution should be significantly shorter than the original text. Don't quote from the text, but use your own words.

You should include the following aspects:
- the scientist Mr Capaldi is talking to the mother of Josie, a girl who is seriously ill and might die soon
- Klara, an android robot or "artificial friend" (AF), arrives at the scene after she has filled in a survey to test how well she knows Josie
- Mr Capaldi has built a life-size "artificial friend" of Josie (the "portrait")
- Klara congratulates him on the design of the portrait and offers some suggestions for improvement
- Klara first believes that it is Mr Capaldi's plan for her to teach the AF Josie
- however, Mr Capaldi informs her that if Josie dies, she should inhabit the new Josie
- Josie's mother still is not fully convinced about the plan

In the given excerpt from Ishiguro's dystopian novel *Klara and the Sun* from 2021, the scientist Mr Capaldi is talking to the mother of a girl called Josie, who is seriously ill and might die soon. It turns out that they have planned for the android robot and "artificial friend" (AF) Klara to embody Josie after her death so that Josie "lives on" for her loved ones.

introduction: author, title, main topic of given excerpt

The android Klara narrates the events from her perspective. First, she just eavesdrops on the conversation between Capaldi and Josie's mother after having filled in a survey which is meant to test how well she already knows Josie. Upon being spotted, she conscientiously reports that she has completed the tasks set her, and congratulates Mr Capaldi on the life-size model he has constructed of Josie, which she had secretly cast an eye on before. On being asked what she makes of the "portrait" and the survey, Klara guesses that it is going to be her job to train the model to resemble Josie. Mr Capaldi then reveals to Klara that actually she herself should inhabit the model of Josie after the girl's death so that Josie continues to exist for her family. Throughout the scene, it becomes obvious that Josie's parents have qualms and are not fully convinced about this plan, yet Mr Capaldi seeks to reassure Josie's mother that it is the reasonable thing to do.

main part: summary of the conversation between Capaldi, Josie's mother and Klara

2 TIPP

In this comparison, your task is to look at the differences and similarities between the two characters Capaldi and Victor Frankenstein. Make sure you back up every point you are making with sufficient evidence from the text at hand and by making efficient use of your background knowledge of the novel *Frankenstein*. Remember, too, that your text becomes more readable if you lend it a good structure. So an introduction, a main part and a conclusion are just as important as clear paragraphs and smooth transitions that walk the reader through the text.

Similarities:
- both characters play God by creating life or continuing life, respectively
- both characters show no moral qualms when it comes to their innovations

Differences:
- motivation: while Frankenstein is seeking scientific recognition and glory, Capaldi's work is devoted to helping a paying client
- approach to work: while Capaldi seems to be level-headed when it comes to his work, Frankenstein is emotionally consumed by it
- openness to feedback: while Capaldi seems to regard other people's opinions as valuable, Frankenstein works alone and in secrecy
- "material" used: while Capaldi creates android robots, Frankenstein assembles actual pieces of flesh he has collected from dead bodies

introduction: reference to the task and the two texts

The novels *Frankenstein* and *Klara and the Sun* have something in common. They are dystopian novels, whose plots eerily resemble modern-day issues. Yet they are also different in as much as the one was set in the 19th century while the other is set in a not-too distant future. Turning our attention to the characters Capaldi and Frankenstein will bring even more similarities and differences to the fore.

main part: similarities between Frankenstein (F) and Capaldi (C) playing God

Let us start off with the similarities first. Obviously, both Frankenstein and Capaldi "play God" in a way by creating life or continuing life, respectively. Furthermore, both seem to be sure that (re)creating life is something that can be mastered by science alone. This becomes evident in Capaldi saying that there is "nothing there. Nothing inside Josie that's beyond the Klaras of this world to continue" (l. 75), and also by the fact that Frankenstein never seems to have bothered about the soul in the creature he was going to create.

lack of moral qualms

What is more, neither Capaldi nor Frankenstein seem to have second thoughts or moral qualms about the long-term consequences of what they are creating. Capaldi flatly rejects the objections of Chrissie, Josie's mother, that it may not be possible to copy her daughter completely, and that she may not be able to love the final product Mr Capaldi is putting together (cf. ll. 65–68). Capaldi clearly shows no signs of wavering when he says that "[i]t's not faith you need. Only rationality. I had to do it, it was tough but now it works for me just fine. And it will for you." (cf ll. 77/78). Likewise, Frankenstein does not worry about the consequences his creation may entail. Instead, he is obsessed with the glory his scientific breakthrough may bring him.

differences between Frankenstein and Capaldi

motivation: glory and recognition (F) vs. helping a paying client (C)

At this point, some differences between the characters come to light. While both seem to be very devoted to their work and convinced of its necessity for mankind, they differ in their motivation for beginning their research in the first place. Frankenstein is in it for the glory. He craves scientific recognition and throws himself into his work accordingly. Capaldi, on the other hand, may come across as self-obsessed and self-confident, but the reason why he creates artificial life is to help a paying client.

approach to work: obsession (F) vs. detached professionalism (C)

What is more, Capaldi's and Frankenstein's approaches to their work are somewhat different. While Frankenstein throws himself into his work to the point that he seriously endangers his own mental well-being, Capaldi seems to have a more level-headed approach. This becomes evident in the way he speaks about his project. When he faces criticism for not having got a certain part of the newly created AF right, for example, he replies professionally, asserting that "[i]t's still a work in progress" (l. 43). In short: while Frankenstein seems to be emotionally absorbed in the project of his creation, Capaldi showcases a certain emotionally detached professionalism.

Closely related to this is another point in which Capaldi and Frankenstein differ. While Capaldi seems to be interested in feedback regarding his work (cf. l. 22) and works together closely with his clients when he is in the process of creating (cf. ll. 30/31), Frankenstein works alone and in complete secrecy. This, you could argue, leads to him creating something which he will ultimately fail to control.

working alone and in secrecy (F) vs. openness to feedback (C)

Last but not least, both scientists differ in the "material" they use for their creatures. Unlike Frankenstein, who assembles actual pieces of flesh that he has collected from dead bodies, Capaldi produces android robots that closely resemble real humans.

creature made of body parts (F) vs. android robots (C)

Looking back at the evidence presented, it is safe to say that *Klara and the Sun* could be regarded as a "Frankenstein 2.0" in many ways. However, we do not learn in the extract whether the AF Josie will eventually be created and what the future may hold for the characters.

conclusion

3 TIPP

In this task, you have to write a blog entry for an online book club. Thus, your text should include a catchy headline that raises curiosity about the topic, and possibly some subheadings. You can also include direct addresses to the readers and, for instance, invite them to leave comments.
In your introduction, you should briefly refer to the quote by Justin Rosenberg and explain it in your own words. In your main part, you must then state your own opinion about it. You can either agree with the statement, disagree or take a position somewhere in between. However, it is important to back up your argument with examples from the given extract from *Klara and the Sun* and other material you have dealt with in class, such as Mary Shelley's novel *Frankenstein*.

The following aspects are mentioned in the sample solution:

- **introduction:**
  - historical example: Industrial Revolution
  - explanation of Rosenberg's quote: technological and scientific innovations can unwittingly lead to far-reaching consequences for the individual, society and the environment
- **main part: arguments and examples supporting Rosenberg's statement**
  - examples of how scientific innovations can lead to unwitting consequences:
    - *Frankenstein:* pushing the boundaries of science and shunning responsibility leads to disastrous consequences
    - genetic engineering: human reproductive cloning as "frontier" of science that could lead to a two-class society

- examples of how technological innovations can lead to unwitting consequences:
  - *Klara and the Sun*: androids replacing humans raise questions about what makes us human and unique
  - digital assistants and "social robots": lead to changes in our social relationships and can gather sensitive data
- **conclusion:** summary of findings and invitation to leave comments

Exploring the limits – the consequences of scientific and technological developments in literature and real life

heading

Writing during the period of the Industrial Revolution, the author Mary Shelley must have been impressed with the changes she witnessed in her lifetime. Scientific innovations like the steam engine had been invented which generated energy and brought about immense progress in manufacturing and transportation. When steam engines were developed, the inventors probably did not think about child labour in the coal mines or women having to work two jobs at the same time, one at home and one in the factory, to eke out a living for their families. The same inventors probably did not plan on destroying beautiful landscapes for extensive mining either. Thus, even if something happens without it being intended, the consequences for the individual, society and the environment can be far-reaching.

introduction: historical example: Industrial Revolution

This example reminds me of a statement by the software programmer Justin Rosenberg, who said that "as the frontiers are pushed further and further, the unintended consequences of how science and technology are used could affect who we are as humans, the viability of our planet, and how society evolves". And once you think about it, there are many more examples from literature and real life that prove that Rosenberg's statement is indeed true.

reference to Rosenberg's quote

The case of *Frankenstein*: science pushing the frontier

The topics of "pushing the frontier" and the unintended consequences of new developments fascinated Mary Shelley. The protagonist of her novel of the same title, Frankenstein, is a scientist obsessed with pushing the boundaries of what is possible, and finally manages to create new life from dead body parts. His creature, just like any other human being, seeks friendship, company and love. However, as it looks rather ugly, Frankenstein and other people reject it, so that it ultimately turns evil and kills several people to seek revenge. Frankenstein may not have intended to create a monster, but by abandoning his creation because it does not look the way he wants it to and by shunning his responsibility for it, he ultimately creates a disaster.

main part: examples of scientific innovations leading to unintended consequences reference to *Frankenstein*

Frankenstein and modern genetics

example of cloning

If Mary Shelley were alive today, her protagonist would probably work in the field of genetic engineering, trying to further push the limits of science. Perhaps he would secretly experiment with human reproductive cloning, which is banned in many countries. If it became a reality, cloning would fundamentally alter our concept of human identity. It could, for instance, lead to a two-class society of "cloned" and "naturally conceived" humans (as Kazuo Ishiguro powerfully depicted in his novel Never Let Me Go).

***Klara and the Sun:* technology pushing the boundaries**

examples of technological innovations leading to unintended consequences
reference to *Klara and the Sun*

In Ishiguro's novel *Klara and the Sun*, people are not cloned, but it is possible to replace a loved one who has died with an android robot who looks and acts exactly like the deceased person. The family of Josie, a girl who is seriously ill, is planning to replace their daughter after her death, but they still have qualms and wonder whether they will be able to love the "second Josie" as much as the first one. Again, the scenario in the novel raises far-reaching questions: what makes us human and unique? Will artificial intelligence ever become so emotionally intelligent that it can actually replace human beings? Can an android robot develop human feelings? The scientist Capaldi flatly rejects the idea that there is "something unreachable inside each of us. Something that's unique and won't transfer" (ll. 72/73) – in other words: everyone is replaceable.

"Artificial friends" in real life

digital assistants and robots

Klara and the Sun is a powerful reminder that we are in the midst of a digital revolution and all sorts of algorithms and artificial intelligence already influence our everyday lives and social relationships. Digital assistants such as "Alexa" and "Siri", for example, have become a familiar part of many households. In Japan, nurse robots and pet robots often serve as companions and are accepted as members of the family. Again, these technologies have positive effects but they also have many negative ones: the machines could collect all sorts of sensitive data about us, sell it to companies and manipulate us into buying certain products, for example.

conclusion: summary of findings

Having looked at these examples, it becomes clear that every innovation produces consequences we cannot quite foresee, just as Rosenberg stated. This makes it all the more important to carefully consider the possible impact a new development may have on all spheres of life.

invitation to comment

What do you think about Rosenberg's quote, and what examples from literature or real life come to your mind when you read it? I'm curious to read your comments!

Niedersachsen Englisch ▪ Abiturprüfung 2023
Erhöhtes Anforderungsniveau

Um Ihnen die Prüfung 2023 schnellstmöglich zur Verfügung stellen zu können, bringen wir sie in digitaler Form heraus.
Sobald die Original-Prüfungsaufgaben 2023 freigegeben sind, können sie als PDF auf der Plattform **MyStark** heruntergeladen werden. Ihren persönlichen Zugangscode finden Sie auf der Umschlaginnenseite, ganz vorne im Buch.

Aktuelle Prüfung

www.stark-verlag.de/mystark